HUNDER

by

Jane Palmer

DODO BOOKS

First published in Great Britain
by Dodo Books 2010

ISBN 978 1 906442 21 7

Other science fiction books by this author

THE PLANET DWELLER
THE WATCHER
MOVING MOOSEVAN
BABEL'S BASEMENT
THE KYBION
NIGHTINGALE

Fiction

BALD WENDY

CHAPTER 1

*God came to Auroal to smite the
Devil's creation.*

Skirra bounced closer to the viewer. 'What are they chanting now?' he asked Ansopha who was lounging on a ceiling buttress, exuding indifference and refusing to translate the droning coming from the artificial planet.

'This is the chant of cosmic resurrection,' the voice of Hunder explained in an unusually patient tone.

Ansopha peered down from its precarious perch. 'Let me know when God arrives.' Then the communicator stretched like a satiated carnivore and closed its silver eyes.

'And what will you do if He does?' demanded Skirra.

'Emigrate to the furthest reaches of deep space.'

'Why not, it's probably where you came from,' the medical scientist muttered.

The limb of Auroal could be seen rising impressively from the satellite's view port. Skirra and Orphanus, the engineer, were too immersed in the ceremony taking place on the screen to notice. At the south pole of the artificial world, species who didn't share an atom of DNA had gathered to indulge in an act of archaic and superstitious time wasting.

Hunder's quantum processor had once computed the likelihood of so many different species agreeing that they worshipped the same God. Given the immediacy of communication, cosmic dissemination of ideas, and close proximity to each other on the space-port, it was inevitable. Lashing out at each other on such a small world over semantics wouldn't have been practical. The bio computer's circuits silently groaned as he realised they were on the threshold of a nonsensical episode generated by the intolerance of consensus while the mysterious Ansopha, who probably came from a corner of the Universe where deities weren't permitted, radiated contempt for the proceedings below.

Having agreed to share God, the inhabitants of Auroal now faced the problem of what to do when He arrived. Blood sacrifices had gone out of fashion long before Auroal had been a glimmer in the eye of the ambitious engineer who had designed the spaceport. Had she been able see what was going on she would have probably kicked her computer for visualising the concept. Her world was supposed to be a galactic point of convergence for several gravity lines, not the gateway to some mythological heaven.

Over generations Auroal's inhabitants had become jaded. Supplying, servicing, and organising space traffic from across the Galaxy could be boring if that was all you and your ancestors had been engaged in. So, to break the monotony, why not join hands with your neighbours, resurrect a few cosmic myths and try them on for size?

Hunder was as old as the artificial planet. He had been designed to control all its systems as well as the gravity lines through which traffic travelled. Systematically up-dated by the elite technicians of Space Command, he eventually developed the capacity to program himself. Being a reasoning bio computer and as a consequence irritable, only to be expected in someone with his cosmic intellect, Hunder was allowed to have his own way because the saving on upgrading him was immense. At one time hundreds maintained the bio computer's satellite. Now it only needed a skeleton crew, mainly to keep a mortal eye on Auroal and Hunder's tantrums. The atmosphere in the satellite's cavernous spaces was only intermittently restored to echo to the footfall of Orphanus as she checked welds and connections, matters too humdrum for the mighty Hunder to bother with.

The bio computer liked company to reassure him of his superiority, yet wasn't so keen on the arguments his existence provoked in lesser intellects, which included most sentient life. Orphanus was no problem. The engineer knew her limitations, although he did have to disarm her when she occasionally threatened to eviscerate an irritating mortal. Skirra was always too busy with medical research and ministering to the needs of the many species on Auroal to be bothered about the bio computer's ego. Then there was Ansopha, an enigma with no origin, gender, pretence of social conditioning, or noticeable bodily functions.

Though the subject was never broached, the crew suspected that their communicator knew more about deities than was healthy for all of them. Ansopha came from the only species Hunder had been unable to categorise or Skirra make medical sense of. Polarising molecules in any creature were pretty unusual, and when that creature used them to become invisible – the only evidence of its presence a faint, rustling sound - evolution took on a new meaning.

Skirra knew that there was no point in interrogating Ansopha about its origins. The medical scientist had even been denied the tissue sample all crewmembers were obliged to surrender before a term of duty, and chasing invisible entities with laser scalpels was not in his terms of contract.

The ceremonial chanting on Auroal grew more intense and the illumination from the massive arena could be seen rising on the planet's limb.

'This is giving me a headache,' moaned Ansopha.

'Serves you right for being a telepath,' snapped Orphanus. She was a Vardel and capable of crushing bones with her thoughts.

Suddenly the chanting congregation below rippled back from the hub of the ceremony as though God had tossed a thunderbolt into his pool of believers. Given the different life support systems and body sizes it was a wonder no one was asphyxiated.

On each narrow layer of the planet the rest of the

population sat in their respective ecosystems, fervently anticipating God's appearance. Ansopha also began to wish He would arrive; emotions this intense played more havoc with its telepathic efficiency than the solar wind could with electromagnetic frequencies.

'Something is happening,' Hunder announced.

'They're going home?' a voice from the ceiling asked hopefully.

'There is an unusual blister of energy forming.'

'How?' demanded Orphanus. 'Artificial planets don't have volcanoes - at least, this one didn't the last time I inspected its core.'

'The anomaly may have used a gravity line - but I never registered it.' Hunder sounded defensive.

'Well hadn't you better find out what it is?'

'Why?' The bio computer knew what she meant. 'No, I'm not going to let you train the satellite's weapons array on it. The thing hasn't made any threatening moves and might take it as belligerence if it is a sentient being.'

'Looks like a proto star to me,' observed Skirra.

Hunder's circuits crackled at the inanities they had to contend with. 'Keep to medicine. If that were a proto star its gravitational field would have torn us apart by now.'

'Well Ansopha, is it a sentient being? Can you sense anything at all?'

The communicator concentrated. 'Only the telepathic equivalent of a bad smell.'

The medical scientist wasn't impressed with the diagnosis. 'What are you talking about?'

'There is something unpleasantly, voraciously... hungry, in its aura.'

Skirra visualised the casualties he would have to deal with if there was an explosion in the middle of a congregation containing ten percent of the planet's population. 'But what is it for pity's sake? Hunder, you should send out a probe.'

'It wouldn't be politic.'

Orphanus noticed a change in the image on the screen. 'Closer, Hunder. Zoom in closer.'

The bio computer did as she said. The blister of energy had become a pulsating mound of plasma. The huge gathering on Auroal milled about uneasily; fear mixed with the adulation, they backed away.

Ansopha peered down with its glinting gaze, unable to believe the thoughts radiating up from the planet's pole. 'Well, well, well,' it announced like a carnivore spying a lunch of poisonous reptile. 'We're having a manifestation.'

Orphanus' approach was more warlike. 'A what?'

'Believe it or not, God has arrived.'

Skirra bounced too high in excitement and collided with the communications buttress.

'Don't damage the sensors,' warned Ansopha.

'Just tell us it's someone's idea of a practical joke,' demanded Orphanus. She didn't relish the idea of meeting anyone's maker, especially the one of any species her ancestors had managed to wipe out.

The manifestation on Auroal continued to grow. A rainbow knife of illumination cut through the velvet sky. Believers wailed in ecstasy and waverers were convinced. Even Hunder's many monitors momentarily blinked. The only creature not impressed by the aura of God's ego continued to limply straddle the ceiling buttress. It loured down with silver eyes and analysed the bizarre thought rhythms of the apparition taking form on the planet below. Of all the species witnessing this, was Ansopha the only one registering the true nature of the entity? Had they switched off their common sense for fear of offending God's manifestation? The communicator said nothing and, however curious Skirra may have been, even he would think twice before chasing the Supreme Being for a tissue sample.

CHAPTER 2

Gladys Hodge stopped wheeling her luggage and put down her case of cameras to pause for breath. She stood on the promenade and enjoyed the autumn air. It had that comforting bite to it, as familiar as the cheap brandy that her sister would now be pickling barely ripe apricots in for Christmas presents, and the cappuccino Mansel Lascelle would soon be serving on a lace tablecloth.

Here came Arnold, taking his wobbly, overweight Labrador for its afternoon walk. Gladys had lost count of the times she had been stayed at Beachview, but there had always been Arnold, always with the same dog. Yet she had never discovered whether there was a Mrs Arnold, lots of little grand Arnolds, or even where he lived.

'Good morning Arnold. How are you?' The elderly man was so short-sighted he would have bumped into her if she hadn't announced her presence. 'Still fit as ever I see.' It was a lie. Telling Arnold he looked as though a herring gull might carry him off at any moment was not in her nature, despite the years as a photojournalist having to deal with impossible people.

The old gentleman doffed his hat and dipped a bow. 'It's good to see you so soon in the season, Gladys.'

'Had the feeling Christmas was coming early this year. Wanted to get out before the seasonal tantrums.'

'Mr Lascelle and his mother will be pleased to see you.'

Gladys managed a tight smile. Mansel's cockatoo was usually more pleased to see her than his mother, and that always gave a bad tempered squawk at her arrival.

'I understand the season hasn't been so good,' Arnold went on. 'Brinton-on-Sea is not exciting enough for the modern holiday maker.'

That's exactly why Gladys came. She had spent too

many years dashing after combat troops through jungles and snapping the crocodile smiles of the world's tyrants. The last thing she aspired to now was to trip over dinosaur eggs in a desolate Mongolian landscape or eyeball some mountain gorilla. Brinton-on-Sea was safe, had comparatively tame wildlife, and the nearest the teenagers got to cannabis were the herbal remedies produced by Nature's Herbal Realm, the local major industry.

Gladys was suddenly aware that Arnold was still speaking and just managed to stop her expression from glazing over in time.

'At least Mr Butterworth is still there and they are hiring out the saloon to the Moonstar Players for the rehearsals of their winter production.'

Gladys groaned internally. The Moonstar Players were the only wildlife she tried to assiduously avoid. This amateur theatre group was so excruciatingly bad they had to bribe the local residents with tea and biscuits to watch them. *C'est la vie*, as Mrs Lascelle would never say, being too crotchety to be philosophical about anything.

Gladys grasped the handle of her luggage, said goodbye to Arnold, and strode off towards Beachview Hotel. With only a few yards to go, she realised that it was about time she took a taxi from the station. No seventy-two-year-old should be lugging things that heavy, even if she was usually assumed to be ten years younger. But then, Gladys had never acted her age - and occasionally managed to forget what it was.

Though only built in the thirties, Beachview looked as though it had been planted, facing the seafront, before the Victorian promenade was even thought about. The hotel was the first facade to be picked out by passing ships. Even the parish church tower, coastguard station, and amusement arcade could be cloaked by the mists rolling in from the sea. Despite them, Beachview flaunted itself like a cross-gartered Malvolio, confidant that its cross-timbered facade was in the best possible taste. Behind the three storeys of bay windows and mock Tudor timbers were ten guest suites, a restaurant lounge, and a saloon large enough to contain the egos of The Moonstar Players.

Mansel Lascelle and his mother lived in the basement flat, though Joabim the cockatoo's domain was the saloon bar. Over the past twenty years, the bird had developed a taste for pretzels, peanuts, and flying at liberty through the timber beams. As a consequence, food was only served in the lounge restaurant by order of the health inspector. Apart from hygienic considerations, Joabim had also been prone to sampling the meals of guests and swearing in French when repulsed. Fortunately his English was impeccable.

Gladys blundered through the front door with her luggage and was enveloped by the reassuring aroma of garlic, freshly ground coffee, and stale beer. Had it been fifteen degrees hotter she might have imagined herself back in an ex pats hotel adjacent to some kasbah seething with radical malcontent. The most rebellious thing in here was the cockatoo that immediately turned its back as she entered, which was just as well because the photographer didn't at that moment want to hear some French obscenity.

Mr Butterworth was in his usual corner of the restaurant lounge with madeleines and Ceylon tea while Mansel, singing some risqué Jacque Briel lyrics under his breath, cleared tables after the regular afternoon customers.

Gladys smiled to herself. His English was superb, probably to annoy his mother, and it was odd to hear him relish his native tongue.

'Bonjour, Mansel.'

The proprietor turned in time to see Gladys catch her camera case as it slid from her shoulder. He pushed the loaded tray onto the nearest table and swept through the chairs like a tug in a gale.

'Mrs Hodge. You are early.' The large man planted a welcoming kiss on both her cheeks. 'You should not see the place in such a mess.'

Joabim now deigned to acknowledge her presence and gave a bad tempered squawk which was probably cockatoo for, 'Not you again? Brought any pretzels?'

Mr. Butterworth came over to shake her hand. He had a bearing of military correctness and, despite him having the most amiable of natures, Gladys always imagined he was about to twirl his moustaches like the Demon Barber. Fortunately, having seen every variation of male stubble, it was obvious to her that he used an electric razor. Several years ago she might have fancied him, but the photographer was also experienced enough to tell that his affections lay elsewhere - though never did find out in exactly which direction.

Everyone engaged in the usual warm banter for five minutes, though all Gladys wanted at that moment was a stiff coffee. The doctor would have banned even those if she hadn't promised to give up the brandy and occasional cigar - another reason for avoiding Christmas. There's no fun in watching everyone else destroying their immune systems if you couldn't join in.

Mansel carried her luggage up to a bedroom overlooking the sea. Gladys followed and, when he had gone, threw the windows open to purge the air of potpourri and rose disinfectant. Mrs Lascelle must have thought they were aromatic, but they reminded the photographer of an Eastern red light district.

No longer feeling her age, Gladys unpacked and set up her chemicals and developing trays in the darkroom adjoining the bedroom. This was the spacious cupboard under the stairs that led to the attic rooms, and where Mansel obligingly stored her enlarger and chemical tanks. Easily made light proof, it was well out of reach of other guests. After she had retired, some of her best work had been printed under those stairs.

Winter on the coast appealed to Gladys' photographic eye, though she would have to pay dearly for her annual rendezvous with Nature by producing prints of the Moonstar Players in their worst throws of the dramatic and carried the infernal digital camera solely for that purpose. Why waste good emulsion on histrionic posturing?

As she checked the chemicals, footsteps pounded up and down the stairs, making the bottles rattle and a developing canister roll onto the floor. By the time the photographer had stepped outside to see what was going on, the culprits had gone.

Mansel descended from the attic with an armful of bed sheets.

'Staff flying south for the winter?" Gladys guessed.

He sighed in resignation. 'Oui, they are moving to some commune in Provence.'

She wished she had kept her mouth shut, but there was no backing out now. 'Do you have anyone to replacement them?'

Out of breath, Mansel leant on the banisters at the bottom of the stairs. 'No, only Mary and my own fair hands.'

'But you can't manage a place this size by yourselves?'

'Mary says she will do the laundry, and the season is over. We will manage.'

The photographer doubted it, though said nothing. Keeping up a place the size of Beachview as well as ministering to his demanding mother would probably help the man shed a few pounds.

Gladys returned to her room to load an SLR, then left to take a few snaps in the late autumn light.

CHAPTER 3

And the Devil's disciple plotted to
set its mark of evil on Auroal.

The blister of illumination domed out and sent an accusing column of light soaring towards Hunder's satellite. Skirra wondered how any optic nerve down there could withstand the glare, but the population on Auroal believed that this was the God who had created them all and the radiance of His Glory had to be endured, along with any other indignities that would have sent rational people screaming to a lawyer. Even the Voba, a species who had logic and litigation written into their genes, were down there grovelling before a manifestation whose only calling card was a blinding ball of light.

Hunder was worried at seeing the Voba give in. He daren't admit it, even to himself, because the admission would have dented the conviction he had about his own infallibility and the bio computer had a feeling that the Cosmos was going to require every qubit of his vast reasoning quite soon. Hunder hated having to depend on his quantum system, but the fluid reactions of his bio circuits were too emotional to face down such an absolute as God incarnate.

Ansopha had no such quantum gates to limit its responses. The communicator dropped from the ceiling perch and the silver eyes glowered at the screen relaying the events on Auroal: no species down there seemed to be suffering ill effects, apart from a surfeit of ecstasy.

'This is going to screw up your calculations about Creation, Hunder,' Ansopha snarled.

The bio computer's higher instincts wanted to panic. Instead, his primary reason circuits compelled him to reply in his most considered tone. 'Given the size of our Universe, such an entity could be feasible. Virtually everything is known about the transformation of matter,

11

except how it was created in the first place.'

'There was no first place. Why do you have to state the facile? There is no Creator, or such thing as linear time.'

Hunder aspired to mortality despite his contempt for other corporeal creatures and wasn't going to let that pass. 'Most mortals fail to comprehend that.'

'So that makes time linear? Their mere comprehension of it?'

Orphanus was beginning to find the miracle amusing. No Vardel had worshipped any deity for long as the energy of commitment could be put to better use. 'What's the matter, Ansopha? Why does "God's" presence offend you so much?'

The silver eyes narrowed to malicious slits. 'Why has it arrived now? What does it want here?'

Skirra was hovering under a ceiling locker and hauling out aeons of cultural junk as though it was festive bunting. 'Does God need reasons? We should be the ones explaining ourselves.'

The others paused in disbelief at his plunge into religious irrationality.

Hunder had always depended on the medical scientist's level-headedness to keep the other two in check. The consequences of him suddenly falling for the God con trick didn't bear thinking about. 'This could just be how some undiscovered species introduce themselves. Perhaps they expect us to burst into balls of plasma as well because it's the only way they can communicate.'

'Well this communicator has no intention of bursting into flames, even to make first contact with the most peculiar species to ever blunder out of a gravity line,' Ansopha snarled.

Skirra had dislodged so much junk from the locker Hunder was obliged to engage a force field to prevent it from falling onto any sensitive equipment.

'It must be God,' the medical scientist insisted. 'What

other species would arrive like this?'

'The species "God" belongs to perhaps.'

Skirra stopped rummaging for a moment. 'What do you mean? How can there be more than one God?'

Hunder's long standing confidence in Skirra toppled over. 'You know quite well that some entities can alter their energy levels and blink on and off. How do we know that this creature isn't of one of them?'

'So where would it get the energy to do that?' The medical scientist pointed at the manifestation on the monitor.

'Well it did take a nibble at our sun on the way in.'

Skirra hesitated. 'You never said anything about it?'

'I don't always mention when I feel a headache coming on either, because I know you won't have the slightest interest,' Hunder lied.

'Don't become emotional at a time like this.'

'You really mean this "momentous occasion", don't you?'

'All right then, if you can prove that He's not the real thing, inform Space Command.' Skirra resumed his search and more clutter cascaded from the locker.

'What are you looking for?'

'A Cittrac. We can't approach God without a Cittrac.'

This one was of the few instances when Ansopha agreed with Hunder. 'You speak for yourself, egg glow. I shall just stand at a respectful distance and mentally project obscenities.'

'Oh no,' warned Orphanus. She had no intention of confronting any God's retribution after her colourful career. 'You're the communications officer. You communicate with it.'

'She's right,' added Hunder. 'It is possible you are the only one capable of making contact. Skirra bouncing towards God with a Cittrac could cause complications even I wouldn't be able to cope with.'

Ansopha turned to look at the screen monitoring

Auroal. There was little movement about the glowing dome of light.

The silence would have continued if it didn't say something. 'All right. What's the atmosphere like, Hunder?'

'Within your tolerance, though could do with more carbon dioxide.'

'If it's that oxygen rich, why are they trying to hug huge balls of fire?'

'I have the dampers on line. Trust me.'

Ansopha had to. 'I'll use the underside gravline. Don't transmit me too quickly. I want a close look before committing.'

As soon as Ansopha was in position, Hunder projected the communicator into the heart of the gathering like a silver dart where it found itself confronting a platform of multifarious praying priests too awe-struck to be any use and, below them, a sea of upturned faces anxious with anticipation.

The congregation murmured, resentful that Ansopha had taken so long to arrive. They shouldn't have been surprised. It was probably the only creature who could remain an atheist when facing God Incarnate.

Towering into the indigo sky, the manifestation radiated like the limb of a small sun. If this was the way some exotic species made first contact, Ansopha wasn't surprised they were unknown. Not many people would have survived the first encounter, including those on Auroal if there hadn't been bio computer of Hunder's capability to shield them from His energy field. And no other planet had a communicator like Ansopha. It had made contact with some unusual species in its time, but this would be like trying to pull feathers out of a furnace with little more than good intentions. The communicator had many intentions. As far as God was concerned, none of them was good. He had detected something about the telepathic agent that sent a surge of indignation through his Almighty Being. The blazing deity was not going to allow Ansopha the luxury of non-comprehension.

His reaction took even Ansopha by surprise.

There was a rumble that shook the platform of praying priests. Ansopha was snatched from the ground and, sparkling like a sacrificial bauble, dangled aloft. However much it may have impressed the crowd, the communicator was just annoyed.

'What are you?' God demanded.

The telepathic question made Ansopha's skull ring like well struck bell.

'If you're God, you should know.'

Wrong answer.

Ansopha was released so rapidly any other mortal would have smashed its legs.

'You are no progeny of mine. You are the work of the Devil!'

This God had obviously been around and was not craving polite first contact.

'I don't know what I am,' Ansopha thought back fiercely. 'Does it matter whether you made me or not? I'm pretty sure the amount of DNA which has been kicking around the Universe for aeons could have thrown up a few species without you knowing.'

Ansopha felt another kick inside its skull. 'Hey, that hurt! Do you think the high priests here spent all this time trying to raise you just to find out what a spiteful monster you really are? They want revelations and something to believe in, not a bad tempered blob of plasma with an ignition problem.'

God decided that He had spent enough time inside Ansopha's head and abruptly withdrew.

As soon as the communicator's wits returned, it glimpsed a ball of energy heading in its direction. Ansopha swept the nearby priests aside - then disappeared.

Though they knew of the communicator's ability to do

this, the inhabitants of Auroal had never witnessed this minor miracle before. "Due to polarising molecules being rapidly switched", was all medical scientist, Skirra could tell them. All the same, seeing Ansopha blink from their sight was more like magic.

God did not like being upstaged. He struck Auroal an almighty blow. The planet shook and the machinery stabilising its inner core stuttered. Throughout the latitudes, buildings toppled, tanks of illicit substances ready to be smuggled through gravity lines overturned, and crèches of newly hatched Fammorans sent into tail chasing fits.

Then the wailing started.

Ansopha thought it best not to stay around, visibly, or otherwise.

CHAPTER 4

Gladys had several promising rolls of film to process, Mansel was recovering from a flurry of early Christmas shoppers, Joabim had just helped himself to a bag of mixed nuts that were now strewn over the saloon floor, and Mrs Lascelle had made one of her rare appearances to hang the front door curtains against the chill sea breeze. As always this time every year, it was business as usual.

The proprietor sat on a stool at the bar and looked mournfully at the remains of the cockatoo's last snack. Mary, his general factotum, bounced in with a tiny Yorkshire terrier in her apron pocket.

'Moonstar Players ahoy!' the jolly young woman warned.

Joabim squawked at her as she let the small dog snuffle up the pieces of nut.

Mansel groaned and tried to concentrate on the fee they were paying for use of the saloon.

'I've left Mr Butterworth's sheets airing in the laundry room and will change Mrs H as soon as she's finished developing.'

'Thank you Mary.' Mansel felt he deserved a stiff drink and poured them both a sherry. 'Your cousin could not manage a few hours each week then?'

'Sorry. Too much seaweed to process. Good crop this year. And the factory had a new consignment of evening primrose, so they won't be laying anyone off either.' She took a swig of her drink. 'Never mind. Something will crop up. How's Mrs Mansel?' she whispered in case the old woman was wearing her despised hearing aid.

'Howling like a tigress because I will no longer cook her tea.'

'Well, it's too much for you. She understands that - deep down.'

'Oui, so deep only angler fish know.' Another

cavernous sigh. 'And now you say the Moonstar Players are coming. Could any man's lot be gloomier.'

From some way up the promenade came a cacophony of voices vying for attention. It sounded like a troupe of high-pitched Tasmanian devils disputing territorial rights. Mansel rolled his eyes and quickly tried to move the saloon furniture into a formation that would defy the Moonstar Players to arrange it into a stage set.

'You pop downstairs for a nap and I'll make their tea,' Mary said.

'You are an angel.' Mansel pulled the tea towel from his shoulder, laid it neatly over the counter, and then darted across the lounge and through the kitchen, down to his basement flat.

'And I wish you were my husband, poppet,' Mary muttered when he was out of earshot. 'Pity about that old bat you have for a mother. Bet she scared off a few likely damosels.'

From her perch on the stepladders, Mrs Lascelle fancied she heard someone take her name in vain. She snapped at Mary to hide her dog.

Mary snatched up the Yorkshire terrier and hid it in her apron just as the Moonstar Players swept in with a theatrical flourish, allowing in a bitter wind that nearly toppled Mrs Lascelle from her steps.

Henny Stenson doffed his wide brimmed fedora with unnecessary affectation. 'Bonjour Mamoselle.'

The old woman scowled. She uttered something from Joabim's repertoire, then closed the stepladders and bustled out.

After all the years they had been using Beachview for rehearsal meetings he should have known better, yet the performer in Henny was still wounded at the proprietor's lack of bonhomie. 'Strange woman.' He turned to Mary. 'What *did* happen to her husband?'

'She probably shot him for collaborating with the human race.'

Loralie Stenson patted the small head peering out from Mary's apron. 'Hallo Louise. You never grow any larger, do you?'

Mary put the woman's comment down to a need to say something, rather than stupidity. With a husband like Henny, she didn't often have the chance to get a word in edgeways.

The Moonstar Players swept into the saloon for their first rehearsed reading. Joabim muttered a few swear words in French and flapped off to a nook in a ceiling timber while Mary left to bring in their tea urn. Under Henny Stenson's supervision, this was a strictly teetotal troupe as beer fogged the mind and weakened that vital spark which should burn brightly in every performance. The only question now was, would a mere two months be long enough to do justice to their production of *A Christmas Carol*?

For fear of attracting attention to themselves and being roped in, a couple of regulars in a private partition put aside their rustling daily papers and tried to slurp their light ales silently.

Having moved the armchairs and sofas into a circle as though expecting an attack from a tribe of critics, the company pulled out scripts and the bloody business of casting began. Henny Stenson had already worked out who was going to play what part. Nevertheless, the pretence of a little democracy helped morale.

Oliver, the company's leading light was, of course, cast as Scrooge. For such a plum role he even didn't mind giving up the velvet collar and medallion to play someone his own age. His partner, Gerald, having suffered fifteen years of his companion, was ideal to take on the downtrodden Bob Cratchit with a minimum of make-up. As he was directing, Henny cast himself as Marley's ghost and Christmas Present - that would allow him to replace his toupee with even more hair - and Loralie had hectored for the part of Christmas Past so she could wear her best silk and carry a diamante wand. Unfortunately she would also have to play Tiny Tim. The Stenson's son was now a fifteen-year-old Goth and would have nailed himself inside his coffin at the suggestion that he play an infant with upturned eyes.

Gloria would have to double as Mrs Cratchit and Scrooge's housekeeper. She was busty and lusty, and totally unsuitable for both parts, but had to be given something. Mavis Brink would have been better in the roles if she hadn't refused to act, preferring to put together all those things like props, advertising, and ticket sales that no production could do without, yet would seldom admit to. She was a woman with hardly any discernible surface. What went on behind those pale grey eyes was deep and carefully thought out. Her conclusions about the world baffled most people, especially the other Moonstar Players who were nothing but surface. There is at least one Mavis Brink in every amateur theatrical company that manages to survive past its inauguration.

Between cups of tea, the Moonstar Players haggled like horse traders, knowing that they would eventually have to acquiesce to Henny Stenson's casting anyway. Whatever their leader's faults, he did have the knack of making the most of limited resources. There was little else the Moonstar Players could do without abducting members from a larger theatre company as they always kept a low profile when Henny Stenson advertised auditions in the local free newspaper.

This left the troupe with one major problem. Who was going to play Christmas Future? Henny could have easily doubled up, but was not prepared to part with his toupee, even to play Death. They also needed a narrator to fill in the gaps and allow for quick changes.

With a tone more suited to declaring the country a republic, Henny Stenson announced that the casting was settled and handed out typescripts from his briefcase. 'Our first reading, just to see how everything fits.'

The cast immediately riffled through the stapled pages to see how many lines their characters had been allocated. Mavis Brink, glasses on the end of her sharp nose, began to calculate the props and sound effects required. She was like a teacher hunting quotations from Shakespeare, her pen working as though she had been given a copy of Hamlet.

Pleased with her latest batch of prints and the world in general, Gladys Hodge unsuspectingly strolled into the saloon, realising too late that the Moonstar Players already occupied it. Before she could double back to the lounge Henny Stenson pounced.

With an expansive flourish of his arms and stentorian tones he announced, 'Mrs Hodge, so nice to see you again.'

'And again, and again, and again,' Gladys muttered to herself, too diplomatic to swear at him in a foreign tongue like Mrs Lascelle.

'Mr Stenson, I didn't realise how near your next production was.' Her mind raced to try and think up some faux pas that would totally alienate the Moonstar Players before she could be roped in as an honorary member. 'What is it this year? A pantomime perhaps?'

The atmosphere became charged with indignation, and faint sniggers rose from the other side of the partition.

But needs must when in a tight corner. 'Dear Mrs Hodge, I take it you will be staying over Christmas?'

'Er... Yes.' She could hardly pretend to break the routine of so many years.

And then it came, with jingle bells on. 'We are one member short for the most vital part. It will not be necessary to memorise lines and can even be given seated. With your resonant tones and commanding presence, you would be ideal.'

Gladys had found more presence of mind when confronting genocidal maniacs with nothing but a SLR.

But this was the Moonstar Players. So mesmerised at the dreadful prospect of becoming one of them, she was horrified to hear herself asking, 'What part is it?'

'The narrator for A Christmas Carol, my dear Mrs Hodge. You would be superb.'

With any other company she would have been flattered, and perhaps even given the proposal some thought. But this was Brinton-on-Sea's answer to the Great McGonagall pursued by the Keystone Cops. Her eyes became glazed as she wished her journalist's way with words would return. They had seen her through hostile checkpoints, ingratiated her to royalty and the Pope, and persuaded psychopaths who had a camera phobia that she was only some harmless tourist with an instamatic.

When faced with the irrational self assurance of an amateur actor, her mental thesaurus could only produce, 'How kind of you to think of me.'

Opportunely Mansel, refreshed after his nap, made an appearance.

'Ladies and gentlemen,' he announced amiably, 'Mrs Hodge is here to rest. Her doctor would not allow such a thing.'

Groans of false sympathy for her delicate condition rose from the circle of players, and Gladys wondered at the accuracy of his guess.

'You have plenty of time to find someone else,' he went on. 'Do not things always work out?'

'Of course they do,' Oliver agreed, wilfully ignoring the fact that most of their productions were usually disasters with or without the requisite number of players.

Gladys gathered up her white umbrella and camera and gratefully slipped out to photograph whatever creatures might have been clambering down the evening beach to escape being auditioned by the Moonstar Players.

CHAPTER 5

And the Devil's agent attempted to smite God.

Skirra hovered over Ansopha, directing beams of healing light at its head. 'The first time in recorded history God turns up, and you have to make him mad. You're too bloody weird.'

'Shut-up. My brain hurts.'

The medical scientist acquiesced. Ansopha's biology was confusing, even for his vast knowledge of everything alien, and he needed to concentrate on what he was doing.

Hunder knew only too well what headaches were and had no sympathy for anyone else's. 'How did God get inside your brain without permission?'

Ansopha groaned. How could a bio computer with Hunder's capacity ask such a banal question?

'He didn't just get inside my brain, He mined it. Every time I gave a wrong answer there was an explosion.'

'You can say that again,' muttered Skirra.

Ansopha resentfully watched the buoyant, round, medical scientist prod his bizarre anatomy with light beams and the occasional hard instrument.

Skirra was the one to talk about weird; the medically adept race he came from were composite creatures - several species rolled into one. Their ancestors had decided, for efficiency's sake, to assume the most useful attributes from a range of alien forms and genetically graft that DNA into their own. This created an egg shaped being with tapering legs and ability to hover. Skirra looked like an inverted teardrop from the massive duct of the Supreme Being Ansopha had just insulted. The medic was oblivious of his own oddity. It seemed quite logical to him. If it was your destiny to treat so many different beings in the known Galaxy, the least you could do was share as many parts of them as possible.

At last Ansopha's head cleared. Being able to blink

out of harm's way faster than a flea meant that its life had been relatively pain free. No entity had ever managed to land a punch on it before, however well deserved, so it was inevitable that the communicator would eventually meet its match. Most mortals would have been gratified to know that it took God Incarnate to do it, but this new experience of pain annoyed Ansopha on a level that surprised even itself.

'Now what?' snapped the communicator.

'The good people of Auroal want to see you fired into the sun,' announced Hunder.

Ansopha hardly expected thanks from the high priests for saving their lives. Historically marginalised as an archaic irrelevance, they had at last found the status they believed their irrational calling deserved and thought that this heretic deserved death at the hand of God.

'Fired into the sun! That monstrosity wouldn't want it polluted with a blasphemer.'

Skirra was puzzled. 'Why would God be interested in what happens to our sun?'

Hunder knew that this was not the time to tell them. He wasn't in the mood to cope with outrage.

Ansopha worked on instincts and had no clue as to where the idea had sprung from. 'It was something I picked up when He was inside my head.'

'What?'

'I can't describe it. A sort of hunger only a mouthful of star could satisfy. Given all the rage swilling about in there, it was difficult to isolate anything much apart from me about to die.'

'It will be best if you keep out of the way. Let any negotiations be routed through me,' Hunder told the communicator.

'Negotiations? What sort of God needs to negotiate?'

'We have to persuade Him not to eliminate you from your illegal habitation of His sacred universe.'

Ansopha rose, despite the annoyed twittering of Skirra who was about to surreptitiously snatch a bio sample. 'It really is going to destroy me?'

'Something about you has certainly upset The Almighty. I can't think what.'

The communicator wished Hunder had never programmed irony into his circuits. From a machine, however sophisticated, it was disconcerting. 'That demented cosmic firework is up to something.'

'As He's not here to sign autographs, keep away from Him until we know what it is.'

Skirra floated over to face the glowing amber depths of Hunder's monitor. 'What does Ansopha mean? Up to something?' he insisted.

There was a demand in the round features that said Hunder ignored the question at his peril, and reminded him that Skirra had the means to inhibit his bio functions if he judged it necessary,

'Readings from the sun's corona suggest that energy is being leached away,' he admitted reluctantly.

Ansopha had already guessed that much. 'What sort of energy?'

'Basic elements.'

'Why?'

'It might be something to do with omnipresence. I'm not going to waste my computing capacity with that sort of data while Orphanus is on Auroal monitoring the entity.'

'Given her ancestral past, very carefully I hope,' observed Skirra.

'The entity doesn't seem interested in individual mortals.'

'Only Ansopha. I wonder why?'

The communicator turned on the medical scientist. 'All right then, why do you think it wants to atomise me?'

Though Skirra had wanted to keep his suspicions to himself for a little longer, honesty appeared to be the order of the day and now seemed the right time to air them. 'I think it's because you don't come from this Galaxy.'

Even Hunder had to pause before responding to the revelation. 'That means Ansopha must be ancient. To reach here, even from the nearest satellite galaxy, would take thousands of years. There is no evidence of gravity lines crossing deep space.'

'As God said, our communicator is not His creation.'

'Then whose is it?'

Ansopha was needled by the dispassionate discussion of its peculiar origins and left the medical couch to do some profound thinking of its own.

It went down to stand in the heart of the satellite and watch the huge fusion reactor powering the satellite where the atmosphere was too rarefied for Skirra to pursue, and lack of pressure would have inflated him like a carnival balloon.

The dreadful feeling that Skirra was right began to gnaw at Ansopha. The medical scientist may have been absurd, but never made a wrong diagnosis. Until then, Ansopha had not taken on board just how weird its own biology - for want of a better definition - was. After all, "weird" was the most accurate medical description the supreme diagnostician, Skirra, could come up with. The communicator could switch its atoms to become invisible and survive environments that would have scorched, flattened or suffocated most life forms. Of course it was bloody weird. It was hardly surprising that an entity with illusions of godhood had taken exception to the communicator.

Hunder and Ansopha appeared to be the only ones who understood that "God" was an energy thief stealing cosmic matter He considered to be His by right and had probably made appearances in other regions. Ansopha was determined to find out where.

Hunder informed Space Command of God's arrival,

and they automatically logged it in their classified files. This was the opportunity Ansopha needed to telepathically lift the access code from Hunder's bio memory and break into Star Command's database. The communicator had hacked into it many times before Hunder had realised and sent a charge to stun the thieving bird like digits.

There was no point in trying to outwit Ansopha. The bio computer had more universal matters to juggle and didn't even bother to ask what the communicator had started to construct in Orphanus's workshop. If he had possessed fingers, Hunder suspected he would have been doing the same thing.

When Orphanus returned from Auroal she discovered a bizarre mechanism sitting in the wreckage of the machines Ansopha had cannibalised. The engineer pushed up the visor of her helmet and glowered at it, unable to believe that one entity, other than her, could cause so much mayhem during such a brief period. The engineer had no idea what the machine was for, and didn't care. Orphanus was better at rage than reasoning. The communicator had anticipated the Vardel's reaction and hidden in the workshop's buttressing to avoid it. Given enough time, she would work out that the machine was intended to destroy God. At first it looked as though she wanted to destroy Ansopha's wonderful toy, then her rage subsided.

'There had better be a good reason for this?' The engineer threatened.

Ansopha could have floated on the bad vibrations wafting up. 'Have you spoken to Hunder?'

'He told me what he thought you were doing, but I didn't believe him.'

'Aren't you happy at the thought of destroying God?'

'That thing God? I doubt it.'

'Whatever this deity once was, it is now vengeful. If we can get rid of it on the cheap, Space Command will give us a bonus and not ask about those odd maintenance jobs you have been doing for the Nemorans.'

Ansopha should have known that it was impossible to blackmail a Vardel. 'I suppose I have a small place in this scheme of yours?'

'To hold my hand while God tries to blast me out of existence.'

'Am I supposed to be enthusiastic about this?'

'Of course. You're a battle-crazed Vardel. You like a good scrap. This creature may well have been the creator of star systems at one time, but now it is a parasite sucking energy back.'

'And it could be multi faceted, with tentacles into every star cluster. I suppose you want me to seize hold of them as well, while you pull its beard?'

'The sooner the creature is dissipated, the better.' The communicator at last detected reason seeping into Orphanus' fierce thoughts and risked coming down.

'You're too bloody odd to belong to this Universe,' she accused.

'Whatever I am, it is my duty to be suspicious while everyone else is losing their reason to a counterfeit deity. We can control gravity, transmit matter faster than light, and touch other dimensions. Why do we need God?'

The Vardel looked at the communicator long and hard. 'You really don't know, do you?'

'Tell me why the thought of confronting a redundant God worries a Vardel?'

Orphanus tapped her forehead with the pressurised glove she had been about to remove. 'Most mortals crave an omnipotent creator to make sense of existence.'

She was beginning to sound too profound for Ansopha. 'Existence? This monster swallows stars, and if its manifestation is only the tip of the real entity...'

'I suppose the most benign deities must eventually turn bad, like any star.' Orphanus removed her helmet and allowed the huge mass of hair she had carelessly tied back in a knot to escape like a nest of enraged snakes.

'All right. I won't ask you to help me.'

'You can't do this by yourself, and the creature's presence will destabilise Auroal's orientation if it stays here.'

Ansopha was dangerously confident. 'And what better bait than the creation of the Devil.'

CHAPTER 6

Orphanus bundled her hair into her helmet and tightened the pressure suit until its armoured carapace dug into the ribs Nature had the foresight to reinforce.

'How do you manage to breathe through that hedge?' asked Skirra, who had decided to wait around until the engineer was safely out of the airlock: she had been known to severe digits in the heat of engineering keenness, and he had become quite used to sewing Vardel extremities back on.

'Orphanus can't damage herself with this equipment. It only emits negative energy,' Hunder told the medical scientist. 'Ending up prettier is the worst thing that could happen to her.'

Skirra accepted the bio computer's word for it, and allowed the engineer to leave for Auroal's north pole which was used as a port for the occasional supply ship too massive to ply the gravity lines. Before they could do anything else, she had to evacuate the area of robot dockers.

The atmospheres at the poles of the artificial planet were stable enough, yet something else bothered Orphanus. Even she could tell that, Ansopha arrived, it wasn't going to be Heaven that was let loose and Hunder's amazing capabilities might not be a match for the reflexes of this God.

The inhabitants of Auroal tolerated Hunder because he controlled the vital machinery that kept the artificial world in orbit and prevented pile-ups in the gravity lines. Without the bio computer the world would have, very messily, ground to a standstill.

Sacrilege was quite another matter.

Through the warm, reassuring amber glow of his monitors, Hunder had painstakingly explained to

Auroal's population the true nature of the entity they had helped to raise. He even showed them evidence of its destructive behaviour in other systems.

No one listened; God only smote those who deserved it, and God was never wrong.

Orphanus felt edgy because her engineer's intuition insisted that God was bound to know a few more things about elementary particle physics than her, and Hunder didn't want to calculate what could happen if Ansopha's idea never worked. What if, instead of dousing God's Majesty, it just enraged Him even more?

Then, true to form, the bio computer's circuits had a panic attack. Space Command must have been mad to trust the security of the Galaxy to him and an insubordinate communicator of unknown origin. Surely this would occur to them before things really got out of hand? It was insane to try and put out God's light. Hunder felt quite justified in having a spasm of apprehension and if it weren't for his uncomplicated quantum processor, all the lights in the satellite would have blinked.

Suddenly Ansopha appeared on the planet, next to the machine it had designed. Hunder's bio circuits now had something to become paralysed over as he realised they had no control over it. How did the communicator create a device even Hunder had trouble making sense of? How did Ansopha know that it would work? None of the tests Hunder surreptitiously made qualified it for a God slaying guarantee. The more the bio computer scanned Ansopha and its infernal machine, the more his quantum system struggled to stabilise his thought processes. That didn't have the capability to comprehend what it was to be mortal and was becoming increasingly irritated at the frequency with which it had to drag Hunder's bio mind back from the brink of mortal breakdown.

To make matters worse, Hunder became aware that

God was watching Ansopha with a wrathful, devouring vengeance.

There was no turning back. Sensing the entity's presence, Ansopha armed its infernal machine. 'Where is He, then?'

Orphanus wondered at the communicator's calculating coolness, which was just as well given Hunder's state of mind. 'How would I know? Could be communing with the stars for all I care.'

'Or eating them.'

Orphanus told her wrist communicator. 'Ready, Hunder?'

The Vardel's harsh voice snapped the bio computer out of his fit of mortal anxiety. There was something in her warrior tone that wouldn't have thought twice about taking on the Universe.

'I'm aligning your co-ordinates.'

Being telepathically linked to Hunder, Ansopha didn't need a wrist link to know that his wits had returned. 'Is there an energy surge yet?'

Hunder detected gleeful anticipation. What was wrong with these two? They should have been experiencing mortal terror. But then, mortality was probably wasted on them.

'Orphanus, you're too close,' Ansopha told its partner in crime. 'You won't stand a chance if you're caught in its photosphere. And Skirra says that your pressure suit is too tight. You could suffer internal injuries in the gravline if you don't loosen it.'

'Where's the point in a loose pressure suit?'

'Don't argue, just do it!' snapped Ansopha. 'And put some distance between-'

'I have a reading!' Hunder interrupted. 'It's moving rapidly!'

Ansopha and Orphanus sprinted for a gap in the spaceport shielding.

The engineer barely made it before a dome of light

blazed from nowhere. The creature at its centre was taking its bearings.

God's attention settled on Ansopha. It was obvious why He was here.

'Spawn of the Devil!'

Ansopha's thoughts should have been immobilised by terror, but some infernal demon had provided the communicator with the mental saliva to respond. 'Doesn't God like a challenge?'

'You are not a challenge. You are an insect.'

'All of which you made.'

'I never fashioned such an abomination. You are an unnatural abhorrence with no right to be in my Creation.'

Ansopha detected that Hunder was still inconveniently trying to claw his way out of his paralysing spasm of doubt. Aspirations of mortality may have been admirable in less dangerous circumstances: then and there, the communicator wished its mind were plugged into a more reliable machine, even one with cogs and a gyroscope.

'Status, Hunder?'

The bio computer managed to control his tumultuous thoughts long enough to reply, 'It's not at its full strength yet.'

God heard the telepathic exchange. He couldn't believe it had anything to do with Him. They wouldn't have dared!

There was nothing else for it; Ansopha had to play for time while Hunder pulled himself together. 'Tell me, God, why am I so unnatural? Plenty of others are insolent or atheists. They don't get struck by bolts of lightning. Why pick on me?'

'My hand has touched all living things - but not you.'

Still no sensible response from Hunder, and the communicator could think of no more ploys to distract God. There was only one option left, so Ansopha threw out its thin arms and called aloud, 'So smite me down!'

God's instantaneous burst of energy was so sudden Orphanus held her breath, expecting to smell incinerated mortal remains when she released it.

Ansopha was faster. In a split second it had gone and reappeared on the other side of God's photosphere.

Hunder at last managed to pull himself together. 'Get ready,' he ordered. 'Another minute and He will be at maximum.'

'A minute is a long time down here. He can sense the molecular trail of my clothes. I only hope this God's targeting system isn't guided.'

'I warned you not to wear anything.'

'If Orphanus can dress for intergalactic battle, I fail to see why I should not cover my modesty.'

'You have no parts to be modest about.' There was still a desperate edge to Hunder's tone. 'Say something to it!'

'I find His conversation boring.'

Thwarted and furious, God felt left out of the telepathic exchange. 'Who is Orphanus?' He boomed.

The plan was unravelling. This was supposed to be a slick operation to exterminate a cosmic parasite, not an argument between a stressed computer and insubordinate spawn of the Devil. Even Orphanus was confused.

God's point of view was more straightforward. 'I should kill you now!'

Ansopha could even sneer telepathically. 'Why don't you? You've wiped out solar systems.'

'They were mine to do with as I pleased.'

'Say that out loud so everyone on Auroal can hear.'

'I explain myself to no mortal.'

'Now!' Hunder's signal was like a balloon popping inside the communicator's skull.

Ansopha pressed the trigger on its neckband. 'Then die, you miserable bladder of omnipotence!'

A missile from the communicator's infernal machine spat out like a furious wasp and zigzagged through the entity's photosphere.

God froze in disbelief, and then tried to swot the device like an annoying insect. But its sting was lethal and He thrashed about as His energy field began to dwindle.

Ansopha was hurled away and caught by Orphanus. The Vardel pulled the communicator into cover where she armed a more conventional weapon - one she understood.

In His death throes, God sent several fireballs roaring towards them. Orphanus easily picked them off.

God dwindled away, unable to believe that a mere mortal would have dared slay Him, even that spindly, silver-eyed spawn of the Devil.

After Ansopha's missile was eventually spent, all trace of The Creator had gone.

Now the stressed Hunder had to tell Auroal's priests that Ansopha had just killed God.

But, as God's assassins left the scene of the crime, another dome of energy appeared. This manifestation was small, little more than a dark red glow, and filtered about like a bloodhound trying to pick up a scent. Hunder was too consumed with self-analysis to bother with it and put the anomaly down to residual radiation from Ansopha's missile. He also needed to analyse the data so he could construct another in case God's relatives came looking for him. The bio computer overruled his quantum memory, too logical to overlook such humdrum matters as mysterious red manifestations. But this new arrival was no mere afterglow. It had an agenda.

CHAPTER 7

Sandra rubbed her freezing fingers before applying the last label to the boxes of evening primrose oil and wished she had chosen the job in the distillery instead. To preserve the potency of the ingredients, the temperature on the production line was always kept on the low side. She could cope with that, but the rooms where consignments were dispatched were open to the elements. It was as much as the Victorian stove could do to keep a kettle warm. She decided to go onto invoicing after lunch; that just involved punching buttons and she could put her gloves on.

The Nature's Realm factory may have retained its cottage industry ambience, complete with draughts and Stone Age technology, but the productivity deals and Christmas bonuses were worth it. Everyone was good company, and dispatching consignments was better than washing seaweed.

In keeping with its health image, the firm employed a vegetarian cook who believed in portions large enough to satiate carnivores. Today the canteen menu included tomato and cheese pasta, vegeburghers, and a concoction that lurked in a dish under scrolls of something that once used to be green, probably seaweed.

Sandra played safe and opted for a mug of tea and nut loaf. She took them to a corner table where general dog's body, Bernard, sat gloomily nursing a mug of Marmite. After the fisherman who trawled up a chest of Spanish bullion only to have it swept overboard, he had to be the most morose man in Brinton-on-Sea. Sandra knew what it was like to have your numbers come up the very week that you forgot to do the lottery. Bernard, arguably, had even more reason to scowl at life.

'Cheer up, love. Christmas will soon be here.'

Bernard grinned ruefully. 'Can't help thinking about Miriam this time of year. It's when she disappeared, you know. Beginning of November.'

'Yes, of course. Sorry. Wasn't thinking. Rather be left alone?'

'No, 'course not. Bit of company might take me mind off it.'

'How long has it been?' From what Sandra could remember, the couple were no more suited to each other than her cousin's Yorkshire terrier and Mrs Lascelle's Persian cat. Absence usually casts a rosy tint.

'Ten years ago now. Should've stopped wondering what happened to her, I suppose.'

Sandra started to tuck into her meal. 'Not necessarily. It was all so bloody odd, her going off like that.' She chose her words carefully given that Bernard and his wife had squabbled like two magpies after the same diamond. She suspected that the woman had taken off with some fancy fellow from Europe. There had been plenty of ferries to get on.

Bernard stared into his Mug. '"On the beach" the last person to see her said. What was she doing on the beach at that time in the evening? She should have been making dinner, not poncing about on the pebbles.'

'Don't let it get to you Bernard. You've got to accept that you may never know and get on with your life.' The words didn't come easily. Bernard was hardly a catch when Miriam had disappeared. Over the years he had really let himself go and was never allowed front of house in case he frightened off the buyers. The nearest to elegance this dog's body was ever liable to get, was soaking his teeth in nicotine remover.

'Why don't you do something to take your mind off it?'

'In Brinton-on-Sea? Like what? Ask a couple of seals out for a pint?'

'Well, Mary says the Moonstar Players are still looking for a narrator and Christmas Future.'

Bernard choked on his surreptitious cigarette. 'What, join that load of poofters? I'm not that desperate.'

'What the hell, they're fun in their own way. Always trying to get Mary to join in. Even wanted to give Louise a part.'

'What, that little terrier thing of hers?'

'Wanted a bit of colour for Pygmalion.'

'They should have auditioned Mansel Lascelle's parrot. It would remember its lines better than any of them do.' Bernard nipped out the end of his roll up under the table and put it in his tobacco tin. 'He still looking for staff then?'

'Yes. I could do a couple of evenings, but he really needs someone full time for the saloon and lounge.'

'Would have thought some youngster would snap the job up?'

'They would, if it weren't for his mother.'

Bernard nodded sagely. Their paths had crossed. 'He'll never get his act together until that old bat's dead and under the ground.'

Sandra wondered what Beachview's proprietor would be like without his mother. Married with a family most probably. 'Mary only copes because she don't pay attention to her. What Mansel needs is someone who can hold their own, because he'll never stand up to her.'

'What happened to that old crow's husband?'

In Brinton-on-Sea, the curious had their own theory about that, rather like the disappearance of Bernard's wife. Sandra's was that, as Mansel never mentioned him, the man must have been guillotined for some horrendous crime and he had moved to the UK with his mother to forget, obviously not taking into account that this was a nation which lived in a soap opera.

Sandra decided not to share her theory about Mansel's father. Bernard was one of those consummate gossips.

She looked at her watch. 'What are you on today?'

'Bottling iodine.' He held up his stained fingers. Not even the nicotine was visible. 'Still can't get used to the smell.'

'Ever tried taking some of the vitamins? Might perk you up.'

'Nah, don't hold with all these fancy health cures.' Bernard gave a lung-convulsing cough and pushed his tobacco tin into his jacket pocket. 'Reckon they does more harm than good.'

Sandra said nothing. As he was now breathing through something resembling flower arranger's oasis, he probably wouldn't live long enough to find out anyway.

'Try not to think too much about Miriam,' she advised.

He got up and pocketed a paper serviette to cough into. 'Probably wouldn't do if I knew where she went to. It's just like she disappeared off the face of the Earth.'

Sandra laughed nervously. 'Oh come on, you don't believe she was abducted by aliens, do you?'

Bernard shook his head. 'Nah. She'd arranged to meet someone, I'm sure of that. I reckon she'd even bought a new suitcase so's I wouldn't know she'd taken some things. I'm not that daft. Some men may never pay attention to what their wives wear, but I could tell that some of her smalls and other togs were missing.'

Sandra gave a tight smile. If someone was determined not to be found, it was easy enough to disappear without trace.

Bernard left the chilly canteen to briefly bask in the bright sunlight filling the courtyard.

When he had gone, Sandra couldn't help wondering about Miriam. If Bernard's wife had found a fancy man she would have told someone, not being the sort to keep good news to herself. And she certainly hadn't been looking for cuttlefish on the beach; that had all vanished years before. Sandra finished the nut roast, then turned her thoughts to what she was going to wear for the photo session that she had promised to do for Gladys

Hodge at the weekend. A sepia tint of her, Mary and a Yorkshire terrier could well be hanging on the wall of some up market photo gallery next year. The idea cheered her up no end.

CHAPTER 8

And the Devil's creature struck out at God's
Majesty, but He did transmogrify it.

Hunder detected an insistent clicking on Auroal's abandoned mining asteroid and he snapped out of his introspective mood.

Shale was cascading down the side of a quarry as dense black creatures blinked into existence. Their armoured carapaces glinted in the thin atmosphere and giant claws snatched at particles rising from the asteroid's long dead interior, trying to catch atom-sized black holes. The inexplicable appearance of this exotic fuel became visible on the electromagnetic spectrum and jammed the receivers of Auroal and its satellite. Incoming transport travelling through gravity lines was blinded while Hunder attempted to supply them with alternative tachyon bands.

It was just as well the only person able to make sense of these clattering arrivals and their bizarre diet hadn't been fired into the sun after all.

Having to deal with such dangerously voracious creatures on the asteroid's volatile crust as well as their jamming of interstellar traffic was enough to send Hunder into another panic attack. As he had only just recovered from the last one, the bio computer managed to persuade Skirra that it was due to a short in his quantum circuits. Whenever Hunder needed an excuse, he always slandered his despised quantum processor. Skirra was busy preparing medical resources for Armageddon and didn't have the time or patience to argue with him.

Just in case Ansopha couldn't get any sense out of these carapaced creatures, Hunder armed Orphanus with the asteroid's self-destruct trigger - it had been a long-standing precaution because of its erratic orbit and explosive mineral composition - then he sent her and

Ansopha down a gravline as the mining asteroid turned towards the sun. The engineer had only just got over her last encounter with an arrival from deep space and, however warlike her species, there were times she would have preferred to knit; a throwback from the period the Vardels had been obliged to calm down to avoid obliteration by Star Command's strike force. Unfortunately Orphanus was the only one who could keep Ansopha out of trouble and knew she would have to revert to her primal instincts sooner or later: Hunder's reflexes were useless when he was having one of his moods.

So the engineer tucked her hair into her helmet and tightened the pressure in her suit yet again. She may have helped destroy God, but had more respect for the seams of dangerous, volatile ores in the asteroid.

Orphanus peered over the quarry rim at the carapaces. 'Where do you think these characters came from?'

Ansopha tossed some spoil at the creatures. They ignored it. 'Hunder insists it wasn't through a gravity line. Their carapaces and respiratory tracts could survive a vacuum, so they might have drifted in from a rogue ship.'

'Why didn't Hunder pick it up?'

Ansopha gave a shrug of its narrow shoulders. The flash of silver caught the attention of one of the black-shelled creatures. Their clattering snatches at atomic fuel stopped.

'Are they trying to communicate?'

'The only thing I'm picking up is "Klitt". I don't think they have brains.'

'They're not machines?'

'Until they start doing whatever their designer or Nature intended them to, it's impossible to tell. They're not giving anything away.' Ansopha climbed over the quarry rim to confront them.

'Be careful.'

'If I can move faster than God, I'm hardly going to be bothered by these creatures.'

'It smells of ambush to me.'

'You have a suspicious mind, Orphanus.'

Hearing that from the most cynical creature to ever fall through a gravity line made the engineer blurt out a laugh. Vardel humour was a vigorous matter and she lost her footing on the explosive shale. Orphanus tumbled through the thin gravity in a slow motion cascade of rubble.

Ansopha half turned to see what she was doing. 'For pity's sake increase your mass before you float off.'

Orphanus stepped up her suit's density a couple of settings and half clambered, half floated back up.

As Ansopha continued its way down, the warrior's instincts still nagged that something was wrong. These Klitt were more than jetsam from an interstellar experimental ship. It was possible the space they took up had exceeded their usefulness and their dangerous diet blocking transmissions couldn't have done much for internal communications. But Orphanus doubted it. Her engineer's mind knew no sensible mechanic would have designed such creatures; no use for welding, loading, exploration or transport. No intellect lurked behind the tiny bead like eyes and their claws wouldn't have been any good for cargo bay operators, even if they had enough brain to tell a consignment of exotic DNA from excavator parts.

Ansopha was wandering amongst the Klitt, trying to find some glimmer of sentience it could slip a conversation into. As the occasional claw snapped too near it, the communicator nonchalantly blinked out of visibility and reappeared somewhere else.

Since Ansopha's dealings with God, it had become over confidant. As something in its manner suggested that the communicator wasn't bothering with its telepathic link to Hunder, Orphanus kept her transmission to the bio computer open.

Thankful to be marginalized, the Vardel sat on a large slab of mining spoil and watched the odd ballet going on below.

The mindless Klitt clattered about Ansopha as he baited them for devilment. It was just as well the atmosphere was thin. The resulting din could have loosened a few explosive rocks.

'What is going on?' Hunder demanded.

'I don't think our communicator is taking this contact too seriously,' Orphanus warned him.

'Well tell Ansopha to stop playing with the creatures until we know more about them.'

'As soon as we find out what they are, Ansopha's last inclination will be to play.'

Orphanus was an unlikely person to make a pronouncement on the basis of instinct. It worried Hunder. 'What do you mean?'

'They're all wrong.'

'All wrong?'

'No engineer who created a machine for any sensible function would design something like these, unless those claws-'

There was a sudden fluctuation in the asteroid's energy level. Something was about to explode.

'Get out of there!'

It was too late. Ansopha could no longer blink out of sight. Hemmed in by the Klitt, a column of energy blocked its escape, and then turned into a blazing, vengeful God. Ansopha's missile hadn't dissipated all the entity; some of His atoms had reformed in the vacuum of space and turned into an even meaner God, with just enough over to manifest the Klitt. They had merely been bait.

Ansopha should have tried to run, but the concept was alien to it and arrogance and the prospect of a good argument persuaded the communicator to stand its ground.

'You again? You don't give up, do you?'

'Jump, Ansopha! Jump!' Orphanus ordered.

It was too late.

God was now a tower of energy throbbing with rage. Conversation was not on His mind. 'You have doubted too long.'

'So strike me dead,' Ansopha dared Him.

'No, that would mean nothing to the spawn of the Devil. You have no fear of death because you do not understand what it is to live.'

Ansopha had no idea what God was talking about. 'So teach me.'

Suddenly Hunder understood Ansopha's true nature.

The thought paralysed his ability to calculate.

'Get us out of here!' Orphanus demanded.

Hunder panicked. 'I can't. Something has locked all the satellite's gravlines.'

'Listen Hunder. You must construct another of Ansopha's missiles. We'll keep the creature occupied.'

Hunder's signal was barely audible. 'But I can't.'

'Can't? Of course you can. You have the capacity to replicate any system.'

'I haven't analysed the weapon yet.'

Orphanus didn't believe him. 'Liar! You're programmed to analyse everything. Not unless-' She groaned. 'Oh Hunder, you haven't broken your programming again?'

'Sorry.'

'Why now for pity's sake?' Orphanus's soul sank to her weighted boots. 'You're having another turn, aren't you?'

'Don't worry. I've retrieved the data and am now working on another missile.' Hunder tried to sound confident despite knowing it would never be ready in time.

The claws of the Klitt surrounding Ansopha were raised skyward in a horribly bizarre ballet. The communicator desperately tried to switch its molecules and become invisible, without success. It's sylph like body was now leaden. For the first time in its existence, Ansopha felt blood coursing through veins and a heart pumping like one of the satellite's generators. Painfully aware of every laboured breath, the communicator sank to the mining spoil.

Satisfied, God filtered away into the vacuum of space.

Orphanus broke cover, swearing non-stop Vardel at Hunder.

The Klitt clattered towards Ansopha, jagged claws raised murderously. The engineer pulled out her sidearm and vaporised the creatures.

Ansopha was astounded to find it could no longer contact Hunder telepathically and couldn't even access the thoughts of Orphanus as she gazed down in amazement at the bizarre transformation. The atmosphere was rapidly becoming unbreathable and Ansopha felt as though it was being crushed as something touched every nerve of its new repellent body and made them dance a jig.

And it couldn't make sense of the Orphanus' expression. 'What happened?'

The Vardel hesitated. 'What in damnation's name what have you become, Ansopha?'

***

'It's hyperventilating and the brainwave rhythms are odd, even for Ansopha.' Skirra couldn't make sense of what had happened to the communicator and was sounding overly professional to hide the panic welling up from the pit of his rotund stomach. He didn't even know what environment Ansopha's new body should be in. The increase in atomic density had been so great it could only breathe with the help of a respirator and, to prevent the collapse of the internal organs, Skirra had isolated his patient in a bubble of low atmospheric pressure.

Orphanus always viewed inconvenient medical problems with the intolerance of a true warrior. 'Well, what happened to the infernal creature?'

The experienced medical scientist felt as though he was at last losing his grip. 'You know more about that than I do. I wasn't there.' Then he snapped at Hunder, 'Haven't you come up with that information yet?'

'I'm still trying to make a match. A similar life form must exist somewhere. This God wasn't in any condition to originate one. It could have been worse. He might have turned Ansopha into primeval slime.'

'Being metamorphosed is a horrible way for anyone to die.'

Something occurred to Hunder. 'Of course...'

Skirra wasn't impressed by his bright tone, as it was the bio computer's moodiness that had caused the misfortune. 'Of course what?'

'It's a riddle.'

Orphanus wasn't impressed either. 'A riddle? So you want me to go back and ask for a clue?'

Hunder ignored her. 'It's called "find the alien".'

'Well find one then!' snapped Skirra.

'He thinks I can't do it.'

'That's right! It's all to do with your wretched ego, isn't it! I should go into your circuits with a laser probe and burn out those delusions of mortality.'

'Don't you see? It's a logical problem,' Hunder explained patiently.

'Well that lets you out. Of all the computers in the Galaxy to get lumbered with, we had to have the one incapable of rational thought.'

'Can't you say anything useful? I need constructive input here.'

Orphanus was amused by the exchange. She was just

thankful that the entity hadn't transformed her into some wimpish creature with domestic tendencies. 'Will Ansopha live?'

'If Hunder stops entertaining delusions of super-being for a moment and finds me a match.' His annoyance exhausted, Skirra hovered over his patient. 'When God transformed Ansopha into this, He was making sure he had a slow death.'

Orphanus shook her mountain of tasselled hair. 'No, He said something about teaching Ansopha what it was like to live.'

'Well, if Ansopha does somehow survive, he's certainly going to feel a few bruises from reality's rich spectrum. I'm not so sure I did him a favour by trying to stabilise him.'

'Him? You mean it's a male?'

'Yes, but we won't know what sort of male until Hunder comes up with a match.'

They continued to gaze down at what God had transformed from the silver wisp of a being into a thin corporeal creature barely able to breathe. The communicator's half closed grey eyes above a long thin nose and high cheekbones gave his features a V shaped appearance.

'I wonder why God decided the best way to punish Ansopha was to alter its atomic mass?' mused Skirra.

Orphanus only half took in what he said. 'What?'

'That's it!' exclaimed Hunder.

'What is?'

Hunder had taken everything into account bar the possibility that the match he was looking for originated in a region of space with different atomic pressure. To people there, gravity lines would be nothing more than inexplicable anomalies, but some dabbler in the dead-end of pointless research must have also found a way to decrease a person's atomic mass. Hunder ignored the others to do a quick search of his quantum memory.

He was right! The Leamt dealt with very strange merchandise for even stranger customers. Minerals from these atomically peculiar regions had densities law-abiding planets would go into battle for. As it could turn around a healthy profit, and they had been able to find a gravity line long enough to reach most exotic pockets of the Galaxy, the space merchants had learnt how to increase a person's mass. Only the Leamt knew how to transport these potentially hazardous goods from higher density regions, so Space Command insisted that they had a pacifist clause written into their contracts. Peace reigned and ten ton rubies remained expensive gewgaws.

'Speak to me?' demanded Skirra.

Hunder dismissed the thought of weighty spangles. 'There are creatures with Ansopha's mass. They are cosily tucked away in a gravitational anomaly God must have thought we would never find.'

'Well tell me?' Skirra demanded. 'Our communicator isn't going to last long here - We are talking about our Galaxy, aren't we?'

'So, what are we going to do about it?' Orphanus seemed to be under the impression Ansopha only needed a few laser welds and bolts tightening.

'The Leamt recruited one of these people to become a freelance merchant for them,' explained Hunder.

'Well, contact them.'

'Bear in mind that her species might well turn out to be as self-centred and mean as most others.'

'Don't you criticise us. Just because you have a few bio circuits, it doesn't make you mortal', threatened Skirra. 'If you ever manage it, you'll soon find out what makes us so self-centred and mean.'

'I always thought it was because you clung to your pointless history.'

Orphanus had no intention of bickering with the neurotic computer. 'Do you think this Leamt merchant will respond?'

'Well, the Leamt might be as devout as any of the species on Auroal. They may not feel inclined to help Ansopha.'

Hunder was right. The last thing the intergalactic merchants wanted was to save the heretic who had driven away God, and they refused to acknowledge his call for help.

There was nothing else for it; Hunder would have to start behaving like a computer. He used his despised quantum memory to search for the life form freelancing as a merchant dealer. Hopefully she was earning massive rates of commission and could afford to ignore her Leamt benefactors. Perhaps someone from such an exotic species wouldn't be so fixated about mono deities either.

Ansopha was being visibly crushed by his own weight as Hunder's quantum memory laboriously sifted through interstellar traffic to at last it come up with a match for their freelance space merchant. Against all expectations, the alien responded to the bio computer's signal and agreed to visit the Auroal system. Hunder warned Skirra against asking for bio samples, then lay in a secure gravity line to smuggle the merchant onto the satellite.

She was an inquisitive entity and didn't share the Leamt neuroses about God. It was that irrationality in her own kind, that and watching junk TV and having a morose mate, which persuaded her to leave. Miriam discovered that Ansopha's unholy predicament was far worse than the one she had escaped. Hers had only been marriage.

Though the interstellar merchant had been atomically adjusted by the Leamt, she was nevertheless large and intimidating, even by Vardel standards. The density of her body had given Miriam remarkable strength invaluable to a species who dealt in goods with a high atomic mass. Her impressive presence had helped close many deals, and it was unlikely the Leamt would have questioned why she was there: this merchant was wealthy and could afford to be magnanimous.

Miriam looked down objectivity at Ansopha. 'He could pass as one of my species I suppose. What's his mass?'

'Ten fold and still increasing,' explained Skirra. 'Even if I could keep him alive, he would never be able to move again. You don't know how ..?'

'How the Leamt restructured me? Haven't a clue. As I've no intention of returning home, it never mattered. I've now got a vocation which is a vast improvement on pounding the husks off exotic seeds and juicing revolting substances.'

Skirra floated closer to the visitor, sampler at the ready. 'I don't suppose ..?'

'You want a tissue sample?'

'Skirra!' admonished Hunder.

'Well, if she doesn't know how the Leamt did it, how else can I be expected to keep Ansopha alive?'

Skirra had a point.

Miriam rolled up a richly embroidered sleeve. 'Go ahead. I've got plenty to spare.' While Skirra deftly removed traces of skin and blood she continued to gaze down at Ansopha. 'Without the help of the Leamt, he's only got one chance, you know.'

Skirra resented his medical ability being sidelined. 'What other chance is there? None of us knows how to unscramble his atoms. Not even our bio computer on a good day could tackle that.'

Hunder didn't see why he should be slighted as well. 'Ansopha is going to survive, even if I have to transmit him to another galaxy.'

'How?' snapped Skirra. 'You don't expect the Leamt to tell us, do you? We've already upset them by contacting one of their merchants.'

'She came willingly.'

'That isn't the point.'

Miriam's laugh registered on her translator. 'The Leamt won't bother me. That's not their way. They invited me to become a dealer. They were scanning gravitational anomalies for merchandise and picked up my brainwaves. Evidently I was ideal merchant material for them, when Nature's Herbal Realm wouldn't even let me apply for a job as a rep.'

'Why did you agree?'

'It was a good career move and worth the aggravation of altering my atomic mass. I doubt it's reversible anyway. And whenever the bickering starts, I can always switch off my translator. Could never do that at home or on the shop floor of Nature's Herbal Realm.'

'This planet of yours sounds a strange place?'

'You should try marriage.'

'Is this some form of induction?'

'I suppose it is. I used to feel like punching my vicar on the nose every time he mentioned the sanctity of marriage, especially as mine was to a smelly baboon. If your computer can save your friend, I'm certainly not going to let on.'

Skirra's resentment now mingled with contempt. 'Hunder save him?'

'I may not know how the Leamt engineered my atoms, but I have an address he might find very useful.'

'You have coordinates?'

'To my home planet.'

'It is possible to open a gravity line into a gravitational anomaly.' Hunder then suddenly had a mortal doubt. 'It's risky, though, and Ansopha may not survive being transmitted through it.'

'I did.'

'Ansopha has never been human. I've no idea what I would be sending him into.' Hunder's misgivings multiplied. 'I don't think I should take the risk.'

'We don't have any option,' snapped Skirra. 'You'll do it Hunder, or I will go down to your bio core with a laser probe and puncture your vacuum.'

Miriam admired the medical scientist's negotiation stance. 'I've been away some while now, but the place I had in mind will never have any excitement unless a ferry goes aground.'

CHAPTER 9

Like a fur fabric toy shot from a catapult, Louise sped yapping after a large black backed gull scavenging detritus from the pebbles. The tiny Yorkshire terrier believed that everything odorous and at nose level belonged to her. Embarrassingly, this often included infants' ice creams, tins of anglers' maggots, and anything that squeaked or bounced. The fact that a large carnivorous bird with a beak capable of opening a tin of corned beef had claimed the decomposing fish head was neither here nor there.

Mary chugged breathlessly after Louise before the bird carried the dog off for a light snack. Fortunately Gladys Hodge was on the beach. She scooped up the excited bundle before it scattered the interesting composition of mussel shells she had just discovered.

'Thanks Mrs Hodge,' puffed Mary. 'I'll have to stop feeding her so much protein.'

'Try cutting out the chocolate biscuits. That's probably where she's getting her energy from.'

'It's difficult telling the Moonstar Players not to give them to her. The last thing I need is a set-to with that lot after turning down a plum role.' She clipped a lead onto Louise's collar. The Yorkie promptly tried to go after the gull again, but yo-yoed back.

Gladys took a couple of light readings. 'I only escaped by the skin of my teeth as well. I wish there were some way of letting them know how dreadful they are.'

'If it hasn't occurred to them after having so many audiences walk out, it never will.'

'Tide's coming in. What are you doing this far down the beach?'

Mary took a package from her bag. 'Sandra dropped in those evening primrose capsules last night.'

'You needn't have come all this way.'

'You're out so much I hardly see you at Beachview

before I go, and Mansel has too much on his plate at the moment to remember vitamins.'

'I want to get as much done as I can before the weather turns.' The photographer read the label. 'Do these things really lubricate the system and rub out the symptoms of old age?'

'Our old grandmum swears by them, and she still goes to the gym.'

'It's too late to emulate Nadia Comanec, but anything which helps keep me upright is welcome.'

'You don't have trouble with your inner ear, do you?'

'Nothing so subtle. It's all down to a lifetime of alcohol, caffeine, and nicotine abuse.'

Mary was envious. To look at the photographer, anyone else would have thought had spent a life of abstinence. 'Bet you had an exciting career?'

'So exciting it's killed most of the other photojournalists my age before they could lose their livelihoods to the Internet and mobile phones.' Gladys pushed the package of evening primrose into her satchel and passed Mary some money. 'I don't need any change.'

'Well thanks Mrs Hodge, that's really decent of you.'

'Getting these things at cost saves a fortune. How are the Moonstar troupe doing? Wrecked the saloon yet?'

'They've only reached Marley's ghost. Henny Stenson is kicking up hell because Scrooge won't give him enough time for a costume change.'

'Why don't they ever pick something with the right number of players, like "Who's Afraid of Virginia Wolf"?'

Mary gave her a circumspect glance. 'Would you go and see them in it?'

'No, but they would be obliged to pay for performance rights instead of Henny Stenson plagiarising the work by a safely dead author. They could always write out a couple of the characters to lessen the audience's suffering.'

Mary winked mischievously. 'I just might suggest

that to them if they start trying to cast me again.' The dialogue between Louise and the black backed gull was getting out of hand so she picked the Yorkie up and tucked her inside her coat. 'I've left some fresh towels in the cupboard if you need them. Mansel managed to talk Mrs Lascelle into the laundry room for a couple of hours, though I've a feeling she's not going to make a habit of it.'

'Thanks again, Mary. Could you tell Mansel I'll be in at four-thirty for my cappuccino?'

'Sure.' Mary buttoned the terrier inside her coat and walked briskly back to the hotel.

After a couple more shots in the thinning light, Gladys took the evening primrose capsules out of their box, tried to read the tiny print on the label that came with them, shrugged and replaced them. It was unlikely that the oil from some flower seeds would have much impact on her condition, yet she was willing to try anything. Surviving her colleagues wasn't enough. She still wondered what it would be like to sky dive at ninety - though drew the line at having an organ transplant from a pig. Gladys failed to see why some innocent porcine unable to sign a consent form should be obliged to pay for her well-deserved furred arteries or failing liver.

A chill breeze rolled in from the sea. The photographer closed the reflecting umbrella and returned the camera to its case. She had stood on that spot hundreds of times before and never felt such an urge to shudder. A leaden red glow illuminated the sky as though a lurid hand had patted the surface of the sea, while the moist pebbles glinted maliciously in the fading light. It wasn't a scene pleading to be photographed. There was a sinister pall over Brinton-on-Sea, a small resort so inoffensive that groups like the Moonstar Players were allowed to go on living and tourist guides described it as the perfect haven for eccentric's on the

South Coast.

Distant rocks clunked in the swell. For a brief instant it felt as though a slice had been taken out of reality, leaving it sprinkled with the hundreds-and-thousands of an alien Milky Way.

CHAPTER 10

Deep in meditation, the Lukon high priest slowly walked from his sacred cubicle on Auroal where he had been communing with God. The Almighty now only whispered His thoughts into the minds of the devout. His full glory was reserved for those who needed to be intimidated. Announcing that He was about to hurl a storm of space debris at the satellite that controlled Auroal's life support and engines had to be done diplomatically. Those about to die needed to understand that it was for their own good, especially as it would be left too late for evacuation.

Hunder easily guessed what God was planning. Low on imagination, He was bound to do something that had all the finesse of colliding asteroids. The satellite's comet deflectors were strengthened and pressure to the bulkheads increased. The vacuum containing Hunder's bio core, the mind that could either cause cosmic mayhem or prevent it, depending on which way his temperamental circuits were making contact at the time, was triple buffered. If that was jarred about, the bio computer could either crash, or evolve into an advanced life form. His designer hadn't seen any point in carrying out the experiment.

Orphanus programmed an automatic firing sequence that would be activated by anything animal, mineral or incorporeal trying to sneak up on them. Picking off more obvious threats would be down to her Vardel reflexes.

Skirra preferred the engineer not to have her firing station quite so near the satellite's self-destruct button. The possibility of Hunder ending up at the end of some gravity line in the hands of a primitive planet about to experiment with social engineering would have begged some serious questions from Space Command. Not that anyone would have survived to answer them.

Skirra hovered high in the operations dome where he could radiate disapproval. Taking defensive precautions may have been necessary, but Hunder and Orphanus didn't have to treat the survivors on Auroal afterwards.

'I wish you two weren't enjoying this so much. I hope you realise that Ansopha won't stand a chance if we lose power.'

Hunder and Orphanus ignored Skirra.

All trace of religious enthusiasm in the medical scientist had been replaced by bad tempered resentment. 'The creature isn't rational. Why did He choose here of all places to throw a cosmic tantrum?'

Hunder couldn't stand the hectoring any longer. 'That's what Gods do. Reason doesn't enter into it.'

Skirra gave up and left to check on Ansopha.

Orphanus was lining up the last battery of missiles when she noticed space ripple. The engineer zeroed in on the black void beyond a cluster of asteroids that had been happily orbiting Auroal's sun for aeons. The anomaly was no gravity line blinking.

Hunder immediately suspended all traffic on the assumption that his satellite would still be there to guide it in when the threat had passed.

'Something happening beyond Auroal at twenty polar degrees south', Orphanus announced.

The anomaly increased and the bio computer knew that his worst fears were about to be realised. Orphanus may have been looking forward to the fight, but she didn't need to keep her brain in a buffered vacuum. In fact, the thickness of the skull Nature had given the Vardel was overkill.

The disturbance developed into a space storm. Asteroids, meteors, and ancient junk that had until then happily been avoiding Auroal churned into a calamity of rocks intent on slamming into the satellite.

Orphanus fired burst after burst, picking off debris in the immediate vicinity and launching guided missiles to take out anything else the comet deflectors missed.

The backdrop of space was soon carpeted with a silent tracery of explosions and asteroid dust. The percussive kick back of so many weapons made Hunder's buffers judder.

The bio computer was the only thing keeping Ansopha alive. Skirra's patient already had most of the life crushed from him and was unlikely to survive even a slight rise in pressure.

'You're killing Ansopha! You have to do something now!' the medical scientist demanded

'We're fighting a battle.' This was one of the few times Hunder chose to sound like a computer.

'If you're ignoring Ansopha just to fight God, you're nothing but a theologist!'

Despite the slur, Hunder was not to be swayed so easily and his monstrous neurosis reared its inconvenient head again. 'Are you aware that we are at risk of gyroscopic disorientation, depressurization, and an all systems failure that would deactivate Auroal's central core? And that we are twenty solar hours from the nearest rescue station? The planet would be dead by the time Space Command reached us.'

'Stop being so bloody melodramatic and do something about Ansopha!' snapped Skirra.

'The only thing I can do is put him in a gravity line, transmit him to the co-ordinates the merchant supplied, and hope God isn't that omnipresent - You do know he's unlikely to survive it, don't you?'

'You should hear the wailing on Auroal,' Orphanus cut in as she released her safety harness. Another meteor struck and sent her spinning. The Vardel regained her orientation. 'They're taking too many strikes. If this doesn't stop, the planet's self-repair systems will undergo a catastrophic failure.' The engineer joined the medical scientist. 'All right Skirra. Let's do it. It's the only way we can persuade God to leave us alone. Hunder, program the co-ordinates.'

The bio computer was taken aback at being given orders by the satellite's underling. However, when he went into one of his moods he might as well have taken advice from the results of one of Skirra's medical experiments.

Ansopha was safely pressurised, and his pod jetted down the two hundred levels to the launch bay.

The turbulence increased.

Hunder lay in the gravity line.

As the next meteor struck, Skirra took one last reading of his patient then hurriedly sealed the transmission chamber. 'Odd.'

'What is?' asked Orphanus.

'Ansopha still makes that faint rustling sound.'

Hunder activated the transmitter that dismantled Ansopha atom by atom and reassembled him on the other side of the Galaxy in an unmapped atomic anomaly only known to the Leamt.

Despite being in the throws of a tantrum, Hunder had remembered to install a telepath's transmitter and receiver deep in Ansopha's brain. That way, the bio computer would at least be able to tell whether the communicator survived.

As soon as Ansopha had gone, the asteroid bombardment stopped.

CHAPTER 11

As she changed her camera's lenses, Gladys Hodge watched an imposing woman delicately chipping at some rocks lower down the beach. At any other time she would have been happy to have gone over and made her acquaintance. Not many people were hardy enough to frequent the shore in temperatures almost low enough to freeze seawater. But there was something intimidating about the stranger. She was like no fossil hunter the photographer had ever seen before, dressed in a cream coat with matching trousers and boots too elegant for clambering about quarries. She wore no hat, hair to streaming about her shoulders like disorganized raven's wings. This regal creature should have been in black leather and on the back of a 1200 cc Triumph.

If Gladys had had been a lesbian, she would have gone over and dropped her handkerchief. However, the photographer's days of trying out anything and everything were over. Her brain and body craved peace and quiet after framing too many scenes of mayhem and carnage. Fortunately, a ricked ankle was the worst that could happen to anyone on the pebbles of Brinton-on-Sea.

Gladys finished taking her studies of frost on pebbles. It was too cold to operate the film's rewind button, so she tucked the camera into her large pocket then clambered onto the promenade and back to Beachview, passing Arnold and his dog on the way.

Also impervious to the cold, the old Labrador and its short sighed owner pottered along their usual route, no doubt guided by the call of familiar gulls and horn of an offshore beacon.

Even Arnold could not avoid noticing the tall woman in cream on the beach below.

It wasn't Gladys. She had just passed him and would have needed wings to double back that fast.

'Good morning, Madam.' He doffed his hat to reveal the stubble left by his wife's last haircut. 'I fancy the air is a little sharp this morning.'

The visitor was fazed for a moment, possibly believing she was too inconspicuous to attract attention.

The woman gave an amiable smile as though she had just worked out how to do it. 'Yes, it is.'

'When you start to feel the cold, Mansel Lascelle's tea-room at Beachview is open all day.'

'Thank you, I will bear that in mind.' Her voice was deep and had a peculiar resonance to it, as though it came from a great depth.

'Travelled a long way, have you?'

'Quite a distance.'

'Very quiet in Brinton-on-Sea. Nothing ever happens here. If you like peace and quiet you've come to the right place.' Then the old man's curiosity got the better of him. 'Looking for fossils are you? Used to be thousands of them before we joined the Common Market.'

The woman's expression glazed for a moment. She was no doubt trying to work out why the French would have launched forays across the Channel steal Brinton-on-Sea's fossils. 'Perhaps the seam containing them was eventually eroded out by wave action,' she offered diplomatically.

Arnold nodded sagely as though he really knew that all along. 'Yes, I'm sure that's it. Enjoy your stay.'

Pleasantries over, Arnold replaced his hat and went on his way, dog waddling enthusiastically after him.

The tall woman tucked the small pick into her belt and started out along the beach, examining ice crystals left by the receding swell. She strolled along the sea front of irregular façades and the amusement arcade where one or two teenagers were playing pinball with fingers too cold to outwit the machines, and then past Beachview and round the small headland where many an unwary visitor had been cut off by the incoming tide.

Fortunately the tide had seen this visitor coming and was going out.

The woman waited impatiently for some time as though expecting half a dozen buses to roll up all at once and rubbed her arms as though being cold was a novelty. All Brinton-on-Sea's buses terminated in the High Street, however. The nearest encounter the headland ever had with public transport was over a century ago, when dubious legend claimed that wreckers lured a packet ship aground.

There was a sucking noise as if a part of reality had been swallowed, and then spat out again. It was followed by a tinkling that rippled along the frozen beach; it sounded like a gazelle galloping through thin ice. Then there was silence, apart from the distant waves clacking the pebbles together.

A glistening heap, like a rare mineral, lay at the base of the headland.

***

Still trying to regain the feeling in her fingers, Gladys pressed the rewind button on her SLR before taking another swallow of cappuccino. Mr Butterworth obligingly removed the film for her.

'Thank you, I wish I had the sense to stay inside as well.'

'Surely you must have taken enough pictures to keep you developing and printing for months?'

'Oh yes, but not the image I want.'

Mr Butterworth preened his moustaches. 'I wonder what you find in Brinton-on-Sea that's so interesting? I like the place because it is so dull.'

'Only if you bother with the view. Try looking between the cracks. Everything interesting happens just below the surface, beneath slabs of reality which it would never occur to the Moonstar Players to turn over.'

'The only things of interest I ever found under slabs

were scorpions and land mines.'

'The limpets in Brinton-on-Sea tend not to explode, believe me. You should get out more often.'

'I might try it when it gets a bit warmer.'

'I'll point out some interesting slabs for you to turn over.'

'What exactly is it you are looking for, Mrs Hodge?'

She chuckled. 'I'll know when I see it.'

'I gave up thinking like that fifty years ago.'

'It's what keeps me going. I've exposed enough film to fill several picture agencies, yet still need that face; that image which will say it all.'

'Don't let Henny Stenson hear you talking like that. He might think he's found a kindred spirit.'

Gladys tugged the end of the film to prevent it disappearing into the canister. 'You may well scoff, but we should all nurse aspirations until the day we die.'

Mr Butterworth wiped the beer froth from his moustaches. 'But I do. Mine is to prevent my avaricious offspring from finding out where I am and trying to get power of attorney over me.'

'I've left everything to a hospital in Africa, several Far Eastern co-operatives, and a dog's home.'

'Mine goes to overseas war widows and a no-longer-so-young lady and her daughter in Mansel's home town.'

'So that's how you know him?'

'But it's a secret.' He chuckled darkly, and then hid behind a copy of the Guardian.

Joabim, perched on the boundary beam between the saloon and lounge, gave a sudden squawk as Mrs Lascelle, sour faced, bustled through with two carriers of shopping. It looked as though Mansel had at last put his foot down and demanded she bring back some of the groceries during one of her forays to the delicatessen and off licence. Unfortunately the bags were full of wine, pomme de tartes, liqueurs, and petit fours not seen on the lace tablecloths of Beachview. The customers preferred food they could pronounce. Until they saw Gladys drinking cappuccinos, the morning regulars who had been out to collect the bread and bacon thought that anything with froth on it was either beer, or been boiled too long.

Mrs Lascelle clattered through to the kitchen - she wore so much dress jewellery that she always clattered - and the comfortable ambience returned. Gladys gave a deep sigh of satisfaction that everything was right with the world.

***

The bundle glistening on the beach had been expecting certain death.

Then the leaden cloud that had pinned him down was suddenly lifted. He could breath, move his slender fingers, and feel the peculiar way his features had been reformed. Then there were the soft garments he wore; compared to the weight he had recently endured, they felt like gossamer. He was unaware of clutching a large, clumsy case until he realised that it was heavy and quickly put it down.

The arrival looked about.

This wasn't Auroal. It probably wasn't reality.

He knew what he had to do - he had no idea how - and picked up the suitcase, which he managed to lug towards the ornamental gates of the bland two-storey factory where vacancies for loading bay operatives were being advertised.

CHAPTER 12

'Damage report,' demanded Orphanus.

'Give me time,' protested Hunder.

'Oh come on. Your quantum processor can work faster than this.'

Hunder refused to be provoked. 'I'm more interested in establishing my link with Ansopha than reviewing the destructive ability of some psychopathic entity.'

Skirra stopped analysing the list of injuries on Auroal. 'Don't you think that we've already paid the price for one blasphemer?'

'Will you two stop being so emotional.' To drive his point home, Hunder switched off the monitors, gravity, and lights.

Skirra was niggled. 'I suppose that's one way of dropping out of an argument.' Gravity - or lack of it - meant nothing to someone who could already float. Bumping into the few things even his dark-adapted eyes were unable to make out was annoying, though.

Orphanus switched on her body torch and floated up to the perch in the ceiling that Ansopha had been so fond of, taking advantage of the zero gravity to stretch out in a parody of the communicator's languorous habit. 'Well, I can't organise any repairs until the robots know what has to be welded back into place.'

'We got off lightly. I didn't think that firing Ansopha into infinity would have worked.'

'The entity was only obsessed with our communicator.' Orphanus gazed out of the nearest viewport. 'An all seeing, all malicious God. That creature's got a lot of problems for something supposed to be omnipotent.'

'And He's probably listening.'

'Not that one. He got what He came for.'

Skirra suddenly looked up. 'And if He is eavesdropping, He of course knows what happened to Ansopha.'

Orphanus lowered her voice. 'As He hasn't given us any more aggravation, perhaps our communicator didn't make it.' She hesitated to wonder why Hunder had been quiet for so long. For a system that liked to hear itself talk, this must have been some sort of record.

Skirra floated down to a seat, no longer able to analyse his samples of human without the light of his scanning screen. Orphanus had never known the medical scientist perch on anything before. Having his own buoyancy, he usually just hovered or attached himself to something when he dozed so he didn't drift off, but Skirra had never felt like this before. Despite being constructed of so many disparate parts, he was unused to this sense of ambivalence and was already missing the heretical, enigmatic, biologically impossible communicator. There had been something reassuring about a colleague that could turn itself on and off like a light and better Hunder with corkscrew logic. Ansopha may have been nerve-racking company, yet was stimulating all the same time.

The medic sighed. 'You know, I never did understand how it managed to switch the molecules in its clothes as well.'

'Well, you're a medical scientist, not a physicist.'

Orphanus knew what the medical scientist really wanted to say, but wasn't prepared to admit being that empathic. It would have tarnished her image as a hard-headed Vardel.

'Hunder's worked it out. He won't tell me though.'

A light on Auroal's communication panel flashed. Hunder ignored the signal.

'Shall I tell them to call back?' asked Skirra.

Orphanus floated down from the ceiling. 'No, I'll get it.' The engineer punched open the circuit with unnecessary aggression. 'What is it? Fire, flood, or just a major systems failure?'

The voice replying was formal and hard-edged. 'The First Section Leader of the third latitude wishes to speak to you.'

'She'll need a communicator. Sorry we can't supply one. We just fired ours into a gravitational anomaly to save your miserable lives.'

Skirra darted over before the engineer destroyed the last vestige of goodwill left between the planet and satellite controlling it. 'Out of the way Orphanus!' In zero gravity he was the stronger and bounced her aside. 'This is medical scientist Skirra. Hunder's circuits are now totally committed to dealing with the damage to Auroal and this satellite. As much as we would like to speak to The First Section leader, we cannot oblige without a translator.'

The discussion at the other end sounded more like a brief skirmish than consultation. Suddenly the First Section leader appeared on the screen. Without warning, Hunder patched in his own translator so Skirra could understand her.

'This cannot wait. Our priests are demanding to know what happened to the heretic?'

Skirra silently swore at the bio computer, and then announced, 'Ansopha was transmitted through a gravity line to an anomaly on the other side of the Galaxy. It is unlikely it survived.'

'On what trajectory?' There was no sense of remorse in the voice. Hunder's translator, for all his aspirations to mortality, had never been user friendly.

'I do not know.'

This was too much for Orphanus. She regained her balance and elbowed Skirra aside. 'What do you want us to do? Send a missile after him to make sure?'

By the ensuing silence she hadn't been far wrong.

'Well it won't work, whatever happened to him – it!

No weapon would remain viable after being transmitted that distance. It's even more unlikely flesh and blood could reassemble itself. So leave us alone damn you!' She cut off the communication with a blow of her fist, rage saying much more about the loss of Ansopha than words.

'So much for diplomacy.' Skirra had an edge in his voice that could have amputated a limb. He glared at one of Hunder's monitors. 'What a relief our bio computer wasn't listening.'

Hunder switched the monitor on. 'If I'd said anything it would have caused a diplomatic crisis. Nobody is going to pay any attention to you two.'

'What about Ansopha?' demanded Orphanus.

'I can't say.'

'You're a bloody bio computer! Of course you can say!'

Hunder ignored her. 'I have now assessed the damage.'

He restored gravity and brought up the lights. Orphanus landed on her console in an untidy heap as a string of locations needing repair appeared on its screen.

'What about Ansopha?' insisted Skirra.

Hunder ignored his demand as well and told him, 'I have also been picking up energy fluctuations in our satellite's vicinity.'

The medical scientist was still too annoyed to take the point. 'So? What's that got to do with Ansopha?'

Orphanus knew. 'Shut-up Skirra.'

'Why?'

'Because I might have to lance that rotund belly of yours with a laser skewer.'

He suddenly realised. 'Oh - energy fluctuations, I see.'

God filtered away from the satellite. So the communicator might have survived after all. Even if it meant going to the end of time, Ansopha was one heretic who was not going to escape judgement.

CHAPTER 13

Beachview's new arrival wore a voluminous beige greatcoat from which he seemed on the verge of emerging like an emaciated butterfly, and clutched a heavy suitcase as though unsure what to do with it. Despite an elegance of movement, his fingers tended to fumble most things he touched. Though no smile crossed his pointed face, Gladys sensed wary warmth deep beneath the defensive layers. She had seen similar expressions in post war populations coming out of trauma, a desperation to believe that the worst was over whilst knowing that a sniper was still on the roof. And that face! Here was the image the veteran photojournalist had been looking for all her career. She gave a sly glance at Mr Butterworth to make sure he hadn't read the enthusiasm in her expression. This stranger's features weren't blasted or ravaged by experience; they were the enigmatic mask of someone who had paddled across the River Styx to treat the Hounds of Hell for distemper. As he moved there was faint rustling, like the breeze through pine needles. No angel, this. He was the elf who guarded Loki's hearth.

Mansel would have greeted his new waiter and barman with a hug, and then decided he looked a little too frail to withstand such Gallic bonhomie. It was unlikely he would be able to carry full crates up from the cellar, or even more than one tray at a time. That wasn't the point. His new employee's elfin features had filled his mother with dread. All she would utter when first setting eyes on him was, 'Le Diable!' before rushing for the sanctuary of her basement flat in a clatter of costume jewellery.

'Mrs Hodge, Mr Butterworth, this is Amiel - Amiel Sopher!'

Gladys thought that the name had a French colonial exoticism to it, although the new waiter was too pale to have been any further south than Bournemouth. 'Good morning Amiel.'

As that had only been his name for a brief time, the waiter was momentarily fazed. Something at the back of his mind delivered a sharp jab and injected the correct response. 'Good morning Mrs Hodge. I hope you will find my service...' He foundered. Whatever was lurking in the back of his mind, it didn't include a thesaurus.

'I'm sure we'll get along fine - Can you make a decent cappuccino?'

'Say yes,' the thing in his mind instructed. 'I'll show you how to later.'

'Yes,' said Amiel.

Gladys was happy enough with that. It was too much to expect him to have poured coffee in some North African souk as well.

'Good man,' Mr Butterworth added. He was more used to dealing with subalterns straight from school.

Mansel picked up Amiel's suitcase as though it was filled with nothing heavier than tissue paper, and whisked his precious find upstairs before he emerged from the cocoon of his greatcoat and fluttered off to more promising pastures. The proprietor had no idea what good fortune had brought Amiel to Brinton-on-Sea, and had no intention letting him find out his mistake.

When Mansel returned from installing Amiel Sopher in the garret suite, he was still beaming.

Gladys could contain herself no longer and was already loading her camera. 'Where did you find him?'

Mansel gave an expansive wave of his arms. 'My little Mary. He asked at her cousin's factory for some work. Sandra thought he looked not strong enough for the loading crates or processing seaweed, so she called Mary who called me.'

Mr Butterworth was a little more suspicious. 'Where did he come from?'

'I will find out when I get his P45.'

'Looks a rum character to me.'

That coming from a retired colonel who had also seen the weirdest the world could offer made Gladys think a little harder about her prospective find. At least Amiel had passed the first test. When a beautiful or interesting looking person opened their mouth, high-pitched gibberish frequently came out. The new waiter had merely been lost for words. At least he knew how to pronounce the ones he could remember. And if the new barman did possess a large intellect, what was he doing at Beachview? Giving his brain a rest? But then, Gladys was only after a picture, not a soul mate. No one had ever passed that test.

As it was the Moonstar Players rehearsal evening Mansel decided not to expose his new find to that baptism of fire so soon. Instead, he sat Amiel in a private cubicle where he could watch the machinations of local culture from a safe distance with a pot of tea.

While Henny Stenson boomed out the part of Christmas past, Joabim fluttered over to join the new waiter. Despite the din of amateur dramatics in full flow, Gladys could have sworn that the bird and bird-like man became immersed in conversation. Joabim seldom joined anyone unless they had peanuts or biscuits to share, and the possibility of the cockatoo being empathic to anyone not rustling a packet of some sort was strangely chilling.

Mr Butterworth interrupted her reverie. 'Well, Mrs Hodge, is this the folder you promised to show me?'

Fazed, the photographer gazed down at the opened flaps dangerously near a jug of milk. Of course it was. Still taking the surreptitious glance at the image of a lifetime, she pulled out a handful of her work.

'He's probably married with ten children,' the retired colonel noted discreetly.

Gladys was crestfallen that she had allowed her enthusiasm to become so apparent. 'No, he fell out of a nest in the Amazonian rain forest,' she said, though the photographer knew more about things that had fallen out of helicopters. She whispered conspiratorially to her companion. 'What do you really make of him?'

Mr Butterworth shrugged. 'Never seen that cockatoo so sociable with anyone. But you're probably right. He does look as though he should have feathers.'

'I reckon they were singed off when he hedgehopped over Hell.'

'My dear Mrs Hodge, what has brought on this Byronic flush?'

She chuckled to herself. 'Perhaps I'm becoming sexually aroused.'

Mr Butterworth spluttered so loudly with laughter that he had to push the photos aside for fear of spraying them with whisky. Even the Moonstar Players looked round to see who was upstaging them.

Recovering his decorum, he whispered, 'I think you should snatch a snap of him before he realises you are a photographer.'

'Why?'

'He's not the sort who'll willingly pose, even for art's sake.'

Gladys felt deflated. Mr Butterworth was probably right. 'How can you tell?'

'He has a history. Can't say what sort, but you take my word for it. Old Mrs Lascelle knew as soon as she set eyes on him. She's a cantankerous old woman and probably has enough things to hide to recognise a kindred soul. Best you keep your camera well hidden if you want to get into his trench.'

Gladys smiled and raised an eyebrow at the insinuation. He was right. But, what the hell, she had a zoom lens.

CHAPTER 14

And God revealed to true believers
the sign of the Holy Spectrum.

The Lukon priest watched the recordings of God's arrival apprehensively and eased back from the monitor. He turned to the Supreme Apostle of the First Coming.

'The Bonarian envoy was right. There was another presence in the shadow of God. It was also detected near His energy field when He first came to Auroal.'

The Supreme Apostle rose from his throne to place a tentative tentacle on the rerun button. The holy Lukons noted the unauthorised blip of energy making a faint dent in the corona of God's Majesty.

'It couldn't have been the heretic, holiness. That was on the satellite at the time.'

'An anomaly generated by His corona perhaps?'

The priest wouldn't have had the temerity to suggest that God would create an anomaly Himself. 'Only the primary computer has the capacity to answer this.'

'Hunder is annoyed at losing his communicator. He refused to respond to the First Section Leader of the third latitude. You could try again, though be prepared to have your fins scorched by an enraged Vardel.'

The priest brought up a spectrograph of the energy flux on his monitor before tentatively asking, 'Should the Almighty be told of this?'

The Supreme Apostle was confident in God's infallibility. 'The Almighty is omnipresent. He must already know of it.' Though subconsciously he needed to be reassured and scrutinised the monitor. 'The anomaly might have been a pocket of dense hydrogen thrown out from a gravity line. There is no limit to the rubble some ships bring through with them.'

'Of course, holiness. I never thought about that,' lied the priest.

The doubting subconscious of the Supreme Apostle of

the First Coming was right. God hadn't noticed the blip of energy that had momentarily tagged itself to His almighty being. He was too busy juggling chaos. The entity seldom lingered so long in one place. Having been invited to a solar system by mortal adulation, it was His habit to promptly drain their sun and go on to next one. In the absence of a resident god, the cosmic parasite was only too happy to fulfil the bizarre desire of mortals for an all powerful maker. Few survived it.

God had, until then, kept to the remoter parts of the Galaxy where Space Command held no sway. It was only because His Almighty Being was becoming ancient and unstable, needing more and more energy to keep Him viable, that He dared venture into their territory.

***

Despite its bold title, Space Command had been created by a hotchpotch of civilisations who had decided to pool their resources. Entities who had evolved beyond technology, watched the machinations of this corporeal coalition with knowing non-interference. They had all been there at some time. The feeling of being threatened was part of evolution after all. First came fire making, and then killing your neighbour because they wouldn't agree with you; later destroying your planet because it was too inconvenient to save and easier to annex other worlds. Eventually came an eternity regretting your mortality, only to find out that it had been an illusion anyway.

Space Command was frequently no more effective than the Medusa's antidandruff shampoo on a bad hair day. Sending them into action was usually a precaution, like reinforcing the urn on the mantelpiece to stop the ghost of a troublesome relative from walking. Fortunately, the worlds of Space Command seldom squabbled amongst themselves and were careful not to tip over the ashes of any troublesome relatives.

God wasn't bothered about Space Command's awesome strike capability. His obsession was with the mercurial communicator who had wreaked such havoc with His sang-froid. Now He had a heretical bio computer to deal with.

God could infiltrate the mortal mind, but Hunder was no ordinary bio machine. He was the astounding intellect controlling space thoroughfares at the centre of a feat of cosmic engineering that offended His mighty Being. God did not comprehend why His devoted worshippers were driven to reach through space time to other parts of the Galaxy, or why they needed such a devious brain to orchestrate the complex gravity lines. God may have been vengeful and all powerful, but He wasn't very bright.

CHAPTER 15

Amiel Sopher woke with a start to find he was in the alien surroundings of Beachview's garret bedroom. In the distance there was the dismal lowing of a foghorn and nearby the lap of waves against the headland's defences.

What had happened to him!

Amiel panicked and fumbled for the switch of the bedside lamp. It was three o'clock on an Earth morning.

Then it all flooded back. He was this bizarre thing called a waiter who was paid to bring food and hot fluids to people who were quite capable of collecting their own nourishment. Amiel also recalled a crotchety bird, and an old woman wearing so much jewellery she could have easily beaten him to death with it, who thought he was the Devil.

Also, there was something in his head preparing him for things that weren't going to happen for several minutes. That could have only been down to the flux in the gravity line.

Amiel Sopher had just experienced his first ever dream. He was being sat upon by a pulsar. It was probably just as well he woke up.

Now, who was he again? A waiter at Beachview. In a seaside hotel. In a small settlement. On a small planet. In a gravitational anomaly. On the other side of the Galaxy. His employer's name was Mansel Lascelle.

He didn't need to be in the kitchen until eight, so why had he woken up when the small hand on the dial of the bedside timepiece was pointing to three? He wondered if other humans had this problem with time, then heard what had roused him.

'Are you all right?' whispered a familiar voice inside his mind.

'Hunder, Do you know what time it is?'

'Of course not. Only Skirra could make sense of your

bio rhythms.'

'I was asleep.'

'Sorry. I had to check on you.'

'Why?'

'I can't work out why you're still alive. My calculations say that you should blink out of existence at any moment. Haven't got any holes showing, have you?'

'Don't work too hard at reassuring me, will you? For all your aspirations to mortality, you'll always be a bloody computer.'

'And my logic circuits say that, even though you survived being transmitted here, the shock of the landing should have killed you. How is your mass transference holding up?' There was genuine curiosity in the bio computer's telepathic tone.

Now totally unsettled, Amiel got out of bed and pulled on a dressing gown. 'How should I know? I'm a bloody human. Their backbones never evolved monitoring systems.' He hesitated. 'Why did God turn me into a human?'

'Probably to ensure you would survive just long enough to suffer mortality.'

'If this is suffering, I could learn to live with it, as long as those lunatics monopolising the saloon stop trying to cast me as Tiny Tim.'

'Tiny Tim?'

'Forget it.'

Hunder paused. 'A vacuum has opened up in the existence of Orphanus and Skirra since you went.'

Amiel didn't believe the bio computer. Orphanus had probably moved into his quarters so she could have a clear view of the weapons battery, and Skirra sequencing the DNA of his sample cells to add "transgenic" to his vast gene store. At least their company was keeping Hunder sane. When a bio computer of his capacity ran out of people to talk to, there was a danger imagination could kick in. Then

Space Command really would have a problem.

Why should Amiel worry about that? He was on the other side of the Galaxy with no hope of returning. He must have had the bio computer to thank for that.

'Tell me, Hunder, how did you manage to send through the winter clothes and full suitcase?'

Hunder was mysteriously silent for some while. 'Clothes? I never sent you any clothes.'

Amiel experienced his first, fearful shudder. 'What about the language and logic map of this place?'

'I barely managed to establish this link with your telepathic implant. How could I have managed all that?'

At three on a foggy morning, about to do some bizarre job he never knew existed was not the best time to face those implications. Hunder was the only bio computer powerful enough to manipulate gravity lines, but something else had been keeping Amiel company. Faintly, just above the dull drone of the distant foghorn and odd rustle of his own movements, he could now feel the other intruder inside his head. It was curled up like an obliging maggot, waiting for the next time he was unable to distinguish a fish knife from a cake slice, or warn him when the small animal Mary kept hidden in her jacket was about to explode into a yapping fit as soon as it saw him.

Amiel wasn't the only alien in Brinton-on-Sea. He shivered and fastened his dressing gown. 'I need something warm to drink. This body's temperature regulation is very inefficient. And Hunder...'

'Yes?'

'Read my thoughts to find out what I'm doing before you butt in. One or two people here already think I'm odd.'

'Just as well they'll never find out how much.'

'The female human below this room is looking for an opportunity to photograph me.'

'Photograph you?'

'Transfer my image onto an emulsion then print it onto silver bromide paper.'

'Oh don't worry about that. It's not as if you can still polarise your molecules - Is it?'

Amiel wasn't sure. They felt stable enough, and he now needed to eat. Even if his atoms were having trouble working out where they were, it was unlikely anyone else would notice.

'Let me know if there's any change,' Hunder told him.

'All right.'

'Where are you going?'

'There are things most mortal bodies need to do - or did you forget to supply your own interactive hologram with a digestive tract?'

Hunder resented being given advice about his precious concept of mortality. Amiel was right, though: the idea of his mortal form having to eat, drink, and defecate was disconcerting to a massive intellect like Hunder's. It had to be more refined before he was prepared to live in it.

'You do know how to urinate in that body then?' the bio computer sniped.

'Go away.'

Hoping a small change in location would lose Hunder, Amiel silently descended the stairs, half expecting a zoom lens to appear round Gladys Hodge's door at any second.

Reaching the ground floor without his image being committed to negative film, Amiel went through the restaurant lounge to the kitchen. He boiled a kettle and made some tea (something that the voice in his head, totally unbidden, had shown him how to do) then took it into the stale warmth of the saloon.

Joabim was in his large cage preening himself. 'Well what about a cup for me as well?'

'I filled your dish last night,' Amiel thought back at the bird. 'After drinking so much light ale, you should be under your perch.' Amiel took a handful of unsalted cashew nuts from a dish on the counter and put them in the feeder. 'Here, have these instead.'

'I want some tea.'

Amiel gave up. He poured some into his saucer, placed it on the bar counter and opened the cage door.

Joabim bounced out and swigged it back.

The new waiter watched objectively. 'I hope all this planet's wildlife isn't as awkward as you?'

'Met Mansel's mother?'

'Briefly. She believes I'm the Devil.'

'What? You? Never. The Devil's ten inches taller and makes dents in the settee.'

A cold, clammy shudder made Amiel put his tea on the counter before he spilt it. 'What are you talking about?'

'Came in last night. You were too busy to notice.'

'If you knew the experiences I've been through recently, you wouldn't make jokes like that.'

'No joke, believe me. The Devil has come to Brinton-on-Sea.'

***

An image started to appear in the developer. Not sure what she was looking at in the infrared light, Gladys fumbled for her glasses. The picture in the bromide looked wrong. She worried the print about the tray for a few more seconds. The background darkened. Despite that, patches of light still shone through Amiel Sopher as though he were a lace doily: other parts of the waiter were just reluctant to come into focus. Had she attempted to simulate the effect deliberately, it would have taken a digital camera and PhotoShop.

After years of being crammed into suitcases, suspended from ledges overlooking certain death and trailed out of helicopters, perhaps her faithful old SLR had at last decided to throw a wobbly. But why now,

when she had only pointed it at some inoffensive elfin
waiter? That was it! Perhaps he was a fairy.

Gladys told herself not to be so senile and checked
the negative against the contact print. It must have
been a freak reflection from somewhere even though
there had been a polarizing filter on the zoom: shooting
through glass at an oblique angle had been the only way
to photograph Amiel without him knowing.

It was no good. He would have to be lured outside
into daylight.

When Gladys went downstairs Mansel and Joabim
were in the saloon wrestling with a box full of ancient
tinsel and gewgaws for the Christmas tree, so Amiel
brought for morning cappuccino to her table in the
restaurant lounge.

Behind her smile, Gladys calculated the possibilities
of employing a concealed camera. She had done it plenty
of times in more dangerous situations; here it felt as
though it would be a betrayal of trust.

The closer that barely discernible rustling came as
Amiel cleared the tables, the more the photographer felt
driven to capture his mysterious aura. She had the
uncomfortable feeling that he knew what she was
thinking so reluctantly pulled out the instamatic
concealed in her jacket pocket and placed it on the table
where he could see it. How far away would she have to
be before he was unable to read her thoughts?

Mr Butterworth came down to find his regular table
taken by two Christmas shoppers and their mountain of
purchases, so he joined Gladys.

As Amiel disappeared into the kitchen, Mr
Butterworth leaned across and confided to her, 'The
damnedest thing happened yesterday afternoon.'

'What was that?'

'You know I usually have a beer and sandwich at
teatime.'

'Yes?'

'For a change I thought I would try a pot of Lapsang and cheese flan.'

Gladys nodded knowingly. 'And Amiel brought them before you could order?'

'How did you know?'

She leaned over so their noses nearly touched. 'He reads minds.'

'Never!'

'Mrs Lascelle has given orders he should not pass the threshold of the basement flat and pinned garlic to the lintel of the door. And, hadn't you noticed?'

'Noticed what?'

'He always goes out through the front, never past the basement window, even when Mary is with him.'

Mr Butterworth chortled. 'Well I never.' To him, there was a rational explanation for everything. 'Think he might have been in a stage act before he came here?'

'Given the way he avoids the Moonstar Players?'

'They did want him to play Tiny Tim.' Mr Butterworth cast Amiel a sly glance as he came back into the lounge. 'Though he could probably get away with it. There's hardly anything of him under that apron and the fancy braces. He couldn't keep his trousers up without them.'

There was a tirade of bad-tempered French from the saloon as Joabim decided to play bombers with the baubles.

'Amiel! Amiel!' called Mansel. 'Will you put this bird in its cage!'

Amiel put the tea towel he carried over a narrow shoulder and went into the saloon. Gladys and Mr Butterworth watched as Joabim immediately alighted on his raised hand and allowed himself to be confined to his cage without so much as a rebellious squawk.

After sharing knowing glances, Gladys returned to her cappuccino and Mr Butterworth to his Guardian.

'Think "cappuccino",' urged the photographer without

looking up.

This he duly did. Minutes later he was presented with a head of froth which put his afternoon beer in the shade. Mr Butterworth sat looking at it for some while.

'Is everything all right, Sir?' asked Amiel.

The military man was flustered. 'Superb – quite superb!'

Gladys nearly asked how much more the waiter earned for being a telepath, and then thought better of it.

Mary bustled in from the kitchen with Amiel's coat, a couple of shopping bags and basket trolley.

'All right if we do the shopping now, Mr Lascelle?' she called.

'Fine,' he called back. 'Remember Mrs Lascelle's liqueurs, won't you.'

'She gave me her list.' Mary lifted Louise from the trolley and tucked the Yorkie inside her jacket.

As Amiel put on his coat, Gladys had to sit so hard on the thoughts going through her mind she could feel her piles.

As soon as they were out of the door she gulped down her cappuccino, and then dashed up to her room to collect her old SLR and a telescopic lens.

CHAPTER 16

A dozen deadly crescents swept across the sky. As they turned, the rays of Auroal's sun glinted on the full splendour of Space Command's battle fleet.

This strike force had never been used in anger because it wasn't programmed to back down. Once dispatched, only an executive decision made light years away could abort its attack. These machines were too costly to have a self-destruct capacity so, if anything went wrong, it would have been more economic to replace the unfortunate solar system.

Responsible for requesting that this terrible power be unleashed, Hunder went into a spasm of self-doubt. Perhaps he should have told Skirra and Orphanus before doing it? The medical scientist would have probably lanced his organic circuits with a laser probe and the engineer taken off to join the strike force.

What else could the bio computer do, though? Most mortals would have been paranoid about blasting God out of existence. Hunder should have paid attention to the logic of his quantum system, accepted that he was more machine than mortal, and seen the wider picture long ago.

If he survived, Hunder was determined to keep working on his interactive hologram so one day he could take off into the tinsel Universe and not have to face these bizarre problems any more.

That was it! The bio computer should have really been sailing the stars, exploring new systems, and going where no rationally programmed computer had ever gone before. The irrational thought eased the tension of the immediate crisis and Hunder drifted off into a soothing reverie.

Orphanus and Skirra worked in silence while

Hunder remained uncommunicative. It was either that or talk to the satellite robots or, even worse, each other. Neither of them would admit to how much they missed the infuriating Ansopha: at least the creature had given them a target for their disapproval. Now that the communicator's atoms were scattered at the end of a gravity line in an atomic anomaly on the other side of the Galaxy, they also felt guilty. They weren't quite sure why.

The satellite was virtually repaired by the time it occurred to Orphanus that Hunder was up to something. She went to the station's hub and burst into Hunder's bio system control.

'Alright!' she blasted at the nearest monitor. 'I don't care if you are working on the meaning of the Universe, why have you tampered with the shielding?'

Hunder initially pretended to be in reconfiguration mode, despite the welding torch the engineer was brandishing, looking as though she could significantly reprogram his circuits. 'It was necessary to double their pressure.'

'Why?'

'They're taking power from the main governor. If the gyroscope slows any more, the satellite will start reeling about like a drunken buthmoth. Skirra already floats most of the time and lack of gravity might make you sweeter natured.'

Orphanus aimed the welder threateningly at the nearest bank of exposed bio circuits. 'What are you up to?'

'Have you ever trusted anyone in your life?'

'No. It's against Vardel ethics.'

'Well you'll have to get used to the novelty.' Hunder shut off the monitor and attempted to return to his reverie.

Orphanus ground her sharp teeth and spat a few threats. It was no good. The satellite's rotation continued to slow. When it began to lose gravity she made for the nearest back jet. Being stranded in the huge chamber housing Hunder's buffers, only to be rescued by the medical scientist would have been too much for Vardel dignity to cope with.

Orphanus was about to return to return to supervising the maintenance robots when an energy counter caught her attention. Its readings were off the scale.

There was no point in hitting the nearest panic button; the core had been totally sound when she had left it minutes before, and Hunder wasn't allowing Skirra enough power to run major experiments. Then Orphanus realised that the energy surge was created by something outside the satellite.

She immediately went to the nearest control port and accessed the weapons station, arming every missile.

The medical scientist, blissfully unaware of what was happening, looked up from the DNA he was mapping and glanced out of a viewport. He dropped the sample he had spent the last three hours working on and it gently tumbled off across the lab.

There, silhouetted against the glare of an active gravity line, Space Command's sinister cosmic deterrent was powering up for battle.

CHAPTER 17

The first performance of The Christmas Carol was fast approaching, yet there was still enough time for the full quota of temperamental tantrums before the Moonstar Players presented their next excruciating offering to the public though, on some subconscious level, they realised that they had providence to thank for unsuspecting seasonal holidaymakers. At Christmas they were usually too full of goodwill and spirits to care that much, and put their productions down to some local, quaint, masochistic ritual.

The first Brinton-on-Sea Seasonal ritual was the bazaar in the community hall.

The Victorian building was the most used and abused in the seaside town. Attempts to demolish or modernise it had always provoked petitions. Even efforts to net the skylights against pigeons had raised ugly murmurs from a primary class studying their nesting habits. The toddlers were persuaded to study herring gulls instead - from a safe distance. The sponge cakes and dainty sandwiches of the hall's clientele now no longer ran the risk of being contaminated by everything a pigeon had ever managed to get its beak into.

So, much to the chagrin of the local authority, and some who preferred the Moonstar Players to pay the realistic hire price for a modern venue to commit their performances in, the battered old community hall remained. At least its foundations were deep enough to withstand flooding from the promised sea surges and its acoustics didn't make amateur productions sound any worse than they actually were.

Beneath its skylights scoured clean of lime stains, people bustled about trestle tables laden with homemade goodies and oddments gleaned from the last effort to tidy the drawer. There was even something huge, ceramic and menacing from the house clearance of someone's ancient deceased relative. No one in the vast family had ever known its true purpose, so they tied a label confidently declaring "conversation piece" to one of its handles.

The Moonstar Players had a modest display of lavender bags sewn by Mavis Brink, jam made by Gerald, and covered coat hangers dotted with sequins designed by Loralie Stenson. Their table was somewhat out-gunned by the Townswomen Guild's sugarcraft village, and designer mirrors by a local craftsman. However, the star exhibit at every the seasonal bazaar was always the table groaning with products from Nature's Herbal Realm. The factory had started out as an iodine processing plant then went on to break into the market for vitamins, herbal cures, and cosmetics, becoming a cottage industry on an industrial scale.

Gladys Hodge relished bazaars, especially ones full of garish, useless junk and anything else that glittered. Her lens loved the haphazard way goods were displayed on trestle tables in jumbles of bad taste. Occasionally she discovered interesting items for her still lifes. Many a picture for up market women's magazines had featured a star model surrounded by super clutter gleaned from places like Brinton-on-Sea's community hall. It was her way of cocking a snook at a world that had a diminishing need for the photojournalist and more for the camcorder and sound bite. How she yearned to once again focus her lens on those experience worn faces in the throws of jubilation and drama instead of plastic fruit, plastic furniture and plastic people. Unfortunately age overtakes all aspirations that require a steady hand and sound knees.

Gladys shuddered. It felt as though someone had just read her mind.

And there she was. The woman she had seen on the beach that morning. She was looking straight at the photographer despite the fact that, next to her, Oliver was performing some rigorous anecdote which Loralie and Mavis were finding hilarious. Behind the coal dark eyes, the woman's expression was difficult to read as Gladys felt her trying to see into a soul she was no longer sure she had. The photographer was not easily intimidated; intuition told her that, whatever abyss lay beyond that enigmatic gaze, a safety line was attached.

The woman was at least six feet tall and statuesquely filled every inch of her cream coat, still remarkably free of green stains despite her fossil hunting on a shore covered with enough seaweed to supply Nature's Herbal Realm for weeks.

Unable to resist a challenge, Gladys manoeuvred through the milling crowd to Oliver's group.

As the thespian finished his story he flourished effete hands at her approach. 'Mrs Hodge, so pleased you could come! You must meet Lucinfer - Lucinfer Brimstone, our latest find!'

Gladys opened her mouth, looked up at the imposing woman, and then closed it. Trust the Moonstar Players to find someone called Lucinfer Brimstone. She had to be pulling their legs, yet the woman's expression betrayed nothing more than the patience of an interested observer at an unfortunate accident.

Oliver ploughed on regardless. 'Lucinfer is not only going to be our narrator, but play the part of Christmas future as well.'

This begged many questions. Some about the gender of the role, most of them logistical.

Gladys asked instead. 'So pleased to meet you. Have you been here long?'

'A couple of weeks.'

Yes, with a voice like that she would not only make an excellent narrator, but a superb Death as well. If this wasn't some mischievous con on her part, how had the Moonstar Players managed to inveigle this extraordinary stage presence into their clutches? Lesser mortals with arthritic knees, like Gladys Hodge, were prepared to sprint a four minute mile to avoid them.

'You must be a professional?' The photographer didn't dare hazard a guess at a professional what, for fear of getting it wrong. How could this woman have been performing on the stage for the last thirty years without her journalistic instincts picking up on it?

Even the leading light, Loralie, wouldn't have dared upstage their new find. 'Lucinfer is very experienced, but decided to leave the English stage some while ago. She's toured, you know, all over the Far East and India.'

Gladys was relieved that not even the Moonstar Players would have dared to call her Lucy.

'I knew you would find the right person in the end.' The photographer wondered whether to back away a few paces and reel off some snaps before the subject had time to complain. 'Where are you staying, Miss Brimstone?'

'I have a chalet on the headland.'

'Bit chilly up there?'

'I find the clean air bracing.'

Gladys saw no point in contradicting her if the bitterly cold air didn't mind being pumped through those splendid lungs.

At this point the encounter became embarrassingly awkward. The Moonstar Players' fund of conversation to impress was about to peter out. Gladys sensed an unvoiced plea that she take Lucinfer off their hands before the smallness of their world became apparent in all its pathetic inadequacy.

Suddenly the amateur actors found other things to distract them. They bustled about, leaving the photographer to deal with this imposing tower of middle-aged womanhood.

'Fancy a cup of tea?' Gladys suggested, half expecting to be crushed by a quizzically lowered eyebrow.

To her surprise, Lucinfer inclined her head slightly

as though consulting some higher intelligence. 'Why not?'

The anteroom with the tea urn and stacking chairs was almost empty. Most of the visitors had eaten their fill of fairy cakes and drunk more than their bladders could contain, so they sat in the furthest corner with a few biscuits and murky instant coffee each.

Without warning Lucinfer announced, 'You are a photographer.'

Gladys wasn't sure whether it was an accusation or observation. 'I still do as much as I can. Odd magazine job here and exhibition there. I come to Brinton-on-Sea for a few months every year to get things in perspective. Place isn't quite like any other. It's as though some huge brothel creeper stamped "stay like this" on it somewhere in the Fifties before punks could get their noses above the parapet. People here only get excited about bus shelters being painted a different colour and the price of a perm going up. Nothing else exists. Even the kids come into the world with "Brinton-on-Sea" written all the way through them.' Gladys was suddenly aware that she was waffling. 'Because things here have been left alone, there are some surprising picture opportunities.'

'You collect faces.' There was still no expression in the powerful features to cue which way she should jump.

Gladys was getting too old for enigmatic conversation. 'How did you know? Have you seen my work?'

'I know of it through collectors.'

She was on the verge of asking if Lucinfer collected souls, when she noticed a humorous flicker in the dark eyes. 'I suppose Henny and Loralie have mentioned something about me.'

'Nothing detrimental.' Lucinfer's tone made it clear that gossip was beneath her.

Gladys put her cup on the table and took a deep breath. 'How the hell did you manage to get involved with those dingbats?'

'They amuse me.'

'Mansel's cockatoo amuses me, but I wouldn't get in the cage with it.'

Lucinfer Brimstone took a considered sip of her coffee, then announced. 'You are an interesting person, Mrs Hodge. Perhaps we could meet for a less corrosive coffee at a quieter venue?'

There was nothing the photographer could say to that except, 'Why not. When the weather's bad I'm always at Beachview. You are welcome to pop in any time you like.'

Perhaps life in Brinton-on-Sea wasn't so predictable after all.

CHAPTER 18

The spectre of God's enemies blotted out
The sun and prepared for battle.

As Space Command's deadly crescents deployed around Auroal's sun the planet's devout rushed to the highest structures to pray, while an increasing number of waverers dashed down to the comet proof shelters, well aware that those battle machines didn't carry mortal pilots their priests could convert to the word of God and even the mighty Hunder hadn't the power to countermand their programming.

Skirra was just relieved that Auroal's population didn't know about the bio computer's dangerously introspective lapses. 'Thanks for warning us that you arranged to have the solar system wiped out, Hunder. I don't know how we'd cope without your massive intellect.'

Hunder hadn't been expecting much empathy from either of the satellite's remaining crew. 'It was necessary. This entity must be eliminated before it destroys any more civilisations.' Then undermined his high moral stance by adding, 'The decision was Space Command's anyway.'

Orphanus wasn't averse to a good skirmish; she just preferred to have an inkling about it before seeing the steel of the opponent's teeth. 'And how do they propose to get God to line up and face them?'

'Shut-up,' warned Skirra. 'He's probably listening.' The medical scientist turned on Hunder. 'Is that why you've been so secretive?'

'There is something else.'

'What?'

'I can't tell you. God may be listening.'

'Why is it I can cure Yuzzanution Fever, multiple trauma wounds, and reassemble bodies from warm pieces, but not find the antidote for the headaches you give me?'

Orphanus looked at the screen monitoring Space Command's deadly machines. 'I think something's happening.' She started to seal her pressure suit. 'Patch into the battle plans so I can deploy the station's fighter, Hunder.'

'No. We're keeping out of this.'

'You are joking?'

'You saw what this entity is capable of. Leave it to Star Command.'

'I've already started the countdown for the satellite's missile batteries.'

'And I've disarmed them.'

Skirra expelled a heart felt sigh of relief that momentarily reduced his buoyancy.

'We can't sit here like buthmoths round a flame!' Orphanus exploded.

'We're not going to,' said the bio computer.

He put out the lights out so suddenly Skirra injected his headache cure into a totally inappropriate part of his anatomy. 'You don't honestly think that's going to fool God into believing we've taken off down some gravity line to see the frozen fountains of Mejadan, do you?'

'The command ship computer doesn't want any unnecessary pools of light to confuse their missiles.'

The Universe seemed to be controlled by egotistical computers: Skirra had always seen it coming and Orphanus had secretly designed processor-crunching pulse weaponry as a precaution.

Hunder activated his telepathy circuits to read what was going through their minds. 'And before you say anything, Space Command is issuing the orders.'

That hardly reassured Orphanus. 'From how many light years away?' She pulled her pressure suit open and slumped down to where she could recall there being a seat. 'Aren't you going to shut down the gyroscope as well?'

'Only the lights.'

Skirra looked out of the viewport to see Auroal rapidly dim like a pomander of glow-worms going out.

'And another thing,' Orphanus went on. 'If God has an appetite for suns, He's going to lap up all the energy that strike force throws at Him.'

'Oh shut-up!' Skirra snapped. 'It was just as well Space Command never trusted you with any secrets.'

Orphanus glowered into the gloom. So they were going to use the negative feedback system invented by Ansopha. It was bound to work, even on a cosmic scale and even she knew better than to announce Space Command's plan out loud.

'What is God up to now?' asked Skirra.

'Appears to be communing with some high priests on Auroal. The spectrograph is picking up His signature at the north pole,' said Hunder.

'Stupid fanatics. Haven't you explained what this entity has done to other civilisations?'

'On all frequencies at regular intervals. That's probably why the rest of Auroal has taken shelter.'

'What about those still on the surface?'

'That's their problem. I'm not programmed to deal with their emotional delusions.'

Skirra groaned. 'Oh come on. I'm the one who'll have to sew the bits back together.'

Orphanus chuckled to herself. 'It's so refreshing to listen to the exchange of massive intellects.'

'You keep out of it! I never had this trouble with Ansopha.'

'No? Ansopha's cynicism could have corroded the main bulkhead.'

'Quiet,' warned Hunder. 'I think God's about to gird his loins for battle.'

Against the dense blackness of space there was a faint flicker resembling the bioluminescence of a deep sea fish. Then nearby strands of dull red light swirled like fumes from a boiling kettle of chemicals.

This wasn't God; He assumed the other manifestation to be a decoy and could see no point in chasing space anomalies when He was capable of hurling enough volts to short circuit a star. All the other players in the arena, mortal, mechanical, and bio computer, were at last focussed on God's next move and, like a Cosmic prima donna, who was He to disappoint them.

God's full Majesty bloomed into terrifying existence.

Skirra would have taken cover in the nearest locker if he could fit inside it. 'Looks as though He's had a top up from the sun.' The hysteria in his flippant comment betrayed his terror.

Hunder didn't answer. Why tell a good guesser he's right when that's the last thing he needs to know?

God ribboned into streamers of rainbow energy and sinuously investigated Space Command's strike force. Unimpressed, He reeled His probing spectrum into an intense sphere of light.

Hunder cursed himself for not being able to behave more like a computer. 'Oh no!'

'What?' demanded Orphanus.

Hunder hesitated. 'He's going to incinerate Auroal.'

They watched, horrified as, God's blazing globe hurtled towards the unprotected world.

CHAPTER 19

'And when she swept through those doors like a tsunami in drag, we knew we had our Christmas Future.' Henny Stenson was putting on one of his performances for the benefit of the mature ladies sipping tea in Beachview's lounge.

Gladys had been enjoying a quiet coffee, not realising that he would be making a premature appearance. She discreetly took her cup into the saloon for fear of being drawn into the coos of admiration echoing like some homely Greek chorus. The man's pouting, posturing, and repartee were magnetic in an awful way. That was probably what had saved Henny and his troupe from being set adrift in a leaky boat years ago. Now they had Lucinfer Brimstone to add to their dreadful magnificence. It was just as well that the woman had a strong back. It looked as though she would be carrying the Moonstar Players from now on. At least the troupe wouldn't be allowed into the saloon until Mansel had finished the Christmas decorations. Banished to his cage for trying to destroy them as soon as they were up, Joabim was nattering to himself in an attempt to confuse the pixie that had recently been invading his thoughts.

The subject of Henny Stenson's eulogising made a grand entrance. In her long cream coat, Lucinfer Brimstone wasn't capable of making an entrance any other way, however unintentionally. The cockatoo's crest described a citrine arch and his harsh squawk attracted her attention to the saloon where Gladys beckoned.

Realising what lay in wait amidst the flowery hats and clinking teacups Lucinfer smiled apologetically at Henny Stenson, and then sailed into the saloon like a huge snowflake on a light breeze. She joined Gladys at its far end where Mansel had festooned the partitions in tinsel and pine cones. Joabim kept a beady eye on the

99

two women from under his wing, malcontent radiating through the bars at being confined to his cage. Amiel was going to have his time cut out keeping the bird away from mischief that evening.

'Changing your mind?' asked Gladys.

Lucinfer gave a deep chuckle. 'About the play? Goodness no. I've learnt the part and wouldn't want to let them down now. It would be like snatching the cuddly toy from an elderly spaniel.'

'Spaniels don't usually inflict their egos on the local population and expect them to pay for the privilege.'

'I would have never expected such intolerance in you.'

'I've lived too long. After fifty, you tend not to bother with life's jetsam.' Gladys looked at the large woman's handsome features and wondered if she had any idea what she was talking about. Lucinfer Brimstone would never be old, however long she lived. In fact, it was impossible to tell what age she was. 'Perhaps you're too easy going.'

'Who? Me?' Lucinfer seemed complemented by the observation. 'My occupation has taught me to take in the local colour, and sometimes immerse myself when required.'

Even though the local colour in Brinton-on-Sea was hardly the bright end of Pantone, Gladys knew what she meant. 'What is your occupation then?' Despite her assertion to have toured the Far East in a travelling rep company, that could have only been a minor phase for such a powerful personality.

Lucinfer leaned back and made a tableau of one against the pine panelling. 'I tidy things up,' she ventured. 'I'm a sort of agent for loose ends. A universal loss adjuster.'

Gladys's curiosity was fired. 'Who employs you to tie up loose ends?'

'It's on a results basis.' She chose her words so carefully; the photographer could have believed Lucinfer

Brimstone was involved in industrial espionage if she hadn't been so conspicuous. Loose ends would have seen her coming and got back into mischief's sewing box.

Amiel brought the companions a cappuccino and black coffee. Gladys was now blasé about his telepathy and put it down to a highly organised sense of anticipation.

'Wonder what he did for a living before coming here?' she mused aloud when the waiter was out of earshot.

'Probably an empath of some sort.'

Gladys gave a small giggle, unsure what job description empaths slotted into. 'Would have been useful in some of the war zones I've visited.'

'Ah, war. A strange concept, don't you think?'

The photographer had never seen bloody destruction in those terms. Being right on top of it robbed an observer of detachment. 'I suppose you're right. Rather like colour prejudice - totally absurd when you think about it with benign logic.' She took a sip of her cappuccino. 'Not many humans are that benign or logical, though. They all have their excuses, their egos to butter,' she gave a half glance at the gathering in the lounge, 'and gods to blame. Goodness, I wish I had a shilling for every time I've heard the name of Jesus being cursed for allowing a war started by some greedy human.'

'That is the nature of mortality,' agreed Lucinfer. 'Everyone needs their gods, however sophisticated they become, even science is obliged to find a reason for the existence of God.'

Gladys nodded. 'Like the Big Bang Theory. If that isn't a lot of evidence looking for a miracle I don't know what is.' She indicated Amiel who was cleaning the bar counter. 'I'd like to know what science has to say about him?'

'He bothers you?'

'Not any more - I think. But I'd be interested in

seeing the brain scan of anyone who has such a rapport with that crotchety old cockatoo.'

Lucinfer gave a wry smile. 'He's just an elfin spirit. Probably took the wrong turning when he lost his way back to his own dimension.'

Gladys said nothing. She had the uneasy feeling that Lucinfer knew what she was talking about.

CHAPTER 20

And God departed Auroal.

The blazing sphere of God embraced Auroal in a grotesque rainbow that seared Hunder's satellite.

Using his infrared vision, Skirra started to program the artificial world's medical stations to accept God's scorched devotees. Because he could see in bands of the spectrum not visible to others, he noticed that Orphanus was radiating disagreeably on several of them. The warrior in her wanted to be part of the action, even though her firepower would have been little more than a sparkler in a firestorm. All she could do was direct her pent up annoyance at the viewing screen.

Space Command's strike force broke formation to tempt the entity away from Auroal. The battleships were more rewarding game and God rotated slowly, releasing Auroal.

The crescent shaped craft angled themselves into firing position.

Missiles primed to detonate negative energy to soak up God's belligerent, blazing Being were launched as soon as He was clear of Auroal. As they struck, the enraged entity belled out a little. God's blazing rainbow sphere went into contortions, threatening the solar system with a cosmic tantrum that would have made His attack on Auroal seem like lightly toasting bread as He was devoured from inside by the invention of the heretic He had risked all to destroy.

The entity started to dissipate. A second volley of missiles and God's sphere glowed angrily like a red sun fighting to keep its atmosphere. Coldly, mechanically, the ships circled the disorganised energy mass, firing wherever it tried to reform.

The mortal aspirations in Hunder winced. It was a hell of a way for any deity to go. Not even he would dare confront the computer controlling Space Command's strike force, which would have been capable of trapping him in his holographic body and expelling it from his comfortable vacuum into the wide Cosmos. No other thing, living or electronic, could have known that the interactive hologram designed to contain his vast consciousness had been perfected, apart from this strike force computer. If it could annihilate God, what hope would he have?

When he snapped out of his self induced, obsessive reverie the onslaught was over. All that remained of God was a faint red hydrogen stain on the backdrop of space.

'Right, now can we have some lights, Hunder?' Skirra was demanding. 'There are only so many useful things I can do in infrared.'

Hunder immediately illuminated the satellite and planet.

Orphanus stared accusingly out of the viewport. 'It was too easy.' Though probably right, it sounded like sour grapes.

As he had called their strike force out, Hunder felt obliged to defend Space Command. 'I can detect no residual energy traces and spectral analysis verifies that the entity has been terminated.'

Orphanus always became suspicious whenever Hunder sounded like a computer. 'That creature would never have gone so easily.' She watched Space Command regroup for a routine search: silver crescents scything through the sparse atoms of space.

'What makes you so sure?'

'Instinct.'

'I do have a little more than instinct at my disposal,' Hunder declared haughtily.

Orphanus felt even more inclined to attack his circuits with a beam laser. 'Then you are wrong. The entity knew what was going to happen. It did same thing to us.'

Deep down in his bio core, Hunder could feel his

argument wobble, but would be damned before a mere engineer bested him. 'I have refined the scanner spectrum analyser since then.'

'It's wrong, all wrong.' Orphanus would have wandered away under the cloud of her own misgivings if Skirra hadn't remembered something.

'Hunder, now you're so sure that God has gone, what was it you couldn't tell us before?'

'Tell you?' The bio computer was obviously having second thoughts. It is strange what someone is prepared to admit to when facing annihilation.

'Good news, you inferred?'

'Oh yes.' Hunder paused. 'Ansopha is alive.'

Orphanus spun back in amazement. 'It's not possible!'

'That's what I thought. According to my calculations, his molecules wouldn't have held together. Then I detected his telepathic implant.'

Skirra wasn't sure what to think. He knew too much about Ansopha's new biology to believe it. 'You're right. His atoms should have drifted apart.'

'Aren't you pleased?'

Orphanus shrugged. 'The creature never seemed that real to me anyway.'

'It might be plausible if we knew about Ansopha's origins. Perhaps its molecular structure was more resilient than we thought. The body chemistry was certainly odd.' Skirra went back to work on his burns treatment programme.

Hunder knew they were only putting on a diffident front to impress each other. With no vengeful God to pursue Ansopha, the bio computer could now at least concentrate on how to transmit a person through the same gravity line again without turning them into atomic pâté. Finding someone to go would be the most difficult equation. In most species, one way or another, death wasn't optional.

CHAPTER 21

Gladys worried the print about the developer. 'I've got you this time and no mistake.'

Only hesitating to briefly examine the emerging image, she dropped the bromide paper into the fix tank and developed half a dozen more images of Amiel Sopher in quick succession. The photographer was late for morning tea with Lucinfer Brimstone. Despite her absurd stage name, the woman was capable of the intelligent conversation that was compensation for all life's humdrum inanities. Who else could extrapolate the meaning of life from a black coffee while a bad tempered cockatoo wittered obscenities under its wing?

Gladys still didn't know where her new friend came from, or whether she really was some bizarre loss adjuster. She didn't care. When offered an intriguing nugget, you don't ask the name of the miner who dug it up. Her real name would eventually be wheedled from her anyway, or Gladys wasn't worthy of her NUJ membership card.

After fixing and pegging up the prints, she dashed downstairs, almost bumping into Amiel coming the other way. As she had forgotten to lock the door to the dark room, he hopefully hadn't bothered to read her mind.

Lucinfer was sitting in a window seat in the restaurant lounge, gazing out at Mansel who was stringing lights through the branches of the old sycamore undermining the front courtyard wall.

'That man loves Christmas,' she observed as Gladys joined her.

'It's the only time he can let his hair down.' Gladys sat in a carver opposite Lucinfer, and then looked about. 'Who's serving, then?'

'Mary said she would come out in a moment. Amiel is not feeling well.'

Gladys hadn't noticed. The waiter always looked the same wan hue to her. 'What's wrong?'

'Apparently came over a little faint.'

Gladys swallowed hard. 'Really?'

'I assumed you would like your usual?'

'Yes. Thank you. Place looks deserted. Where is everyone?'

'As it is so bright, Mr Butterworth decided to take a stroll on the front and the regular ladies are probably making paper chains and mince pies.'

Gladys detected irony. 'You're not another one who detests Christmas?'

Lucinfer smiled at some private joke. 'I haven't been around for enough of them to make a judgement.'

For a woman of intellect, she had apparently managed to avoid quite a lot of life's essential punctuation. The evening before, she had even let slip to a rep from Nature's Herbal Realm that she had never bothered to try make-up, though with her striking features it was hardly necessary. Lucinfer was probably being ironic again. What actor didn't know about greasepaint? Gladys blinked at the thought. Perhaps Lucinfer wasn't an actress after all? But she had to be! A thespian, loss-adjusting giantess with a profound grasp of life's meaning. The photographer told herself to stop thinking like that. She had retired as a journalist long before all the proofreaders had been made redundant.

Lucinfer allowed the lace curtain to fall back into place and turned to Gladys. 'I think it will be an interesting Christmas this year. I can feel it in my bones.'

'Please don't mention bones.'

With her magnificent bone structure, Lucinfer was never likely to suffer from osteoporosis. 'Trouble getting up?'

'Every bloody morning.'

'No HRT?'

'Would you want periods when you're seventy two?'

By her expression, that was something Lucinfer hadn't thought about. Her hormones must have been too intimidated to give her aggravation.

Louise yapping at her heels, Mary delivered their beverages, then scooped up the Yorkie and put her in her apron pocket. 'Just shout if you need anything. I'll be in the kitchen with the laundry until Amiel comes down.' And she bustled out.

Lucinfer could tell that Gladys didn't want to discuss female biology. 'I suspect you are an agnostic?'

Gladys was thankful for the change in subject. She was more at home with politics and religion. 'More out of laziness than anything else.'

'And yet you are a creative artist, not a scientist?'

'God is a matter of opinion. Artists make their living by visualising different points of view. Scientists are slaves to experimental proof. They get their illicit kicks by having beliefs, the more irrational the better.'

'I don't follow?'

'Virtually all useful discoveries are made by scientists having an irrational leap of imagination. The most irrational is that some deity created everything. Of course, the Big Bang might be a bit more than an act of faith. As we know so little, scientists are only here to claim that we know everything.'

'If God is the Big Bang, that must mean that the Devil is a black hole.'

'Now wouldn't that let a lot of people off the hook.' Gladys took a sip of her cappuccino. Amiel was able to put a much better head on them. 'Why are you so interested in the existence of God?'

'Don't you find the premise fascinating?'

'Should I?'

'What if some being, far more advanced than anything a humdrum mortal could comprehend, decided to prey on their desire to believe?'

'More fool them.' The cappuccino was too hot so Gladys

replaced the cup in the saucer and wiped the froth from her upper lip. 'What would this advanced being get out of it?'

'Perhaps it feeds off energy.'

'Emotional, fusion, photosynthesis ..?'

'All of them.'

The photographer shrugged. 'Rich pickings in a galaxy this size.'

'And a galaxy this size overlaps so many other dimensions.'

'You sure about that?'

Lucinfer corrected herself. 'Probably does. All this entity needs is someone to invite it in.'

Logic told Gladys not to be spooked by Lucinfer's mischievous God bashing. She shuddered all the same. 'Just as well all the religions here are too busy at each other's throats to generate enough belief to catch its attention.'

'That is very true. Very true.' Lucinfer Brimstone looked at her watch and sighed.

'Moonstar Players time?'

'A brief sojourn into the absurd.'

'Have they decided on the costumes yet?'

'Most of the charity shops have been divested of their brocade curtains and lacy nylon blouses.'

Gladys grimaced. 'Stop talking like that. It reminds me of Henny Stenson.'

'Delving into the unfathomable depths of the props mistress's universe helps anaesthetise and realign the brain. Why do you ask about the costumes?'

'I'm always expected to take some pictures. I prefer to do it before everything unravels into its component parts and Loralie has an accident with her heels or hairdo, or Oliver's toupee takes a turn for the worse.'

Lucinfer's expression glazed for a moment.

'Oh,' chuckled Gladys. 'Such wonders do await you, believe me.'

CHAPTER 22

*God answered the prayer of the high priest of
Fammora and entrusted to that devoted servant
the Sacred Casket containing His essence.*

The Fammoran high priest silently watched his scorched devotees being stretchered to treatment centres. After wrestling with his conscience for a few moments, His Eminence's sense of self-importance won by a knockout and submission.

The dignitary lifted his ceremonial tail from the debris of burnt offerings littering the spaceport and climbed into the waiting carriage. He ordered the vehicle to Fammora's secret temple dedicated to the Last Coming and swept past the mournful spectacle caused by God's carelessness.

As Hunder restored Auroal's light, the high priest travelled over the other latitudes of the planet where the residents were emerging from their shelters. Now they had received a taste of their deity's true nature, most of them were sadder and wiser. A vociferous minority was ranting on about being visited with retribution for the sins of their ancestors. Not even the high priest of Fammora could find room in his narrow view of the Universe for that one. Any sins available to ancestors on the tightly controlled planet of Auroal were very limited.

In the depths of the sanctuary shielded against Hunder's prying sensors, the high priest lit the sacred flame. He stood before it in a trance, double-thumbed hands outstretched to invite the thoughts of God. As no one else was listening to Him at that moment, they came pretty quickly.

God wasn't taking any chances after his almost fatal encounter with Space Command. 'Why have you summoned me?' He demanded warily.

The high priest rocked back in ecstasy. He was now the only true believer. Those hoards of freeloaders trying to monopolise sacred revelation had wavered before the Majesty of His rage and were found wanting. It was the aspiration of every religiously susceptible mortal to don a gown with holy symbols and intimidate fealty from a sceptical hoi polloi. The Fammoran high priest alone had stayed the course.

'I ask you to witness that my faith has not been shaken.'

God hesitated. How could any mortal still be so gullible after what He had done? The entity had no more use for the devout of Auroal and had only needed them in the first place to summon up enough belief to allow Him into their dimension. Like a Christmas pet, they had quickly become tedious. He usually shook such weaklings off like annoying fleas. Perhaps it was another trap, but this time God could detect no spying Hunder.

The high priest's mind was devoid of betrayal, as well as common sense. It seemed to be crammed with intellect's poor relation, cunning - a lot of it - peppered with ambition and self-importance. An ideal combination for God's needs. The high priest, with his tick-like tenacity, was not going to be shaken off like an annoying flea and could prove useful after all.

'Are you willing to demonstrate your dedication?'

'Command me.'

'The treacherous entity who defied me still lives.'

God could only be talking about Ansopha. 'It lives? But how?'

'It was transmitted to the other side of the Galaxy by the heretic, Hunder.'

The high priest suspected that the bio computer was capable of attempting something like that, though wouldn't have believed that he could succeed: only an entity like God had such power.

'How did the communicator survive?'

God wasn't going to admit fallibility by saying He

didn't know. 'The bio computer maintains contact with it.'

Visions of a glorious crusade to hunt down God's enemies fogged the high priest's thoughts. He could raise a fleet of ships for the quest and become the most important priest in the star cluster. 'This treachery must be avenged. I will start an uprising and bring down this accused machine.'

God always had trouble dealing with irrational minds. They were usually destructive and didn't have the faintest idea how to do something useful. It obviously hadn't occurred to the priest that Auroal wouldn't function without Hunder.

'No. Do you have a program technician who is totally trustworthy?'

What? No crusade? The high priest hesitated; he didn't want to share his glory with anyone else. Unfortunately, being in holy orders, knowledge of machines was forbidden to him. 'Tollin of the engineer's guild is the best Fammora possesses. She is of the true blood.'

'How true?'

'She is not cowering below with the rest of the population. She is a secret devotee. Such members make a pledge against their own death if found wanting.'

God was not surprised at such irrationality in a scientist. Though few in numbers, they were the hardest to fall when finding religion. It usually blossomed into a quest to scientifically prove that some monotheistic entity made everything, from black holes to fairies. It was much more complicated than that of course. This God had certainly made bits and pieces of the Universe in His heyday but, as His power had waned over the aeons, it was now payback time. Some of His creations had evolved minds of their own and wouldn't be so willing to surrender their sun as easily as these Fammorans.

'You must summon Tollin to this sanctum.'

This unsettled the high priest. Only the ordained were allowed to enter the inner sanctum.

'What is wrong?' demanded God.

The high priest fluttered like a feeble moth for a moment. 'The un-ordained would defile your holy place.'

'Where else are you shielded from Hunder?'

'Only in the inner sanctum.'

'There is a way to cleanse it afterwards.' The temperature suddenly shot up and the high priest's tail was scorched on the searing stone.

'I'll get her! What do you want done?'

'I would like her to slip a little program into Hunder's memory without him knowing, that's all.'

Gladys dutifully went to Brinton-on-Sea's community hall and took one or two snaps of the Moonstar Players in the throes of their chaotic dress rehearsal. Just to be awkward they wanted them in black and white which obliged the photographer to waste precious emulsion. The one thing the laptop Mansel had loaned her didn't have, was PhotoShop, so she tried to persuade Loralie Stenson that colour would flatter her expensive silks. Nevertheless, these pretentious mayflies somehow realised that mono prints were more in vogue.

Gladys wanted to get some shots of Lucinfer Brimstone. Unfortunately, as Christmas Future, she was totally concealed under a black habit and, as narrator, relegated to the shadows at the side of the stage. Trust the Moonstar Players to marginalise the best opportunity they ever had for a favourable sentence in the local rag. However much they valued their find, the fear of being upstaged still loomed large. At least with Lucinfer in the production it wouldn't be the usual embarrassing charade; like the time they attempted a "socially aware" version of Babes in the Wood. Most of the elderly audience went away assuming that they must have dozed off just before the songs and pantomime dame, only to wake up when Henny Stenson's young son was being raised heavenward into the flies on an unstable, primrose decked bier. Fortunately the hall's technician had insisted on a safety line, otherwise the boy would never have survived to become a Goth. (He now preferred to frequent basement clubs like *The Crypt* and the shell shop that sold new age crystals and rings for parts of the anatomy a fifteen-year-old had barely developed enough to pierce.) Such tedium was a high price to pay for a complimentary biscuit and a cup of tea, and it had been impossible to empathise with the other, much older, sixteen-year-old babe with bovver boots and acne.

Back at the Beachview Hotel, Gladys flipped the film out of her camera. When she took it into the darkroom the photographs she had pegged out that morning caught her attention. Dealing with the Moonstar Players egos had made her forget about Amiel Sopher.

She tossed the film into a canister and switched on the light.

This time there was no mistake.

Gladys gazed at the pictures she had secretly snapped from the first floor window of an empty room with a zoom as the waiter and Mary walked towards the hotel's front entrance. Amiel's voluminous greatcoat was crisply focused but, above the turquoise scarf, the bird like features had barely registered on the emulsion.

It wasn't low blood pressure that made the photographer reel. She was so widely travelled the only thing left was to interview a vampire. Could this be her great chance? Judging by the image barely registering on the negative or emulsion, it seemed so. Yet Amiel was no vampire. He wouldn't have stood a chance with the amount of garlic in Mansel's kitchen. He was certainly elfin. Little short of emailing Titania, it was unlikely the photographer would ever discover what sort.

Had Gladys been thirty years younger, she would have immediately toted the prints about to find the highest bidder. Now, she wondered how she had managed to be so ruthless.

The one benefit of age was that not many things surprised her. That was probably it. The photographer wasn't so much surprised at her discovery, as put out by its implausibility. The very subject she had been waiting a lifetime for was apparently fading away on the only wavelengths her SLR would recognise.

Now realising that there was something profoundly wrong with the new waiter, Gladys wondered whether she should go down and show Mansel the photos.

Perhaps not such a good idea - not until after the Christmas rush anyway.

The only other alternative was to confront Amiel Sopher. Whatever condition he had, it might have been receiving treatment and could have been the reason he had to leave his last position so mysteriously.

Gladys needed somewhere else to think. She pushed the prints into an empty bromide envelope and took them downstairs. The last customer had gone and the photographer sat in the lounge while Amiel cleared away the saloon.

Under the light of a table lamp, she minutely examined each picture with a magnifying glass, careful to turn them over as she finished and not think too loudly. Whatever ailed Amiel wasn't natural: to her certain knowledge there was no condition that could make a person literally fade away.

Gladys was so immersed in the paradox she didn't hear the soft footsteps. The roots of her hair stood on end as she turned to see Amiel gazing down at the photograph in her hand.

'Want to explain?'

Amiel reluctantly sat opposite her, still gazing at the picture. 'You wouldn't believe it.'

'I know I couldn't have taken a picture like this accidentally.' She tapped the photos. 'There are at least a dozen here.'

Amiel averted his silvery grey eyes. 'I don't know how to explain it.' He looked back sharply. 'Are you going to tell Mr Lascelle?'

Gladys shrugged. 'Tell him what? That you're disappearing? He's got enough problems.' She hesitated. 'Just let me know what's wrong with you?'

The waiter half closed his eyes. 'I have a peculiar molecular condition not known to medical science. It is very embarrassing.'

'Did old Mrs Lascelle have the horrors because she

sensed it?'

'I do not understand what upset her so much. She was probably reminded of her own inconsequence to the rest of the Universe.'

Gladys laid the photograph face down on the table and leaned forward. 'Look Amiel, the last thing I'm going to do is cause Mansel any grief. If you do want to talk to anyone about your problem, you can come to me. I've been around and seen things the average person wouldn't believe possible and, since I had to give up overseas assignments, life has been pretty tasteless. I'm not averse to the occasional stimulation, however incredible - as long as it doesn't involve jogging or alcohol.'

Amiel gave a thin smile. Not even Gladys Hodge would believe how incredible his situation was. He wanted to take her into his confidence, but how do you tell someone you are an interstellar heretic banished to the end of a dimension because God is out to get you?

'Thank you,' he said, and then rose. 'Will you want Ceylon with breakfast, or orange juice?'

CHAPTER 24

Skirra was still too busy transmitting medical treatment to the casualties on Auroal to listen to Orphanus' misgivings about Space Command, and Hunder was immersed in a program that would safely send someone in and out of the gravitational anomaly Ansopha had been catapulted through.

Auroal was in turmoil. Without a telepathic communicator, Hunder's quantum circuits were obliged to translate the slanging matches about who was responsible for provoking the wrath of God. Apart from the slanders about him, Hunder resented wasting his valuable capacity on recriminations more suited to an end of the world party. What did they think he was? The entity that kept the planet in its orbit or a mundane receptacle for the world's venom? Now he had experienced the aggravation Ansopha had been obliged to cope with, the communicator's cynicism was understandable.

Orphanus tried mediating on Auroal, only to cause more conflicts than she managed to settle.

The bio computer also gave up trying to calm the situation and before long he, Skirra and Orphanus had to admit that they wanted the delinquent member of their team back. Hunder continued to focus on finding a solution for Ansopha's gravity line. It was only when his quantum circuits stopped trying to reason in a hundred disparate tongues he detected the intruder. An electronic maggot was worming its way into his circuits.

Without warning, the Hunder shut down all non-essential systems and once again sent Orphanus spinning for her jetpack.

'What now?' she snapped. 'God's not back, is He?'

'I have to suspend all incoming traffic. Something is

tampering with my memory.'

'That's impossible.'

Hunder didn't answer so Orphanus jetted down to Skirra.

'Done it,' the medical scientist announced as she entered his lab.

It was so dark she had no idea what he was talking about.

'Done what?'

'I know how to stabilise Ansopha's atomic mass.'

'That's a fat lot of good to him now.'

'What happened to the lights?'

'Hunder's got the horrors about something snooping about his circuits. He shut down the gravity lines.'

'That will no doubt please Auroal.'

'They're still too busy arguing.' Orphanus looked over Skirra's shoulder. She couldn't make out much, even by the light of her torch. 'How did you manage to do it?'

'By altering the spin of the electrons in some cells.'

Orphanus sent him a circumspect glance in the gloom. 'How do they keep their molecular integrity?'

'It's simply a matter of balancing the compression. After all, we consist mostly of space held together by a positive charge.'

Orphanus had no idea what he was talking about. 'Is that how the Leamt engineered their human?'

'No doubt something like it.'

Orphanus wandered about in the darkness. She felt like a useless appendage once again. 'So you can now stabilise Ansopha?'

'Assuming we can get the treatment to him.'

Orphanus' eyes narrowed. It looked as though she wasn't so obsolete after all.

CHAPTER 25

Oliver contemplated the ornate scrolls Gerald had painted on Scrooge's desk. They were bound to distract the audience from the marvels of his performance. Their maisonette had ended up the same way. Despite Oliver's aspirations towards rhinestone minimalism, as soon as his back was turned in would come Gerald with the velvet drapes, framed pictures of Tremeloes, and carved salad bowls. The man may have been a mouse to Oliver's Top Cat, but he was so insidiously persistent it was enough to make Liberace shed his sequins.

As though on the summit of a mountain, wondering whether it was worth bringing down the graven tablets, Lucinfer was looking on with a detachment that could not avoid appearing lofty.

Loralie was busily tacking Gloria into her Mrs Cratchit costume and Mavis Brink was rummaging through a box of knick-knacks and gewgaws with a vigour that would have bent the beak of any magpie. The jet jewellery was so cumbersome there couldn't have been much work done on it between mine and display case; and the candlesticks - only an orang-utan on heat could have put those twists into them.

Before encountering the Moonstar Players, Lucinfer had never felt superfluous. Too imposing to merge into the half painted wings, she felt impelled to do something.

'How many tickets have we sold so far?' Her question cut through the air like a delta winged bomber.

When the buzzing in their ears stopped, the cast turned to her as though asked who had used the last sheet of community hall toilet paper.

Loralie declared brightly, even though her soul had sunk to her size four shoes, 'We sent out fifty tickets to friends, and Mr Guha has put a hundred booking forms on his counter.'

With a wicked pang of satisfaction, Lucinfer deduced that this meant none. With the first performance in a week's time it was unlikely they would fill two rows.

'I can't promise anything, but I might be able to sell one or two.' Lucinfer declared with melodramatic magnanimity.

The Moonstar Players were suddenly transformed from egocentric artistes into fawning lap dogs. Even Oliver stopped disapproving of his lover's artwork to concede a gaze of wonderment.

Henny Stenson thrust a large batch of the bright red tickets into Lucinfer's hand.

She looked down at the garish bundle with infuriating detachment. 'I take it there are deductions for parties?'

The question set him back for a moment. Audiences arriving in parties were unknown to the Moonstar Players.

He rallied magnificently in the face of her diffidence. 'Of course, of course. Terms are on the back of each ticket.'

'Would you mind if I slipped out for an hour?' asked Lucinfer. 'I think I have my part sewn up.'

Loralie's paranoia saw it as a snipe at the huge, black cowl she had designed for Christmas Future. She let it pass. The woman was twice her size after all, and promising an audience.

Henny hated to admit it, but Lucinfer Brimstone was the only one who didn't need any more rehearsal. The prospect of unloading half a dozen tickets was compensation enough. 'Please feel free.'

Mavis Brink felt excluded from the excitement and called over from the props table, 'If you do sell a batch of more than ten, remember to make a note of their sequence numbers, won't you?' She had rehearsed that instruction for more than fifteen years.

'Of course.'

'We might even collect enough numbers to use in the next lottery draw,' Gloria muttered darkly. Even Lucinfer's huge confidence could not pin her cynicism to the dartboard of hope.

Lucinfer pulled her cream coat over her shoulders and went out into the mild winter air. She crossed the high street and strode the short distance down to the front where several of Mansel Lascelle's regular morning customers were waiting in one of the promenade shelters, the sunlight sparkling on their Christmas hat trimmings.

'What did they say?' Connie Andrews, woolly hatted and practical, was the keenest of the group, and had thought up the scheme.

Lucinfer read the terms on the back of a ticket. 'Concessions: OAPs, children and students, £4.50, parties of ten or over, £4 per head.' As Lucinfer counted out forty-two lurid red tickets an opportunist gull hovered overhead, anticipating a snack of raw meat. 'I, dear ladies, will let you have them for nothing.' She handed them to Connie who had never had any problem with sums.

'But - that's £168? Who's going to cover the cost?'

'Don't worry about it. If there is one thing that fills me with dread, it is the prospect of performing to a hall full of stacking chairs. Just persuade the mobile residents of your mother's nursing home to turn up.'

The ladies cooed in appreciation. They had never been averse to the odd play, however bad. It was just that in the Moonstar Players case they resented paying for it.

Lucinfer lifted a finger to her lips to ensure their discretion, and then strode off along the promenade, cream coat flapping about her and black hair streaming in the breeze. A flock of gulls rose at her approach and circled until she had passed, before returning to the detritus on the beach.

'What a strange woman,' Connie observed admiringly. 'I wonder where she comes from?'

'Well, Brimstone must be a stage name,' chuckled Alice. 'And Lucinfer sounds like a near relation of the Devil to me.'

'Yes, now you come to mention it, it does, doesn't it.'

CHAPTER 26

*And God's disciple did send the shaft of His
Wrath through the crack in time to smite
His deadly enemy.*

Tollin wasn't expecting the kickback that hurled her from the terminal and into the pond of the Last Coming.

The high priest of Fammora was too startled to accuse her of sacrilege and the sacred creatures weren't quick enough to fasten their fangs into the technician. She was out of the scolding water before the overspill could hit the ground and there followed a tirade of abuse about a certain bio computer that usually wouldn't have been heard in a merchant's trading cavern, let alone a holy inner sanctum.

With difficulty, Tollin regained her composure.

It took longer for the high priest to find his voice. 'What happened?'

'That bloody Hunder! He intercepted my signal.' She rubbed her numb hands. 'He sent a surge through all my thumbs.'

The high priest wasn't concerned about her thumbs. 'But did you relay the program as The Almighty instructed?'

'Oh yes. There's no way Hunder can intercept it. It will ensure that the heretic continues to dissolve. Not even Hunder can help the blasphemous communicator now. That will teach it to have polarizing molecules.'

***

Hunder had been silent for some while.

'Well?' demanded Skirra.

The bio computer displayed on a monitor the signal he was picking up. 'Very faint, but I have his brain wave patterns.'

'They're erratic.'

'Deteriorating rapidly.'

Orphanus pretended to be concerned. 'So now what?'

Hunder sensed the ambivalence in the Vardel. 'You're the only one who can decide that.'

Orphanus looked at Skirra who was trying too hard not to look at her.

'Everything's ready if you want to try it?' he asked.

Orphanus switched off the manual she had been studying and did a tour of the control chamber. 'Do we really need Ansopha back? What would the creature be use for? Even if you do manage to stabilise its mass, it would still be a human. Can a brain that small retain all the languages needed to perform a useful function?'

'The capacity will still be there,' Hunder said.

'And it'll have to carry around its own atmosphere in places it could previously stroll through.'

'He will also be an odd colour, prone to blackouts, and hair loss!' Skirra snapped. 'Do you want Ansopha back or not?'

Orphanus threw herself into a seat. 'Oh all right. Let's do it. But don't blame me if it comes back as vegetable hash.'

Skirra floated over to the medical screen. 'Right. First things first. We'll have to stabilise his molecular integrity.'

'There is something else,' Orphanus suddenly announced.

Skirra was already working on the formula. 'What?'

'How did some Fammoran priest find out that Hunder was in contact with Ansopha, and why would he go to the trouble of destabilising the life support link? I know Ansopha was hardly their number one citizen, but the fact that this heretic is on the other side of the Galaxy should have been enough for them.'

Hunder had been working that out for himself. He wasn't going to admit his conclusion to lesser intellects. 'The Fammoran church is wealthy enough to employ the best programmer.'

This was the bio computer's way of saying that she was a lesser intellect, so Orphanus decided to accept his explanation for the moment. A more ominous one was already spreading its dark wings in the back of her battle-ready mind.

'How will I get to him?' she asked. 'Are the natives friendly?'

'Before I lost contact with Ansopha, he said that someone would meet you.'

Orphanus gave the monitor a sideways glance. 'You are joking? I hardly look like a human, will need molecular restructuring, and a pressure suit to go through the gravity line into that anomaly.'

Skirra continued to tap instructions into the medical computer. 'I can program in molecular alterations. They will only be stable for a short time.'

Orphanus was well aware that these "molecular alterations" involved increasing her mass tenfold. Vardels may have seemed dense to most people, but they weren't stupid when it came to self-preservation.

'And how do we get Ansopha back without crushing it?'

'First things first. When he's been stabilised I can make the calculations. Let's just get you there and back.'

Orphanus slumped down in her seat, misgivings doing a tango with her suspicions. Dense or not, she seemed to be the only one who suspected that a certain entity was not as extinguished as Space Command believed.

CHAPTER 27

'That's the crackers and wine glasses!' Mary called from the kitchen. 'Just leaves the Dundee cake and trifle. They can come out after the main course.' She appeared at the lounge door, 'How's Amiel?'

'I think he'll be all right in a couple of days,' Gladys lied. 'Will Sandra be able to cover?'

'You bet. She needs the money. Shouldn't Amiel see a doctor, though?'

'I don't think so. He just has to rest if he's going to survive Christmas. He's not very strong to begin with, you know.'

There was a long, low coo from the saloon.

On the whole, Mary was an animal lover, but Joabim had often tempted her to contemplate "parrotcide". 'What is the matter with that bird? Since Amiel took to bed he's been more bad tempered than usual.'

'I think Amiel has an affinity with dumb animals. Even Arnold's old dog knows what he's saying - and that's deaf.'

The coo turned into to the skirl of chalk on a blackboard.

'Shut-up Joabim!' snapped Mary.

Gladys went to a table to finish folding serviettes. 'When does Sandra arrive?'

'A couple of hours. We only need her for silver service. Mr Lascelle will be cooking.'

'I won't want a cappuccino this afternoon if that's any help.

'Oh good, Amiel makes a much better job of them anyway.'

'I would like to take a few shots on the beach before the sun sets. Is there anything else you want me to do before I go?'

Mary glanced over the party spread. 'No thanks, Mrs Hodge. I think we've cracked it. It was good of you to help out like that. Feel free to come back whenever you like. We'll always have a table for you and Mr Butterworth.'

Gladys rose and pulled on her coat. 'That's all right. I may have someone with me. I'll go straight up to my room.'

***

The Moonstar Players fourth dress rehearsal was chaotic: the number of tickets Lucinfer Brimstone sold had unnerved the company. If it hadn't been for her stabilising presence there would have been bloodstains on the cyclorama against which Henny Stenson had threatened to hammer his, and everyone else's, head.

Worn to an emotional frazzle, the Moonstar Players retreated to various corners of the hall with a cup of coffee or in a cloud of cigarette smoke. No one dared to communicate for fear of what would be said.

Lucinfer noticed that Gladys was waiting at the foyer entrance. She discreetly went to the chair where her costume had been neatly folded and rolled the black robe even tighter to push it into a carrier bag. Loralie looked up from her coffee, arched eyebrows demanding to know what was going on.

'Mrs Hodge is going to press it for me.'

Logic wasn't the wardrobe mistress's strong point so she didn't question why a professional photographer would offer to do anyone's ironing. She was more put out that she hadn't been asked. After all, she had the steam iron and all the time in the world.

Gladys took the carrier to the promenade. She went past the amusement arcade and Beachview, towards the headland.

By the rock face there stood a figure wearing an articulated pressure suit resembling the carapace of a Devil's coach horse beetle.

The alien removed her helmet as she waited. A huge

mane of tasselled hair that had been tied back in a knot cascaded about features fierce enough to frighten off any black-backed gull trying to assassinate the wildlife in the immediate vicinity.

Arnold and his old dog tottered and wobbled respectively, to the end of the promenade. They were about to turn back when the fearsome creature caught the elderly man's short-sighted eye. His dog may have been deaf, but could see well enough and plunged onto the beach to hide beneath the nearest pile of seaweed.

Arnold lifted his hat. 'Good afternoon, Madam. The breeze is picking up, I think.'

Orphanus was so surprised to understand what he had said that she let out an amazed gurgle which he took to be agreement.

'You would do well to get off the beach before high tide. Treacherous place, that. Been no end of visitors cut off down there.' Without waiting for a reply, he doffed his hat again and turned to walk back up the promenade.

Orphanus felt unreality permeate every tissue. Being blown up to ten times her size was bound to make even a Vardel feel dizzy but, under any conditions, this place would have been bizarre. Over the beach's shallow stone rampart she could see a brightly illuminated cave from which issued sudden blasts of music and the rapid fire of primitive weapons. The noise reminded her of the run-in she once had with some bio mechanical vermin in the spares store. These creatures infesting the cave didn't look metal, though. They were fleshy, oozing bodily secretions, and could well have been parasites. Nevertheless, in this weird place they were probably some parent's child.

The dim light reflected two terrified eyes watching her from a pile of seaweed.

Orphanus snarled. Arnold's dog shot off after its master, nearly bowling over Gladys who had no idea a

Labrador that old and fat could move so fast.

It looked as though Amiel Sopher hadn't been having her on after all.

<h1 style="text-align:center">CHAPTER 28</h1>

God's enemies did contemplate defeat.

Now that Orphanus was safely out of the way Skirra demanded, 'All right, just where did the Fammoran high priest get the idea to sabotage your link with Ansopha?'

Hunder hesitated, despite knowing that Skirra was too perceptive to be fobbed off.

'There is only one entity who could have realised that the link existed.'

The medical scientist slowly revolved in mid air to gaze out of the viewport. 'God?'

'I'm afraid so.'

'Is Orphanus in any danger?'

'It's unlikely. God's had more than one chance to crush her and never took it. Probably break His teeth. She's only a small irritant compared with Ansopha.'

'I know Ansopha was always a pain, but for an entity this powerful to go to these lengths is paranoia.'

It was no good. Hunder had to admit his suspicions, otherwise his emotion circuits would have seized up. 'I'm not so sure. Ansopha's ignorance of its own origins was totally genuine. Even Space Command has no record of them.'

'And they trusted it as communicator on this station? I know it takes a rare sort of detachment to crew the satellite, but Ansopha could have been a liability - was a liability.' Skirra floated down to sit in front of Hunder's monitor and lowered his voice. 'If Ansopha didn't come from this Galaxy, there was only one other explanation for its presence here.'

The bio computer was curious to know if the medical scientist had reached the same conclusion as him. 'What?'

'It was planted.'

'Why?'

'You're the brain; you should have worked that out by

now.'

'I'd rather not, especially if God's listening in.'

Skirra fell silent. His litter was happily prospering without their male parent at that moment. If God recovered and parasitised enough energy to become a galactic menace, none of his progeny would survive to spawn.

On the other hand, perhaps the medical scientist was being paranoid. 'Can He get through the gravity line to Ansopha?'

'I hope He doesn't try before Orphanus comes back. The flux in energy would disrupt it.'

Skirra floated out of his seat. 'What a mess. I should have stayed with the litter.'

'Thought they took you for granted?'

'They did! I'd just sooner live to be a downtrodden grandparent than stretched out on the singularity of destiny.' He watched a large Antoran vessel waiting for Hunder to open a gravity line. It had been suspended for ages between two asteroids like some cosmic executive's toy. 'We're all damned, you know. We'll never rid ourselves of this thing, whatever Star Command throws at it. It'll consume suns, system after system until it reaches the next dimension, then probably start on that.' Skirra thumped the console in frustration. 'Just what is this creature, Hunder?'

'Unknown to any physics I'm programmed to comprehend,' Hunder admitted, 'More advanced civilisations would understand it.'

'And when was the last time they spoke to us?'

'We're probably part of a game they play to help pass eternity.'

'Then keep your voice down. They're probably listening as well.' Something occurred to Skirra. 'Oh, I see! This is resentment. You believe that these cosmic super beings should already be communicating with our mighty bio computer.' Skirra could almost feel Hunder's circuits crackle as he spelt out the truth. 'How many frequencies have you tried to raise them on?'

'It's my function to explore all possibilities!' snapped Hunder. 'The fact that there was no response was not due to an emotional episode on my part.'

Skirra gave a hard laugh. 'We're stuck with "God" then, and you've got to work out what He really is all on your own.'

'By rights He shouldn't exist, so He might as well be God.'

Streamers were flying and glasses clinking as Gladys peered into the lounge. Had there been another way to reach her room she would have taken it. Unfortunately the only other route was through the back door and past the ever watchful Mrs Lascelle, who had probably bolted it against wandering guests anyway. There was no other option but to cross the floor where the first of the season's parties was in full swing.

Sandra looked up as a she served trifle to the revellers and saw a tall figure covered by a voluminous black cloak following the photographer. 'Been busy Mrs H?'

The waitress had fortunately assumed Orphanus to be a photographic model with a mountainous hairpiece, and the floating of her movements learnt on the catwalk instead of being caused by lack of atomic density. Gladys sighed with relief. She hadn't been too sure she would get away with it. Thank goodness sober people are capable of supplying their own explanations.

'Just a few shots upstairs and we'll be done,' Gladys called back. She noticed Mansel had taken a break to sip a liqueur at the saloon bar, and decided to push her luck. 'All right Mansel?'

'Of course, Mrs Hodge. Use any room you like.'

Joabim was perched on the partition watching the party. Head tilted to one side, he fixed Orphanus with a quizzical gaze, and then uttered a squawk loud enough to unnerve even a Vardel. The sound exploded through the alien's delicately balanced molecules like a bolt from a beam blaster shattering glass.

Gladys ushered Orphanus upstairs before the cockatoo decided to snatch off her hood.

Stairs had never given the warrior engineer trouble before; running up and down vertical ladders was second nature to her. But they weren't covered with an insecure, yielding fabric. Gladys steadied Orphanus. It was like pushing wheels on air.

Doors were also something that had never given the Vardel aggravation. Having never encountered the hinged variety, she walked into the one of Amiel's room when it didn't slide aside and her escort had to open it for her.

Amiel hadn't moved since the photographer left him and was barely able to speak.

Gladys locked the door behind them so Orphanus could throw off Lucinfer's cloak.

The sight of the alien in the harsh glare of the electric light set the septuagenarian back on her heels for a moment and made her wonder what she was doing, smuggling into Beachview a huge hawk on a bad feather day. Clad up to the neck in an articulated pressure suit, Orphanus could have been the hallucination of an ancient Egyptian priest after discovering the recreational properties of yeast.

So Gladys hadn't seen everything after all. In a Universe peopled with creatures like the Vardel that probably wasn't a bad thing. Fortunately Orphanus was bemused and light-headed enough by her molecule expanding experience to be on her best behaviour.

She pulled a fine cobweb from her hip pouch.

'What's that for?' asked Gladys.

'It should restore his atomic integrity.'

'Why did he lose it in the first place?'

Time was short. To explain the difference in cosmic atomic pressures to a human would have taken a week. 'Being sent from such a distance requires adjustment to a person's mass. Ansopha's was never that dense, but my atomic structure had to be radically adjusted so I could be transmitted here.' She omitted to add that Gladys was actually ten times her size and could have kicked her over Beachview if the inclination took her.

The photographer tried to look interested. Her short-term memory blanked and refused to retain what the Vardel had said. 'Oh.'

Amiel lay on the Beachview rose tinted sheet like a jellyfish stranded on a pink sandbank. Now barely tangible, parts of his body were fading as his stretched molecules attempted to hold hands.

Orphanus had hoped the patient might have at least mouthed some familiar abuse at her but, as she watched, he seemed to fade even more.

'Why was he sent here in the first place?'

Instead of receiving another answer that would baffle her, Gladys was handed one end of the fine cobweb.

She looked down at it as though waiting for the lace-making manual. 'You want me to plug it in?'

Unused to operating medical equipment, Orphanus was determined to appear professional. The last thing her Vardel honour needed was to appear incompetent in front of a human. 'Help me lay it over him.'

With a life of its own, the filigree web blossomed out in a gossamer sheet and trickled its way over Amiel's slight body before transforming him into a shimmering cocoon.

'What's happening?'

Orphanus took a reading from her wrist monitor. 'It's adjusting his atomic mass.'

'Does that mean you will have to alter in again when you take him back? Mansel has ten more functions to cope with over Christmas, you know.'

Had the Vardel known about Christmas, it was unlikely she would have been able to grasp the concept of angels, tinsel, and virgin birth. 'His body will need to adjust to its new biology before that is attempted.'

'New biology?'

'Human biology. Your species is quite frail.'

As a seventy two-year-old with dangerously low blood pressure, arthritis, and diabetes, Gladys could only agree. 'Tell me about it,' she muttered.

The cocoon encasing Amiel faded, and then dissipated into thin air.

'I'll say this for Skirra, he may be a preposterous bladder of hot air, but he does know his job.'

'Can he cure piles?' asked Gladys, ever the opportunist.

Amiel suddenly twitched. His silver eyes flashed open and he looked up to see a Vardel. He turned to Gladys to make sure he hadn't skipped dimensions again.

'It's all right, Amiel,' the photographer reassured. 'You should be fine now.'

Somehow Amiel found the strength to round on Orphanus. 'How the hell did you get here?' he demanded in their common language with some difficulty because of his human vocal chords.

'Stick to human, Ansopha,' Orphanus chided. 'We don't want there to be any misunderstandings, do we.'

'Am I meant to understand what's going on?' asked Gladys. 'I was hoping all this would be over my head.'

'Ansopha will explain everything to you now.' The Vardel gave him a crocodile smile that would have knocked Joabim off his perch.

Amiel tried to rise. 'But I don't know what's going on?'

'Then Mrs Hodge will explain everything to you.'

Gladys took off her glasses and rubbed her eyes. 'I need a drink. Do you think a couple of brandies will stop me hallucinating?'

'There are too many layers of reality for one mortal mind to comprehend. Because ours does not fit your experience, it does not mean that you are hallucinating.' Orphanus heard herself speak, and wondered how Hunder had managed to put the words into her mouth. That was as near to a profound observation the Vardel ever wanted to get.

Gladys looked the hawk-like alien straight in the

diamond eyes. 'You've never met the Moonstar Players, have you?'

'Is this some sort of night time manifestation?'

The recollection of them trying to cast him as Tiny Tim swilled through Amiel's disorganized thoughts. 'And you should meet the parrot.'

Orphanus felt uneasy. How was she going to tell Hunder that the communicator he had just invested so much in saving was becoming irrational?

Gladys sensed that the Vardel needed a way out. 'How long can you stay?'

'I must leave right away. The gravity line is only viable for a short time.'

'But how-?' Amiel started, and then thought better of it. He still couldn't make sense of what was going on, and Gladys was bound to ask as soon as she had downed a couple of brandies.

'We will come back for you as soon as Skirra has calculated the compression needed for transfer. In the meantime, Hunder has to suspend telepathic link.'

Amiel's expression fell. Removing his link with the bio computer would be like excising part of his mind. 'How will I cope without him?'

Gladys was becoming more and more bemused. At any other time this would have sounded like a good story, even if she dropped the "alien". WAITER CAN ONLY SURVIVE WITH BRAIN LINKED TO MACHINE; the sort of article you only wrote with one eye on the invoice and mid summer slump in sensible news.

'You seem to have picked up the hang of things here, Amiel. What's the problem?' Gladys tried to reassure.

She was right. Now his atomic integrity had been balanced, Mansel's new waiter could make it as a human being if he remained permanently stranded on Earth.

All the same, Amiel was still horrified at the thought

of losing Hunder. 'Why is it essential for him to suspend the link?'

Orphanus was reluctant to tell him. 'It was intercepted,' she nevertheless admitted. 'That's why your metabolism could not be stabilised.' She didn't add that he shouldn't have survived in the first place because of the questions that would beg.

Amiel gazed at the Vardel with a tinge of resentment. 'I suppose you're relieved to be rid of me after what happened?'

Orphanus would have preferred him to say something offensive to give her a good reason to change her mind and leave him there.

'I have to go.' The engineer handed him a tiny case. 'Skirra sent this. If you have any problems, it will regulate your metabolism until it has fully adapted. Hunder will be in touch eventually.'

To avoid the embarrassment of a fond farewell, Orphanus put the black robe on and pulled the hood over her head.

Gladys led the alien back downstairs.

They passed through the streamers, laughter, bursting balloons, and squawks of the cockatoo that made Orphanus fizz inside like a vigorously shaken bottle of carbonated water.

Gladys walked to the promenade to ensure that the Vardel found the transmission point near the turning tide. She was disappointed that the alien didn't disappear in a cloud of sparkling molecules or wavy lines. One second she was there - the next gone. So what did the photographer know about faster than light tachyon transmission? In her next incarnation perhaps...

Gladys returned to the saloon and, after two stiff brandies and chat with a couple of deep-sea anglers, went back upstairs to tuck Amiel in. If he survived, she could at least look forward to a decent cappuccino in the mornings.

CHAPTER 30

'That hurt!' Hunder snapped as Skirra went into his bio core with a probe.

'I told you to shut down your bio circuits.'

'That's where the headache is.'

'Trust me, I'm a medical scientist.'

'Then tell me what brought it on?'

'Probably a few loose neurones. You are getting on after all! The longest serving bio computer in the star region.'

The bio circuitry of Hunder's memory was like the entrails of a huge star cow pulsating with heartburn. However familiar Skirra was with the bio computer in his routine dealings with him, down there it was salutary to be reminded of the entity's true nature. This half machine, half biological system had the power to open gravity lines, move planets, and throw tantrums capable of deflecting asteroids. And yet a mere mortal had tinkered with Hunder's circuits without him knowing. When a brain the size of a planet insisted that it had a severe migraine, it hadn't been triggered by a slight increase in atmospheric pressure.

Skirra methodically scanned each neurocircuit cluster until he came to part of the bio system that shuddered at the light of the probe.

This was bad.

Skirra sat tight on his thoughts, even though it was unlikely his patient could have read them at that moment, and feigned professional bonhomie. 'Here we are. Looks as though there's been a sudden flux that sensitised the neuro-connections.'

'How?'

'You probably downloaded something that should have been dealt with by your quantum memory.' Then he muttered to himself, 'Colliding pulsars! What happened here?'

That close, Hunder could have heard bacteria chewing. 'You tell me, you're the one in my brain?'

'This wasn't caused by random switching.'

'Tell me what you've found.'

Skirra hesitated. How could he tell Hunder that something had taken a chunk from the centre of his brain? 'A large region of your bio processor has been burnt out,' he eventually admitted.

Hunder didn't believe him. 'That couldn't happen without me knowing about it.'

'Run a check with your quantum memory to see what's missing.'

Hunder switched to the qubits of his cumbersome universal register. 'Random images of incoming traffic... Some backup data -' Suddenly the bio computer was aware of the void in his memory. 'Oh no!'

'What?'

'I've lost Ansopha!'

'How?'

'The link with his implant! It's been erased!'

'Didn't you have it duplicated in your quantum back-up?'

'How could I? That's not telepathic.'

'How did it happen?'

'I don't know. The link was suspended when Orphanus returned. I was going to restore it as soon as you had finished.'

There was nothing Skirra could do about retrieving the lost data. He replaced his probe in its sterile case and floated up into the bio computer's control while Hunder speculated through the migraine.

'It was just as well I stunned that Fammoran programmer before she could do any more damage, but something else might have filtered in before I had chance to close the link.'

'Does this mean we've lost Ansopha?'

'We still have the gravity line.'

'Is it stable?'

'It could take several time cycles to re-establish.'

'How long?'

'It's subject to the same laws as the other gravity lines. Compensations have to be made for their movement and Ansopha is so far away galactic rotation is too great to keep it aligned.'

Given the length of time the medic had been gone, Orphanus realised something was wrong and dropped through the control's hatch to join them.

'Hunder's telepathic link with Ansopha has been burnt out,' announced Skirra.

The engineer gave a wry smile and leaned indolently against a bank of anxiously blinking indicator lights. 'It's started then.'

'What's started?'

'You know damn well. Just because I use a welder instead of a surgical laser, it doesn't mean I've got the intellect of a reinforced bulkhead. Space Command never wiped out God after all, did they?'

'All right,' Hunder admitted. There was no point in denying it any longer. 'It appears that this entity only needed a few viable atoms to reform. As soon as that happened He wasted no time in tracking down Ansopha.'

'Why didn't you realise that this was happening?' Skirra demanded.

'I don't have the energy map of every entity which decides to run amok,' snapped Hunder. Then he calmed down, even though his titanic headache was increasing by powers of ten. 'He could be related to the energy forms that evolve from the ionised atmospheres of gaseous giants. Once viable, they develop extraordinary capabilities. I've never heard of one leaving its planet to start tapping the power from stars, though.'

'Could He be from another galaxy?'

'If the entity travelled that distance, it would explain why He was so bad tempered and ravenous. Our sun just might have had the bad luck to be sitting at the end of the first gravity line He encountered.'

'But the entity claimed it created us?' protested Orphanus.

'His molecules were probably addled. The creature no doubt created somebody when He was in His prime. Though I doubt that they are in the immediate vicinity, or still exist. When you're God, one life form must be very much like another. He had no doubt become senile and vindictive because He was so ancient.'

Skirra felt embarrassed at ever believing in the fraudulent manifestation. 'God is a very weird creature.'

'How long before the entity reaches Ansopha?' asked the Vardel.

'Depends on His mass,' explained Hunder. 'My guess is that He won't attack our sun again. He's still vulnerable.'

'He had enough power to get into your bio memory,' said Skirra. 'Seems God wants to isolate Ansopha.'

Orphanus sneered. 'I wonder why.'

CHAPTER 31

And God reached out with His hand of vengeance.

There was a disturbance at the end of the gravity line Ansopha had been transmitted into.

Being unable to do anything about it didn't improve Hunder's throbbing headache.

Something was inside the anomaly, threshing about on the border of another dimension like a comet trying to escape a gravitational whirlpool.

It crossed Orphanus' mind that she had narrowly escaped being trapped inside the gravity line with it. 'What is that?'

Hunder gave up attempting to stabilise the anomaly. It was draining power from the satellite's core and the Vardel was heartily sick of becoming weightless every time its rotation slowed down.

'At a guess, I would say it was an embryo God,' admitted the bio computer bitterly.

Skirra and Orphanus gazed at each other. For once their perceptions, so often alien to each other, entertained the same thought.

Skirra was furious. 'How could you have let Him through?'

This was no way to cure Hunder's headache. 'Me! All you two needed to do was look out of a viewport and see Him coming.'

'How should we know what an embryo God looks like? And I could have hardly looked out of a viewport while I was poking around in your miserable bowels! You're supposed to be the Galaxy's ultimate computer. Why didn't you detect Him?'

'With your laser probe up the rectum of my bio circuits?'

'Shut-up you two!' Orphanus was amazed at the authority in her tone. Skirra was usually the one trying to tranquillize her away from someone else's throat. 'If that is God, everyone on the other end of that gravity line is in very real trouble - and Ansopha is as good as dead. Try to re-establish the link, Hunder.'

'Too much of my bio memory is missing.'

'Does that mean we've lost Ansopha for good?' There was no reply so Skirra went to the medical screen. 'Pity, now I know how to stabilise his atomic mass.'

'That's the last of my worries,' confessed Hunder. 'Since I opened up a gravity line to that Leamt merchant's home world, a new region of space is now at risk.'

'You have told Space Command?'

'Of course.'

'Well, can't they transmit a warning?'

'Not in any binary code that would be understood. The only messages the people on the other end would understand are strictly at the, "Me have four legs, three arms and two heads" level and it would take them aeons to pick it up.'

'What will God do to Ansopha?' asked Skirra.

'I'd rather not think about it.'

CHAPTER 32

At the foot of Brinton-on-Sea's headland there was a loud thud that reverberated throughout the district.

As it was only three in the morning, woken children thought Father Christmas had collided with the cliff, and their parents went downstairs to make sure that the turkey hadn't exploded before realising that Christmas was still a couple of weeks away.

For a moment the cliff glowed, and then the shingle on the beach rippled as though a huge pebble had hit a bowl of risotto, shattering quartz and making it glint like magical hundreds and thousands. The region was shaken by a low frequency vibration that registered on seismometers. Then everything was calm again, apart from a few woken gulls, a small Yorkie running in circles about Mary's bedroom, and the sea slurping in and out of a huge hole where part of the cliff used to be.

Lucinfer stood by the veranda window of her chalet, looking out over the inky sea at the faint tinsel gleam of the Milky Way. A dome of light rose over the headland. It briefly flared like Hell's sparkler, and then gave way to the moonlight.

***

As the hazy sun rose, Gladys was in Beachview's laundry room. She pulled the black robe from the tumble drier and started to press it. Just in case the Vardel had carried some exotic bacterium bold enough to make its home on Lucinfer, the garment had been washed three times. The only thing to come out of it, though, was black dye and Gloria's tailor tacks.

In the adjoining kitchen, Mansel and Mary were clearing away the debris from yesterday's party. Knowing that Amiel was not going into terminal decline after all had cheered the proprietor no end. He launched into song. Louise joined in from her basket in the basement flat's hall. Mary decided it was time to go upstairs and vacuum.

Only when Gladys entered with the neatly folded robe was there a lull in the cacophony.

Mansel lifted his sudsy hands from the sink. 'Mrs Hodge, I did tell you that the next week's cappuccinos are on the house, didn't I?'

'Why thank you Mansel. What have I done to deserve that?'

'Amiel. He would not have recovered so quickly without you.'

'I only took him the occasional powder and hot drink,' she lied. 'He has a delicate metabolism. The sea air must have come as a shock to it. You will be careful not to overwork him?'

'I will treat him as gently as a mushroom soufflé. I also owe you Christmas dinner for helping Mary and Sandra.'

Gladys laughed. 'Don't be ridiculous, Mansel. You won't make any profit at all if you carry on like this.'

The proprietor plunged his hands back into the sink. 'You must humour me.'

Gladys was usually discreet enough to mind her own business when it came to kitchen matters yet, after spending so many Christmases at Beachview, she was unable to keep quiet any longer. 'Mansel, have you ever thought about getting a dishwasher?'

By his expression, Mansel obviously had. 'Would that not scratch the glasses?'

'If you only used if for plates and dishes it would still save you hours, not to mention your hands.'

He sighed as the thought of the inevitable hurdle loomed before him. 'Ah, Mama Lascelle, she would not like the vibration on her ceiling.'

Gladys had also seen that hazard coming. 'If it's by the sink it would be over your hall. And modern machines don't make that much noise.'

That must have been all Mansel needed to steel his resolve. He burst into a few bars of some obscure ballad, which usually meant he had made his mind up, and then nodded towards the robe. 'How did your photo session go?'

'Very well. She was an extraordinary model.'

'I think Joabim would have liked to play with her.'

Gladys giggled nervously. Lying was hard work. 'I suspect he would have done given half the chance.' Unable to keep up the charade any longer, she went into to the lounge where Lucinfer was waiting for her costume.

Christmas Future pushed the black garment into a carrier bag.

'Can I buy you a coffee?' asked Gladys. 'That robe was more help than you can imagine.'

'Why thank you.'

Gladys was baffled by her friend's lack of curiosity in not asking what she had needed it for, or even a promise to see the photographs of the model who had worn it.

Lucinfer looked about. 'Isn't Amiel any better, then?'

'I told him to stay in his room for the day, just in case. Mansel will be out at any moment.'

They went to a window seat.

'You look wan.' Lucinfer sounded concerned.

'Probably just a little chill.'

After last nights escapade it was hardly surprising that the blood had left the photographer's face. Gladys thought it even more surprising that she hadn't lost her sense of reality as well, but was worldly wise enough to know it was not a good idea to tell anyone she had met an alien, let alone that another one would be serving her a cappuccino the next morning. Lucinfer had a broad outlook, yet it would have been unreasonable to expect her to believe in a Vardel.

'Mr Butterworth has taken another morning walk,' Gladys said, 'I think it may be developing into a habit.'

'Good idea. Where's the point of coming to the seaside if you don't see the sea?'

'What made you come to the Brinton-on-Sea, Lucinfer?'

The woman raised an eyebrow as though caught out in espionage. 'Just a break from my usual routine. I found I was beginning to take things for granted. Getting a little stale. Started to make the odd slip.'

'Not to escape Christmas then?'

'Never really thought about it. Is that why you come?'

'Every year. Playing the maiden aunt to my sibling's gruesome family is not my style. After ignoring you all year, they have this need to display goodwill. They have this picture of me in their minds as an elderly, crabbed creature huddled over a one bar electric fire.'

'I suspect you are wealthier than all of them put together?'

There was no way Gladys could duck the acuity of her new friend. 'True, and none of my seasonally attentive relatives are going to get their hands on it. When I go several good causes overseas are going to benefit instead.'

'In places you have no doubt covered as a journalist?'

'Places I know would make good use of everything which comes their way and not blow it all on another car, second home, and skipful of inane DVDs.'

Lucinfer leaned back, saying nothing. She knew that something more pressing than family relationships was on the photographer's mind.

It was no good, if Gladys didn't say something, however ambiguous, she would probably explode. 'Tell me, Lucinfer, do you believe that there is life on other planets?'

Given the way their conversations were wont to veer, her friend must have been anticipating the question. 'In this Galaxy?'

Despite being a journalist, Gladys had never

confused the Galaxy with the Universe. 'Can't get my head round the idea of anything larger.'

'This would not only be a unique world if there were not, it would also be very peculiar.'

'Intelligent life?'

'As intelligent as you like. By the law of averages it must cover the whole spectrum, from ants to super-beings from the intergalactic void.'

'If beings were that intelligent, why would they want to visit a place like this?'

'Would they?'

'I meant-' Gladys faltered. 'I meant, is there anything special on this planet that would interest some super-intelligence?'

Lucinfer leaned on the windowsill and gazed at the rising sun. 'Humans might seem like ants to them and, if not accidentally trodden on, be ignored altogether.'

'What do you believe?'

'I believe that if a being is that advanced they can see into the mind of an ant. Perhaps even become one.'

Gladys felt her soul retreat a little. This was eerie stuff. 'So, if super-beings exist, they could already be here?'

'Not necessarily disguised as ants.'

'Surely they must perceive time differently?'

'Time? It might pass at a frantic pace to some, and crawl to others. The Galaxy is probably banded into zones accordingly. Though personally, I doubt that there is such a thing as "time". The Universe is a pond filled with the lily pads of expectation. Very few know how to tiptoe across them from one time zone to another.'

'I wish you didn't sound so sure.'

Mansel bustled in with a cappuccino and coffee.

'They're both on me, Mansel,' said Lucinfer as Gladys gazed absently at the dawning sun.

Mansel was concerned by Gladys' detachment. He wondered if he should have allowed her to clear so many tables for him. Lucinfer raised a reassuring finger to her lips and he went back to the kitchen.

Gladys eventually gave a deep sigh. 'What if these advanced beings are able to transmit themselves about the Galaxy through some gravitational anomaly? What reason would they have to come here then, do you think?'

Lucinfer raised an eyebrow. 'I think you need a stiff drink and some fresh air.'

Gladys suddenly laughed. 'Sorry. These things never used to bother me when I was young.'

'Congratulations, you've probably just come of Cosmic age.'

'At seventy-two? I can die happy now.'

'I think fate has a few more adventures for you yet.'

Gladys cast her a sideways glance. Lucinfer didn't sound ironic enough for comfort.

'If you're going into town I'll come with you, but I want to pop upstairs and see that Amiel is resting before I go.' The photographer shook her head. 'You must think I'm going doolally?'

'On the contrary. You're the sanest human I could ever hope to meet.'

CHAPTER 33

The ritual wail of mourning engulfed Auroal on every available electromagnetic frequency.

Orphanus couldn't disguise her scorn, even if she wanted to. 'At least they think God is dead. And thank God for it.'

Skirra was puzzled. 'I didn't think they would make it official so soon. I wonder what convinced them, Hunder?'

Hunder didn't reply; he was too busy calculating the consequences of his own mismanagement. His aspirations for mortality were playing havoc with his quantum circuits, which had trouble keeping up with his bio system at the best of times. If they had their way, they would have allowed Hunder his mortality so they could be free of him to create a genuinely useful traffic control system.

Skirra was used to Hunder having a reply for everything - when the he wasn't sulking, that is. 'What's he gone quiet for?'

'Guilty conscience,' said Orphanus. 'Being responsible for what happened to Ansopha, not to mention finding God a cosy new home to devour.'

'Pity we can't contact someone there.'

'Even if they were able to receive Space Command, they'd probably think the signal was coming from a pulsar.'

Skirra floated away from Hunder's monitor. 'I hate to admit it, but I am going to miss Ansopha. It may have been a cynical, self-opinionated and undisciplined creature, but it was company.'

'And wasn't afraid of anything,' Orphanus added reluctantly.

'If Ansopha had been, it would still be here.'

Orphanus shook back her jungle of hair. 'No it wouldn't. We'd all have been wiped out when God devoured our sun.'

The rituals on Auroal went on for two more rotations of the artificial planet as the newly formed Cult of the Rainbow was celebrated. Even those who were glad to see the last of God joined in. Now He was gone, they could save face without encouraging the dangerous entity.

The Fammorans brought out artefacts hoarded away in their Hunder-proof sanctum. As the bio computer and his mercenaries believed they had destroyed the Creator they felt justified in flaunting every holy symbol they could lay their appendages on. Even the Fammoran ceremonial tails were garlanded with anti-Hunder slogans.

God's death had united many species on Auroal who had never been on friendly terms before, and the bio computer was just relieved that they hadn't turned on each other instead. Without him as a common foe, it would have happened soon enough. Now Hunder was free to perfect his interactive hologram and emigrate to some distant star cluster where creator gods hadn't had time to evolve.

Many found it a relief to release pent-up energy after being confined for so long on a space dock at the end of nowhere and, as night descended on one longitude, each species raced their holy reliquaries after the setting sun's rays. It was a wonder the artificial planet didn't tilt in its orbit.

'Are Space Command going to send us another communicator?' Orphanus asked without warning.

Hunder was caught out by the question and forgot he was sulking. 'I haven't asked for one.'

'You're never going to get Ansopha back now. You have to admit it. You know that.'

'Vardels don't have periods of mourning, do they?'

Orphanus shrugged. 'What goes, goes. Mourning doesn't bring it back.'

'No, I didn't expect they would. Probably unfurl a few banners to celebrate a glorious death. Can't imagine many of your species dying of natural causes.'

Skirra felt an irrational pang of empathy for Hunder's predicament. 'Losing Ansopha wasn't your fault. You did what you had to. If you hadn't, the entity's reaction would have been catastrophic.'

Hunder lapsed back into his sulk to avoid a deep, meaningful conversation.

There was still one thing that puzzled Orphanus, and she knew that Hunder wouldn't explain it, so asked Skirra. 'I still can't comprehend why God was so determined to pursue Ansopha? Nothing about it makes sense.'

'God never made sense.'

Orphanus recalled something the entity had said. 'God insisted that the communicator was the work of the Devil. If what we encountered was God, I wouldn't want to meet that other delusional deity.'

Skirra gave an uneasy laugh and wished Ansopha had been there to make some acidic comment to put things into perspective. But even perspective was beginning to have negotiable parameters.

During his sulk, Hunder had detected atoms moving less randomly about space than was mathematically comfortable. He would have ignored them if they hadn't been so near the gravity line to Ansopha. It could only mean one thing. God had decided to come back and destroy Auroal before devouring the star system in the atomic anomaly. Getting rid of the Devil's disciple hadn't been enough for Him; now that God was getting His act together, His capacity for vengeance was becoming indiscriminate.

Having spread the lie about God's death, Hunder could hardly tell those mourning for Him on Auroal that

He had returned to devour the planet.

There was no time to recall Space Command. Only Hunder could save Auroal, even if its residents were prepared to hold God's coat while He sent the bio computer back to the great programmer in the sky. If Skirra and Orphanus had known how he intended to do it, they would have immediately pulled his plug, left things to his acquiescing quantum circuits, and summoned a Space Command evacuation fleet. Unfortunately that would have only arrived in time to gather up the carbonised remains of the planet, its inhabitants, and Hunder's satellite.

The bio computer had no choice but to act before God stabilised Himself. The entity would zero in to anything that generated energy, but he could hardly switch off Auroal's life support systems.

Taking the artificial world to another solar system would be too slow, and easy for an enraged entity to overtake. There was only one place where it could be safe and Hunder would have to collapse the gravity line as soon as Auroal was through it. The bio computer quailed at the thought, but there was nothing else for it.

A suspicious number of alerts for damaged systems and medical emergencies on Auroal began to bombard the satellite. Orphanus and Skirra couldn't ignore them and were obliged to go down to the artificial world.

The medical scientist packed enough medical equipment to interfere with the shuttle's stability and insisted that Orphanus leave behind some of her weaponry instead. Who was liable to attack the only effective medical relief Auroal had? The Vardel had no answer. She thought the worst of all life forms, including her own.

When they arrived Auroal's inhabitants were so immersed in mourning for God only a few alert atheists noticed that there was something not quite right with their planet's alignment. At first Orphanus paid no attention. When she did call Hunder to stabilise Auroal's gyroscope, she received static. From a pole observatory viewport it was possible to see that the bio computer had shut down his satellite, its limb only visible against the sun's light.

Now what was Hunder up to? For all his moods, tantrums, distorted logic, and program overrides, he was only a machine after all.

Orphanus took a team of engineers down to Auroal's core. There was nothing wrong with the systems stabilising the planet and only one explanation. Only one other person who could confirm her suspicions without having a fit.

Hunder had found Skirra so many patients, his team had no option but to sedate and place them on racks according to species, despite the protests that there was nothing wrong with them. The medical scientist really didn't need to discuss engineering with an agitated Vardel warrior at that moment.

'Why can't I raise Hunder?'

'Look, we're busy!' snapped Skirra. 'Hunder's probably having one of his moods.'

'This is no mood! Auroal is leaving its orbit!'

Skirra slowly put down the scanner he was calibrating for yet another life form. 'Are you sure?'

'Auroal is heading for a gravity line.'

'What?'

'Hunder has charged the core with enough power to last a generation and opened a gravity line. He's sending Auroal into uncharted space, Skirra!'

The medical scientist bounced in alarm and hit the ceiling. As they didn't know what he and Orphanus were talking about, his Auroal assistants accepted this behaviour as normal for a weird species.

'Why?'

'I knew he was keeping something from us.'

Skirra nervously glanced about at the wide

assortment of puzzled expressions. 'God?'

'Must be.'

'Why the hell didn't he say something?'

'Would you have wanted to know?'

Skirra went to his medical case and took out a canister. 'Can you access all the atmosphere systems simultaneously?'

'Yes. Why?'

'Because total chaos will break out as soon as everyone realises what's happening.'

Orphanus took the tube from him. 'You don't need to do that. I can disorientate everyone by manipulating the rotation.'

'Including the Aubrins?'

'Aubrins?'

'They don't need gravity. They were the species my people acquired our buoyancy genes from. As soon as we've done that we'd better get to a shuttle. I don't want to end up at the other end of a gravity line having to deal with planet wide hysteria.'

'Where will you go? Hunder has shut down his satellite and the nearest system is out of range. Do you really want to be out there in a shuttle with some insane entity who's decided it's payback time?'

Skirra came down to the Vardel's eye level. 'Do you really think that this gravity line will be deep enough to hide from God?'

'Hunder must have thought of that.' Orphanus paused. 'You've been away from your litter for ages. They've probably forgotten what you look like. And I could do with a change of scenery.'

'I'm not sure I want to see what you can get up to in another dimension, but it doesn't look as though we have any choice. Let's stun the planet.'

CHAPTER 34

Gladys and Amiel waited patiently while Mavis Brink wrestled with the community hall keys.

'Of course, I will only need Amiel for the one evening performance to fill in for my sister. Did I tell you she has to go to London? It's our mother you see. It was really my turn, but with the production - I couldn't very well leave The Moonstar Players in the lurch, could I?' The other two were more interested in getting out of the cold than the machinations of her dreary family as the amateur company's treasurer and general factotum wittered on like a worried budgerigar. 'It's just that I can't manage the graveyard flat by myself and need another pair of hands with the feast of Christmas Present.'

At last the tumblers of the lock turned and they could enter into the relative warmth created by ancient radiators that should have been sent to a museum to demonstrate how global warming came about. They pumped more heat through the draughty roof, doors, and windows than inside.

'Wouldn't it be easier for Amiel to sell programmes and me to help backstage?' suggested Gladys. She was afraid the poor man - or whatever he was - would not be able to survive an evening of the manic theatre group stampeding around the furniture.

'Oh no, I think it's much better we have a strong male to do this.'

Amiel looked uncomfortable and wondered about this human obsession with that other strange alien, Superman.

'He has just been ill, you know,' Gladys reminded her.

Mavis Brink managed to drop her brimming prop's satchel just in time to drown out her words. 'I'm sorry?'

'And Mansel can only part with him for a couple of

hours.'

'Oh what a pity,' Mavis said absently. She scuttled to the far end of the hall and rummaged in some boxes on the stage. 'We were going to have a party afterwards,' she called back over her shoulder.

Leaning higgledy-piggledy, as though some mighty hand had been playing knucklebones with the set, were the flats. All the stage furniture was groaning under yet another layer of paint and, with the unnecessary number of props, in the dim hall light it looked like a charity shop having a clear out. Being a photographer, Gladys knew the wonders judiciously placed lights could work. If it hadn't been for the community hall's resident electrician, the Moonstar Players would have literally faded from view long ago.

Mavis pulled a handful of folded pink pages from a box. 'These are only twenty pence each. Almost at cost because the pictures of the cast were scanned in by a friend of Oliver's.'

A groan of despair rumbled about the photographer's soul when she saw what dire work could be committed with an instamatic, bad make-up, and PhotoShop illiterate designer.

Gladys asked herself why she had agreed to sell programmes, and replied that it was because Amiel could not be exposed to the full glare of a Moonstar Players' egos without some support in case he started to disappear again. Even they wouldn't have been able to upstage that.

Mavis pottered about like a hyperactive crab tasting morsels on a crowded beach. 'Over here, Amiel. This is the props table.' As most of the props were stacked in mounds about the set after the Moonstar Players had squabbled about where they should go, there were very few items left on it. The dowdy woman then lifted a small flat to prove how light they were, despite being held together by little more than layers of emulsion. She suddenly popped her head round a canvas tombstone to ask Gladys. 'I say, did you hear that dreadful bump in the night?'

Gladys had been woken by it and wondered if Amiel's alien friend had crash-landed, thought better of it, and gone back to sleep. 'No, when was this?'

'About three. Did you hear it Amiel?'

It belatedly dawned on Gladys that the wretched woman was tipping her cap at the waiter. Not the sort to compete for a man herself, it hadn't occurred to the photographer before. She wasn't sure just how alien Amiel was, or whether he understood what the human budgerigar was doing.

Amiel shook his head. 'I have been sleeping very heavily lately.'

'And I'm sure it came from the direction of Beachview. I almost phoned Mr Lascelle to make sure you were all right.'

'Oh, I was all right.' Amiel was able to pick up enough vibes from Mavis Brink to know he should run for the door. He could also sense Gladys's his hackles rise. He wasn't sure why, only recently having had to cope with the novelty of being male.

Mavis was totally oblivious to the emotional explosions she was causing. 'It would be so terrible if anything happened to you now, just when the Moonstar Players have discovered you.' She giggled. 'Who knows, in a couple of productions time you might even feel like treading the boards.'

Amiel assumed that was some alternative expression for walking the plank. He backed away from the enveloping cloud of Nature's Herbal Realm perfume. 'I do not have a very acute sense of balance.'

Mavis Brink pursued the waiter. 'Oh, don't worry about that, they'll always be someone to catch you.'

Amiel picked up the detonation as Gladys' patience exploded.

'Well thank you for showing us what we have to do, Mavis,' she said firmly. 'Now we must get back for lunch. Amiel will be needed.'

They left Mavis Brink sorting props to walk along the chilly promenade in silence.

Amiel at last commented. 'I don't serve lunch unless there are more than five tables? Mr Lascelle insists it is the best time for him to socialise with the customers.'

Gladys stopped in exasperation. 'Are you really such a dingbat or do you put it on?'

'I prefer not to read people's thoughts, though sometimes they escape with such violence I cannot avoid it.'

Gladys realised. 'Of course. Now you haven't got Hunder, you're not too sure how to react.'

'I am a quick learner, but where else in the Universe would I encounter a Mavis Brink? If you were to ever witness the birth of a star, you would never see in its atoms the potential for anything like that strange woman.'

'Or you, come to that.'

Another baffling human response. 'Why not?'

'Well, you obviously can't help what you are.'

Amiel hesitated. 'I've no idea what I am. I might have been one of those bizarre entities that created itself.' Gladys looked puzzled. 'On some worlds, beings can spring into life when the solar wind is at its maximum - similar to the way flowers in the deserts of this planet burst into bloom when there is rain.'

Despite herself, the journalistic irony that had helped her survive over the years managed to escape. 'Good grief! Mrs Lascelle was right. You're a pixie, albeit an intergalactic one. What was your true incarnation like? Did you have wings and magic wand?'

Amiel stopped. 'Don't ask me to be myself, please.'

This sounded more like the real Amiel. 'Why not?'

'You wouldn't like it. You really wouldn't like it.'

'You're not such a shrinking violet are you?' Amiel daren't reply. 'Why are you here?'

Amiel shrugged. 'Because I can't go back.'

Gladys nodded. That was logical enough. 'Why not?'

'We've lost the time line.'

'What does that mean?'

'What you call "time", moves at different speeds.'

'As in Einstein's Theory of Relativity?'

Amiel looked puzzled. 'Probably not. The Galaxy has different time planes as well as atomic densities.'

Gladys felt the hairs on the back of her neck rise as she recalled what Lucinfer had said about time.

Amiel went on, 'It's like stepping off a bus. However hard you run, you will never catch up with it so you have to wait for the next. If you want the one you just missed, you have to wait until it comes around again, probably with a different driver.'

'So you're waiting for the next bus?'

'On no. Hunder is. He's a bio computer. He will live long enough to catch the next time line and return to the same place.'

'So it's unlikely you'll ever see him again?'

Even the Ansopha in Amiel couldn't answer that.

CHAPTER 35

Life could be short for the unwary technician who probed the insides of powerful bio computers. Unfortunately this was the only way to prove the existence of God. It was salutary to discover that all the legends about Hunder had been true: the switching that controlled the bio computer's thought processes was so finely balanced he had needed a total vacuum to protect him from the nudge of random atoms.

As she poked and prodded about the unending mesh of bio circuits, Ongal was glad that the processors inside the satellite had been inactive for millennia.

When the technician reached the tangled micro connections that radiated from Hunder's bio core it was like encountering an alternative reality: none of the circuits seemed to make logical contacts.

Ongal carefully probed deeper. These organic machines were known to have had an attitude as well; so much so, they had been relegated to museums where the only conversations they could hold were with mentally unstable, closely guarded, geniuses.

The bio computer's core at the very centre of the satellite was surrounded by massive buffers to protect its vacuum. It was possible to see how Hunder could have rebuilt himself from that dormant tangle if catastrophe had taken out his other circuits. Ongal shuddered. The technician's sophisticated instruments would have been useless if Hunder woke and resented her presence. It was just as well that these monstrous bio systems had gone out of fashion centuries before.

The technician put away her probe. Breaching that sealed vacuum was the job of an experienced medical scientist. Being at the mercy of a bio computer capable of rebuilding itself when so many light years from anywhere else did not bear thinking about. But, for all the care she had taken, Ongal must have touched one of

Hunder's erogenous zones while probing his radial connections.

In a pulse of ultraviolet light, the deep well of bio circuits above her lit up and the technician tumbled into the shaft containing Hunder's quantum system. She only just managed to find the control of her backpack and prevent herself colliding with the battery of control circuits powering up.

'Orphanus,' skirled a disjointed voice. 'Is that you?' Not receiving a reply, the tone became more lucid. 'Skirra? What kept you?'

The technician froze in terror and could only guess what the bio computer was saying. 'My name is Ongal. I am a bio technician. Do you understand my language?'

Hunder paused, and then demanded, 'Speak!'

Ongal understood that, and waffled something about his circuits being in an immaculate condition considering their great age.

Hunder riffled through his memory until he came across a similar dialect. Time had altered Ongal's language and he instantly worked out what had happened.

'Skirra is dead?'

'You went into suspension seven solar centuries ago.'

'Oh shit! Of course. I've missed all the fun. Did God come back then?'

Ongal reeled slightly. She had never encountered a processor with personality before, let alone a bad attitude. The temperament of bio computers used to frequently interfere with vital operations, leaving civilisations in limbo while they were counselled out of some tantrum or other. At least Hunder's disposition seemed healthily realistic.

'So Skirra and Orphanus never made it back?'

Ongal could only answer. 'No idea. How did you manage to power up after so long?'

'Sensors programmed to detect body warmth. While

that sun shines, I have all the energy needed to activate myself.'

'Why do it now?'

Hunder became secretive. 'Can't remember.'

The technician forgot to be afraid. This bio computer didn't vaporise interlopers, just argued them to a standstill. 'Of course you can remember. You've got unlimited capacity in your quantum memory.'

'Probably dust on a contact somewhere.'

Ongal gave up. Greater minds than hers would have to sort out the machine. At least Hunder hadn't taken exception to her poking about his entrails. It would have been easier to ask how the bio computer felt, rather than check all his major circuits. Unfortunately, this one was probably so self-obsessed, listening could take forever.

'Why have you waited all this time?' Hunder demanded.

Ongal paused. The bio computer might have had a telepathy chip, so she decided to humour him. 'Some influential people have decided that the God question be settled once and for all.'

'Oh that.'

'They also believe that, somewhere in this jungle of circuits, bio contacts, quantum backup, and laser gates lays the answer.' Ongal paused. 'So who were Skirra and Orphanus?'

Hunder fell silent. To him, all this had happened yesterday. The technician couldn't be expected to understand. She was seven solar centuries too young and everything was safely stored down there in his memory. He didn't need to access it to find out whether God existed. There was no doubt a gospel that explained everything.

CHAPTER 36

The light of the spectrum penetrated the Sacred Prism, searing its colours onto the towering altar.

In robes perversely diaphanous for such a profound order, the Witnesses of the inner sanctum of the Sacred Prism wafted in and took their places before the Holy of Holies, careful not to break the prism light. That had been punishable by death before the regional government grew tired of the complaints about burning flesh.

Uneasy and embarrassed, Ongal and her superior took their places well below the Holy of Holies. The technician would have preferred the company of Hunder; despite his extraordinary powers he sounded in no way as grandiloquent as this gathering.

The chanting in mystic tongues and prayers to His Almighty Being, not to mention eulogies to His resurrection, were enough to intimidate a Vardel army. All the same, the metabolism of Ongal's superior was so sluggish, he became overpowered by the incense and began to doze off.

Ongal wished her species had developed the same ability. They only slept when necessary, refusing to waste a micro second of a valuable existence filled with so many conundrums to unravel. Unfortunately, she was the one expected to waste precious time answering a string of silly questions without laughing. The Witnesses of the Sacred Prism may have been absurd, but they were also pompous, powerful, and paying for her services.

The Meaning of the Universe should have already been unravelled after aeons of research by millions of scientists on various rungs of the technological ladder. The Grade 1 civilisations knew what it was all about, yet it was unlikely they would seep through the cracks of reality to satisfy the futile whims of lesser species and explain it. Watching the corporeal trying to work it out no doubt introduced a little light relief into their interminable existence. So, it still boiled down to the chanting and trances to induce divine enlightenment. Numerous adepts had reached it of course and, having achieved it, kept it to themselves. An eternity of research by some unenlightened science theologians eventually came up with, what seemed to them, a plausible explanation. The meaning of life was accepting it as it was because you were bound to find out in the end anyway. That neatly brought everything back to religion.

Ongal silently sighed. If Hunder could help solve the God question once and for all the religious squabbles in the star cluster would have to stop so everyone could get down to something worth while, like designing a probe that would find out what was at the bottom of a black hole. Even when facing the Holy of Holies, Ongal still thought like a technician.

The shroud was lifted from the Gospel of the Sacred Prism and the holy book ritually offered to a shaft of sunlight directed down into the inner sanctum. This had happened thousands of times since the discovery of the Gospel by the first prophet tending shaftan on the hills of Oron. Its covers had been bleached to a pearly patina in the intense rays of a star that necessitated those who lived under its zenith to evolve horny scales. The Witnesses, who spent their lives in sacred contemplation, were expected to preserve their soft, lily-white skin. If accidentally presented to sunlight, these elite became painfully scorched. The resulting burns were used as a litmus to prove how devout prospective members were. Many failed candidates deliberately burned themselves to prove that they had been wrongfully denied entry into the order.

The Gospel was withdrawn from the stream of sunlight before it burst into flames and the devotees filed from the inner sanctum, their diaphanous robes dancing on the scrolls of leaden incense like drugged butterflies.

Ongal's superior suddenly woke up. He nudged the technician to get to her feet and make abeyance while the holy crocodile filed past. He knew his assistant's atheistic tendencies and wasn't going to allow the Regional Technical Corps to offend the influential Witnesses of the Sacred Prism. They may have believed creation was magic, but their computer working to prove it needed regular upgrades.

Ongal switched on the communicator that linked her thoughts to Hunder's and reluctantly followed the ponderous crocodile into the outer sanctum.

Her interrogation consisted of questions in theological gobbledegook translated by a dowdy little priest. It was obvious that some believed the presence of the technicians defiled their temple.

Ongal found it best to let her brain idle in first gear, taking time to think up answers that I didn't offend the delicate sensitivities of the Witnesses of the Sacred Prism.

She was almost relieved when obliged to open her telepathic link with Hunder. Being a technology free zone, the temple of the Sacred Prism wouldn't allow in the electronic hardware required to make conventional contact with the bio computer. Telepathy was the chosen, more mystical, way to discover the whereabouts of the Holy Casket that would prove God's existence. Only when they knew where it was, would the holy order finance the quest to retrieve it.

Ongal was unnerved by Hunder's telepathic ability. She had encountered many exotic, powerful, and intimidating systems before, yet never one so close to mortality that she could actually detect a pulse. It may have been one of Hunder's strange affectations. However, having probed about his entrails, Ongal suspected that it was genuine. It was not something she wanted to share with the Witnesses as she relayed his claim to know the whereabouts of Auroal. The holy order immediately deduced from the admission that the infernal computer must have also had something to do with God's expulsion, and it was much better for them to believe he was no more than a mere machine, however powerful, artful, and without scruples.

The devotees cracked eggs into a ritual omelette to read the swirls in the setting albumen. The patterns it made confirmed their doubts about Hunder and the silent anger filling the outer sanctum scared even a Galaxy wise technician like Ongal. This wasn't mere annoyance, but deep rage welling up from centuries of conviction. It was just as well that Hunder's satellite was out of missile range; the Witnesses of the Sacred Prism had precise ideas about how to deal with heretics, mortal or otherwise, and that did involve hardware.

As she listened to the replies Hunder relayed through her, Ongal began to wonder if she would be allowed to leave unscathed. According to the Gospel, God's followers on Auroal had been the keepers of the Sacred Casket. Fortunately Hunder was the only one with the answers they needed and knew the gravity line the artificial planet had disappeared down and immolating this heretic, or his telepathic conduit, would have made no sense. Without that knowledge, the Witnesses could not send out trained seekers to search for the world that would lead them to the Sacred Casket in which God's atoms had been preserved.

The logic of God having mortal atoms had conveniently escaped theological debate; proving that God WAS came before questioning His nature.

Being kindred spirits in an odd bio fellowship, Ongal and Hunder let the telepathic link remain open so he could find out what the priests were planning.

After more rituals, a Witness turned the Sacred

Prism in the shaft of sunlight and the garish spectrum was diverted onto the outer sanctum's walls. The devotees lapsed into a dutiful chant.

At last the mumbling stopped and attention once again turned to Ongal.

She pretended to reopen her link with Hunder.

'Does this bio computer know the origin of the silver-eyed heretic?'

The question needed no elaboration: Hunder knew who they meant. 'No. Ansopha had been delegated to Auroal's satellite. The communicator was so exceptional I did not ask for references.'

'Exceptional? A creature who sneers at the holy Cittrac and defies God Himself!'

'I'd call that exceptional,' noted Hunder and Ongal wished that it hadn't come from her mouth.

An ugly murmur filled the outer sanctum.

Ongal quickly explained, 'This bio unit is very old. Due reverence to the Almighty was not programmed into these machines.'

The atmosphere remained charged.

'Can nothing be done to modify its tone?'

'I wouldn't like to try. These bio computers could be unstable. Corrective tampering might damage his memory. I'm afraid you're stuck with his point of view, however sacrilegious.'

Hunder was relieved to still be his old temperamental self. It felt good, so he went on, regardless of how much it embarrassed Ongal.

'Ansopha may have been sent by the Devil, of course. That's if entities such as God and the Devil really exist.'

The Witnesses' sharp intake of breath nearly depleted the sanctum of air.

Ongal was beginning to wish she was somewhere else, preferably another dimension, as she continued to elucidate the bio computer's anarchic view of the Universe.

'A communicator was essential to control an artificial world like Auroal. All those different species on neighbouring levels had to interact. They managed it pretty well until God turned up and turned their minds to vacuous mush.'

The senior Witness hissed with rage.

Hunder carried on regardless. 'The occasional argument broke out with the endless traffic arriving and departing from gravity lines. Docking crews on different latitudes needed a communicator like Ansopha who could converse in every dialect on the planet.'

'This creature was a malevolent influence.'

'What sort of Hell do you think Ansopha came from?'

Another Witness of the Sacred Prism was becoming restless. Protocol forbade him to speak before his senior gave permission. When several other members showed the same impatience, their superior was obliged to dismount his high horse to cut off a stampede of questions.

'What happened to Auroal, computer? We demand to know.'

It was morning and a crowd had gathered at the headland. Behind the plastic ribbon cordoning off the site, men in fluorescent yellow raincoats and wellingtons stepped over pebbles forming concentric ridges radiating away from the centre of a deep hole. A local astronomer was poking around at the bottom of it for the remains of a meteorite. Rubble started to cascade down the sides of the hole. He was unceremoniously hauled out and told to wait for the real experts.

Arnold's dog knew more about the strange goings on at that part of the beach than any expert from the local council. While his owner shakily snapped away with an ancient Polaroid camera, the Labrador remembered the Vardel it had recently seen and hid behind Arnold's coat.

'Well, was it a meteorite?' called down an official who had just parked his car perilously near the edge of the promenade.

'The astronomer says he can't tell', called back a small man in overalls and outsize wellingtons. 'Whatever created the hole burnt up. We'd better check the area. There won't be a high enough tide to fill this in for weeks.'

'Okay, but I don't want any men working on this over Christmas.' The official pulled out his mobile phone and held a long, professional sounding conversation.

Gladys looked blankly at the site of the impact, nursing suspicions that were going to last long enough to ruin her Christmas dinner.

Then a voice behind her declared in a matter-of-fact way, 'I've been evicted, you know. I'm going to stay at Beachview.'

Gladys wasn't surprised. 'Hallo Lucinfer. I'm glad whatever it was didn't come in at a higher angle.' The practicalities of the immediate situation were more pressing than her foreboding. 'Like a hand with the luggage?'

'Lucky it didn't hit the chalet. I'd have landed on the ring road. Doubt that I would have got my undercarriage down in time.'

It then occurred to Gladys that there was something different about her friend. Her coat was so red even the promenade's Christmas lights couldn't compete.

'You're wearing a red coat.'

Given her height, Lucinfer could have probably been seen by passing ships.

'Felt like a change. Must be the influence of the Moonstar Players. Pity none of them are here to see this.'

'Mavis Brink heard it last night. She's taken such a shine to Amiel I wouldn't put it past her trying to hold his hand right now.'

'Goodness. I'm sure she's not his type.'

'Can't imagine who is.'

'He probably left someone behind to wonder what became of him.'

Gladys gave a tight smile. 'Well, whoever it is, let's hope the snaps I took of him don't end up in the national press.'

Lucinfer's ebullience waned a little. 'You took photographs of him?'

'Several. Some with the Moonstar Players.' Gladys was suddenly aware of what she was saying. 'They came out much better than the first batch,' she added quickly.

'They did come out, though?'

'Fine.'

Lucinfer sounded relieved and promptly changed the subject. 'Understand we're going to see you tomorrow night?'

'I'm selling programmes and Amiel is helping Mavis. You will keep an eye on him for me, won't you?'

'You like him, don't you?'

'He won't give away enough for me to tell.'

'There is no reason to sound so glum over it, unless you fancy him of course?'

'I wish I still had the hormones.'

'Cheer up. It's already happened.'

Gladys wasn't so sure.

The wind began to bite so they walked back to Beachview.

'Mansel has given me a room overlooking the front. Hadn't much to pack. Just as well they're not letting anyone return to the chalet. The sideboard and hat stand will probably be delivered in a corporation van any moment now.' Lucinfer stopped prattling; she wasn't very good at it. 'What is the matter with you, Gladys?'

'Ever had the feeling the world's about to end and you're the only one who knows about it?'

'Not that I can recollect. Is the world about to end?'

'I'll be fine if someone with a forceful personality would just tell me I'm imagining it all.'

'You're imagining it all.'

The photographer shook her head. 'Didn't work.'

'Tell me about it?'

Gladys came to a decision. 'I'd like you to see some photographs.'

She felt it was a betrayal of Amiel's trust, but things were getting too bizarre for her to cope with. Put the photographer in the middle of a major uprising with bullets describing a cat's cradle about her and she would have been in her element. But interstellar visitors with dissolving atoms and hedgerow hairstyles? Now holes in the beach where yet another alien had probably landed? If this was the end of civilisation, she would much rather Lucinfer announced it to the world. At least she would give it some gravitas.

***

As Lucinfer examined the last photo Gladys couldn't detect so much as a flicker of surprise or disbelief in her friend's expression.

Lucinfer returned them to the bromide envelope. 'Amiel's at the community hall tomorrow night, you say?'

'From seven to nine.' Gladys could contain herself no longer. 'Well, what do you make of them?'

'This has something to do with what you needed my robe for, hasn't it?'

'Yes.' The photographer sighed heavily. 'Please don't ask me to explain that as well - not in the same day anyway.'

'At least I now understand your sudden curiosity about the supernatural. Don't worry about it, Gladys. At least three inexplicable things happen to everyone in their lifetime. Yours have just arrived all at once like the proverbial buses.'

'You don't think that any of this is odd then?'

'Of course it's odd. So are most things without apparent explanation. In a couple of centuries someone will blunder onto the answer and not think twice about it. Just look upon it as a trick of time.'

'Time, again?'

'Yes. Imagine all humans live inside a bottle of clouded glass, unable to see what is really going on all around them.'

For a moment the reassurance was totally plausible, although it sounded more like a variation on the theory of crystal spheres long believed in before the telescope. Lucinfer had credibility built into her voice. When she became Christmas Future, some elderly members of the audience would no doubt see the shadow of death and remember to cut some irksome relative out of their will before it was too late. And Lucinfer's reaction could have been worse. She might have dashed for the phone to get Gladys' peach-bottling next of kin to cart her away.

Lucinfer glanced at her watch. She was late for rehearsals. 'Would you ask Mansel to keep a look out for my luggage? The muse calls.'

Gladys waved the envelope of prints with a flourish of futility. 'Of course.'

Lucinfer reached the door, and then turned back. 'It's probably best you don't show those to anyone else. If the local papers got to hear of them, Amiel might feel obliged to leave.' She was right of course. 'I'm only across the landing if anything else worries you.'

Gladys gave a thin smile. Her friend was too open-minded to agonise over the perplexing minutiae that immobilised ordinary mortals, though might have been less blasé if she had encountered Orphanus.

CHAPTER 38

During Hunder's hibernation, God had described the original orbit of the long vanished holy planet Auroal with the ghostly rainbow of a planetary nebula as though he had every intention of returning for the rent like an avaricious landlord.

Now the Witnesses of the Sacred Prism realised that the artificial planet had been sent into oblivion by Hunder, there was a risk that they would disable his satellite for the sacrilege. Bearing this in mind, the bio computer was thankful that his interactive hologram had almost been perfected. When it was ready he wanted to inhabit it as soon as the opportunity for escape arose. If the Witnesses of the Sacred Prism found out the recollections bubbling up through his bio circuits - so disconcerting his quantum memory would have nothing to do with them - it would need to be soon.

***

The Neekite were fearsome little creatures; short lived and frenetic, they had no time for sex and perpetuated their existence by cloning off single offspring. Because of their static genes there was no opportunity for good manners to evolve. Hunder was glad that Skirra had never encountered the species. The medical scientist wouldn't have approved of beings able to procreate exact copies, complete with nasty thought processes and sharp teeth.

All the same, the Neekite had their uses. They were ideal for deep space exploration because death and ageing held no terrors for them. Whenever they started to run down, they simply cloned off a replacement. As long as their appetite never overcame their curiosity, their offspring could be guaranteed to find the odd life form other expeditions had overlooked. Fortunately the Neekite were being sent into an unmapped gravitational dead end to find an artificial planet. As Auroal's support systems had been dependent on Hunder and could have only remained viable for one generation without him, it was likely the artificial world would be derelict and have no life forms for them to devour.

To Hunder's chagrin, the Witnesses of the Sacred Prism had been fired with hope by his account of the multi-layered world and its inhabitants. The last thing he had wanted to do was give credence to the myths in their Gospel, especially the one about him being responsible for Auroal's disappearance.

The Witnesses of the Sacred Prism, much to Ongal's relief, allowed a program to be written so Hunder, blasphemies and all, could commune directly with them.

First, despite the bio computer's indignant protests, the Neekites were sent in to make sure the Sacred Casket was not concealed on his satellite.

The frenetic little creatures felt like a nasty infestation of gibbering parasites in his intestines and Hunder would have opened all the air locks and jettisoned them if there hadn't been a danger of the sudden change in pressure interfering with the delicate vacuum that buffered his bio core.

The little ferrets did find something. Before Hunder could work out what it was the Neekites swarmed back to their ships and were gone.

Hunder almost had a panic attack and had to tell himself to grow up and behave like a computer. Then he realised how mortal he had become during his hibernation. If the Witnesses discovered how much, he wouldn't just be switched off; after settling all the external threats to their huge alliance, Space Command now had a sizeable battery of Hunder-sized missiles.

Did bio computers who overrode their programs get to Heaven? Hunder hoped not. God was bound to be waiting for him.

CHAPTER 39

It was well past one in the morning.

After washing the plates from an evening party, Amiel still had the saloon to clear. Mrs Lascelle had decided to have one of her "I'm a poor old woman - nobody loves me!" moods and promised to throw a fit if her son did not spend several hours humouring her instead of working in the restaurant.

Despite his slight frame and bird like fingers, Amiel had learnt how to manage awkwardly loaded trays and carry four tankards in each hand. Perhaps he had found his real niche in life after all - from telepathic interspecies communicator to pot carrier. Perhaps he had dreamt his previous life and only just woken up. If Gladys hadn't taken those photos of him, Amiel would have been quite happy with the notion that he was no more than an irritating pimple on reality's backside. The human race craved too much excitement for his comfort. He would have even tried to humour Mansel's gruesome mother, though that carried the risk of having a toasting fork run through his heart.

Not tonight though.

He threw the tablecloths into the washing machine with a misaligned drum in the hope it would reverberate about the basement flat and annoy the crotchety old woman even more. Then he loosened his bow tie and went back into the saloon.

Joabim gave a long, low whistle.

'Don't you start,' warned Amiel. 'I've about had it with this Christmas thing.'

'What? No Christmas where you come from?'

'No,' Amiel thought back fiercely at the bird. 'Just bloody stupid aliens prepared to worship anything that drops in and calls itself God. Believe you me, that's nothing to celebrate.'

'Perhaps they need a little Jesus.'

Amiel seized as many glasses as he could and put them in the sink behind the bar. 'Why don't you get back in your cage and lay an egg.'

Joabim's crest flashed mockingly. 'Who's a disgruntled little alien, then?'

Amiel turned on the bird, jabbing a finger at it despite another armful of glasses. 'Do you know what I'm getting in exchange for doing this?' Joabim was only a cockatoo. Why should he need to know? 'All day off so I can help out the Moonstar Players!'

'Lucky you,' whistled Joabim. 'That Mavis Brink wants you to get inside her knickers.'

'And the last thing I need from a bird is instruction on human mating habits. I never used to have this problem, and don't intend to start now.'

Joabim hooted like a train and swung on a paper chain that promptly broke. Amiel ignored him and continued to pile glasses in the sink.

The bird rolled over and bounced across the saloon carpet. 'What sort of alien are you really then?'

'A bloody tired one.'

'I bet Dan Dare never had to wash up.'

'Who's Dan Dare?'

'Thought you knew everything?'

'My well of useless information dried up rather abruptly.'

'He lived in a comic a long while ago.'

'A geriatric bird like you reading comics?'

'Mansel's pen friend used to send them to him when he was small. His mother confiscated them and used Dan Dare to line my cage. Paid that spaceman a lot of compliments in my time.'

Amiel noticed his reflection in the mirror behind the wine shelf. Nobody should look like a startled muntjac caught in the headlights of a car, even if he felt like one. Once again he wondered what he was doing on this bizarre world. He had no useful answer, so carried on washing glasses.

An onyx ornament fell to the floor with a resounding thud and narrowly missed Joabim.

Amiel turned sharply. 'What was that?'

Joabim's crest had risen in alarm. 'It leapt off the mantelpiece!'

Amiel dried his hands. He wearily picked the ornament up and replaced it.

'Got a poltergeist! Got a poltergeist!' crowed Joabim.

'Shut-up. You're beginning to sound like a parrot.' Amiel rubbed his aching back as he rose and wondered how many more painful treats like this his human anatomy had in store for him. 'Lucinfer Brimstone is just above us, so keep your squawk down. I wouldn't fancy getting on the wrong side of that woman. Positioning her graveyard flat presents problems Orphanus never had to face.'

'Is that alien really your girlfriend?'

The thought filled Amiel with dread. 'No she isn't!'

'Why did she come all that way to visit you then?'

'Shut your beak.'

'Look out!' screeched Joabim as a half-empty bottle of light ale whistled past Amiel's ear.

The waiter froze. He hadn't felt such terror since being disconnected from Hunder.

'Poltergeist!' Joabim insisted unhelpfully from his new perch on the festive merry-go-round. 'Must have been raised by those two students who played around with that Ouija board.' He would have said more if some invisible hand hadn't flipped him over.

'Get in your cage,' Amiel ordered.

The cockatoo promptly obeyed and closed the door after him.

Then all hell was let loose.

The empty bottles and glasses rose in a clinking chorus, remained suspended for a few seconds, and then rained down on Amiel. He ducked under a table just as they exploded in the air above it. Joabim bobbed up from the bottom of his cage to glimpse decorations being wrenched from their Blue Tac and paper chains and baubles whirling in a tangled mass about the saloon like a frenetic cartoon.

But this wasn't Bugs Bunny.

The furniture started to thud towards the table where Amiel cowered. The waiter vaulted the lumbering settee and made for the front door.

Glasses, Christmas decorations, and bottles crashed down on him, drawing blood before he could release the bolts. When the door was opened, he dashed outside and across the deserted road onto the promenade.

As he searched for cover, Amiel was engulfed by a livid ball of light and tossed onto the shingle like a half deflated beach ball.

Then a voice reverberated in his mind. 'There is no escape heretic! Your friends cannot rescue you now. You will suffer the extinction all offspring of the Devil deserve.' It was low, malevolent, and forced something inside Amiel to remember who he was.

He spun round on the pebbles and faced the entity now towering above him in a pulsating pillar of energy. 'This is not your territory, you malignant parasite on the underside of Creation! You have no place here!'

'I will leave when I have tasted their sun. It is mature and ready to be absorbed.'

Amiel tried to think straight. It wasn't easy. 'All right then, kill me and have done with it.'

'I haven't come all this way merely to kill you.'

'What then?'

'All in good time, "Amiel Sopher". All in good time.'

The pillar of light faded. Amiel sank to the pebbles, exhausted by terror.

CHAPTER 40

The Witnesses of the Sacred Prism insisted that Hunder reopen the gravity line he had collapsed after sending Auroal into an unmapped region of space.

Hunder hoped that the planet had remained stable long enough for the population to discover new worlds to settle on. Torn between defiance and the guilty need to know what had happened to Skirra, Orphanus, and Auroal's two million inhabitants, the bio computer activated his traffic control system and scoured its registry. He found some pretty exotic visitor records, logs of species long extinct and, amongst all the ancient clutter, his quantum backup had preserved a link his bio circuits had attempted to delete. It sat like a minute nugget of recrimination in the bedrock of superseded data. Should the bio computer activate it and re-establish the gravity line Auroal had disappeared down? There was only so much the Witnesses of the Sacred Prism would put up with from blasphemy incarnate and it was either that or face one of those Hunder sized missiles from Space Command. So, with much prevarication, he opened the corridor to that gravitational abyss into which he had sent the artificial world.

The mean little Neekites with their spiky attitude to all things fleshy were first sent to find Auroal. Hunder hoped that some creature at the other end of the gravity line would think they were a light snack but no monster, however exotic, was likely to make that mistake. To compound his resentment of a species who didn't deserve the mobility Hunder craved, the Neekites immediately blundered into the artificial world as soon as they entered the region of space so remote it virtually bordered reality.

Auroal rotated ponderously like a cracked eggshell against the backdrop of an uncharted maroon sky.

The Neekites burrowed through its levels like hyperactive shrews to find deserted cities, spaceports, temples and living complexes preserved in the vacuum of space. Everything else had been destroyed by meteors crashing through the outer shell.

Various forms of space vermin scuttled about in residual pockets of atmosphere. They were encased in iron hard carapaces not even a Neekite would risk breaking their teeth on.

The Witnesses of the Sacred Prism waited anxiously for their first report, resenting the fact that their sacred quest was so dependent on Nature and technology's rejects. Until then it seemed as though the very Devil was dealing every hand. But that would all change once God returned and cleansed the Universe of these riffraff. As they had discovered the planet of the Sacred Prism, the Order was obliged to forget that the Neekite were Nature's ultimate carnivores though, on their triumphant return, they did put the lid over the sacred pool before debriefing them.

Now it had been established that Auroal was no myth, the Sacred Casket that contained the atomic traces of God Himself had to also exist.

After some consultation, a senior Witness demanded to know if the holy relic could be brought back from the depths of the gravity line. Hunder resented the dismissal of Ongal and having to collaborate with these zealots, so he decided to have a mood and play hard to raise. How could he usefully communicate with anyone who had committed their lives to spreading the word about God's loving nature? A description of the entity's true character coming from a computer would only confirm what they already believed. So Hunder blew a few connections and created some static to put off the inevitable. He couldn't keep it up forever without doing himself permanent damage and giving his quantum system the opportunity to take over. That would have acquiesced to anything, even a missile straight up the satellite's loading bay tubes.

But Hunder found himself dealing with an adept Senior Witness with enough conviction to bend light and had trouble blocking him from his telepathic circuits.

This disciple of the Sacred Prism seemed to inflate like an indignant toad before the pyramidal screen which was supposed to safely contain the contagion of the heretical bio computer. 'What happened to the inhabitants of the holy planet, computer?'

It was no good; resisting the devotee's thoughts was giving Hunder a headache. 'I hope they baled out before the main gyroscope lost power.'

'The Neekite found no mortal remains.'

Hunder was thankful for that; at least Skirra and Orphanus had survived.

The priest sensed his relief. 'How could the inhabitants have escaped your infernal crime?'

'Auroal was a massive space port, more ships docked on it than the Inter Star's Space Fleet port.'

'Inter Star Space Fleet?'

'Don't tell me they went under? I thought they were investing too heavily in the tachyon end of the market.'

The Senior Witness took an exasperated breath. 'Could the casket containing God's essence have been removed?'

Hunder hesitated. Why did they expect him to know anything about this Sacred Casket? 'I don't know.'

'Who were Auroal's most devoted?'

The bio computer knew only the Fammorans had the capacity to be that irrational. He blocked every pathway to the thought. 'No idea. Anyone could have it now - if it ever existed.'

'Of course it exists. Have you no soul at all, machine?'

Hunder could have taken this as an invitation to throw another mortal tantrum, though would have been a waste of time with these virtuous defenders of the

Faith; to them, immortality was no excuse for being uncooperative.

The bio computer was suddenly aware of his isolation. What was his function now? Orphanus and Skirra, who had given him a sense of purpose, were long gone. His only reason for existence had become to assist a group of fanatics to find the whereabouts of a star-devouring entity. Perhaps having a small fit wasn't such a bad idea after all.

CHAPTER 41

The elite seekers of the Sacred Prism were a diverse bunch. Each was named after a colour of the visible spectrum - except Indigo who was quite sinister, and not always visible. Some believed she had to plug herself into the nearest power source to be seen. Indigo was also the only one to demand remuneration for her services. Unlike the other seekers, her commitment to the Quest for the Sacred Prism was negotiable, yet she had far more experience than the others put together and was mercenary like the Neekites, only to be used as a last resort.

All the seekers came from different species and were prepared to travel to the ends of space to plunge a lance through the neck of the Devil's dragon.

Hunder had misgivings about these holy warriors with a martyr fixation. However, now he had opened up the gravity line, no one in the Order of the Sacred Prism was asking his opinion. The Witnesses were only keeping his link to them open in the hope the blasphemer would learn something.

Now the Witnesses had all the proof they needed to dispatch their warrior seekers on the holy quest to find the casket that contained God's atomic signature, the Neekites were paid off and hastily dismissed after their hungry gaze had fallen on the blessed bird of the resurrection.

Rituals at last over, the youngest of the seekers, Violet, was ceremonially handed the Order's armour, tailored to accommodate her four neat breasts and winged ears. Being unmapped, searching the mysterious region at the end of the dimensional cul-de-sac Auroal had been sent down would be interminable without Hunder's help. Unfortunately for the seekers, the Witnesses were determined to stand by their principals sooner than allow the help of that heretic, so the other seekers were placed in suspension until Violet returned. Except Indigo. She had better things to do.

Warrior seeker or not, Violet looked such a vulnerable little thing to Hunder. He was torn between curiosity and the risk that God's molecules had a long memory, feeling the need to point out the most likely worlds the diverse population of Auroal might have colonised.

Violet a gleeful innocence under all that top-heavy commitment and should have really been playing skittles with her friends on one of her home planet's ice plateaux, not going on a hazardous quest into uncharted space. She only had a standard on-board computer to help her find the way about the mysterious region that waited at the other end of the gravity line. How could Hunder allow such a delicate creature to travel into the depths of the unknown with a processor he wouldn't have allowed to monitor his satellite's vermin levels? He didn't particularly want a missile up his satellite's loading bay, but this bio computer had guile.

While Violet's craft was docked in his satellite's launch chamber, Hunder spoke to its on-board computer - and had the last word. Apart from a brief power surge as he usurped its circuits, the Witnesses, monitoring the launch from their inner sanctum, noticed nothing.

Hunder opened the gravity line. Violet's craft briefly hung over the churning vortex gaping like a dragon with a belly full of stars, and then was swallowed into a dimension where space, time and matter ceased to be relevant. Losing all sense of time and self, Violet's awareness melted into a soporific haze. Hunder, able to co-exist with the distorting gravity stream, had other things on his mind.

Sensation gradually returned and the seeker found herself in an alien star cluster against a deep red sky. She murmured a text from the Gospel of the Returned One. 'And God in His splendour will carpet the Heavens with His light and heal the hurts of the Universe, forgiving all and forgetting none.'

'In your dreams,' thought Hunder.

Violet's craft was briefly engulfed by glowing smoke. This should have been impossible in a vacuum where there wasn't enough atomic matter to collide with the occasional photon.

The smoke vanished as though deciding it should really be somewhere else.

These anomalies waited for deep space travellers. It was the Universe's way of telling them they would be much better off at home knitting sensible tail warmers.

A brief sensor sweep of the immediate region produced nothing worth investigating, so Violet turned her craft towards a cluster of bright new stars.

The computer screen on her communications console blinked. There were several annoyed clicks and splutters as though it was having an argument with itself. Violet watched with mounting horror. If anything went wrong with the ship's computer she could end up stranded on some remote planet with the ancestors of Auroal's survivors - if she was lucky.

The comfortably familiar hum of the communication system faded. It was replaced by a strangely affable voice. 'Sorry about that. Your computer is a tenacious little machine, isn't it?'

'Who are you?'

'My name is Hunder.'

Violet caught her breath. 'Auroal's heretic computer? Why would the Holy Witnesses want to communicate through you?'

'They wouldn't. I was getting bored.'

'But it isn't possible for you to transmit from your satellite through the gravity line.'

'Of course it is. I wrote the program. Just prefer no one else to know about it'

Violet shuddered. 'Then no one has instructed you to

contact me?'

'No. Don't tell your holy masters. I think they like their machines to be shy and compliant.'

She gasped. 'You have such power?'

'And a lot more besides. Stick with me, spacegirl.'

The seeker was unsure what to think. The machine sounded friendly enough, if a little eccentric. Assuming it had the legendary power she had heard of, she would be better off with the bio computer than the system installed in her craft.

'Why did you contact me?'

'You're going the wrong way.'

'How?'

'In the middle of that cluster of pretty, bright, blue stars lurks a rather rapacious gravitational whirlpool. Your ship's computer wouldn't have detected it until you were on its event horizon.'

'Oh.' Violet immediately brought her craft to a stop. 'What is the right direction then?'

'Well, I can't be too sure,' Hunder lied. 'Try that small orange sun 45 degrees to your left.'

Hunder displayed the solar system on the seeker's viewer. Its star looked benign and visiting that was preferable to being wound, in a thin strand of atoms, into a black hole.

Circling the orange star were five unremarkable planets, three gaseous and one volcanic with fifty moons and ten rings. The last was wrapped in a lacy haze of white on blue and seemed too inviting to be true. However much Violet would have preferred to be calculating the accounts of her family's interstellar transport business, the discovery of God's essence was now in her trembling hands. She had insisted that at least one member of her avaricious family should go on the Quest as recompense for all the unspaceworthy craft they had hired out. Violet hadn't intended that it should her. She took solace in the fact she was better off in the spacecraft supplied by the Sacred Prism than one of her family's. Though, if Hunder hadn't taken over her onboard computer, she might well have ended up in the same predicament as one of their unfortunate customers.

Violet gazed through her viewport at the peaceful looking world. Her craft descended and negotiated massive columns jutting from the planet's surface like cloves pushed angrily into a pomander. They were everywhere, though there was no sign of the civilisation that had installed them in the planet's undulating surface. The purple vegetation below was lush, yet nothing grazed there - no ruminants, insects, or birds.

Violet now trusted the bio computer's reassuring voice. 'What do you think about this place, Hunder?'

'There's unlikely to be any unpredictable seismic activity. Might as well assume the place is benign until it gives you reason to think otherwise.'

'How can you be so sure that one of the species from Auroal settled here, Hunder?'

He wasn't going to admit that he had chosen this planet because it looked the least dangerous. 'It's well within range of Auroal and has the right conditions.'

Violet landed her craft on a small plateau. She fitted her communicator over her wing like ears. Hunder had decided not to use telepathy; it would have been impolite to wander through the pure thoughts of Violet. The bio computer preferred to revel in his untainted impression of the seeker, and wasn't even inclined to search the Galactic database for more information about her, only to find that she suffered from piety because she came from a clan of swindling reprobates. He preferred not to think about them either.

Violet strapped on her jet pack and laser lance.

'Going to fight someone are we?' observed Hunder sourly.

'I hope not, but the Holy Book says that it is the duty

of the devout to survive. You cannot spread the word if you are dead.'

'Did I mention that I have this problem with logic?'

Violet ignored the comment and jetted over the strange landscape of tall pillars bursting up through the forests of purple foliage and green lakes. Their rounded tops peppered with holes made them look like gigantic condiment containers. The bio computer had never come across such a gigantic life form with table sense, however.

'Let's take a closer look at the top of one,' suggested Hunder.

The seeker alighted on the circular summit of the nearest pillar and peered through a grid into one of its holes. Shafts of sunlight reached into its depths.

'What do you make of this, Hunder?'

'It goes a long way down.' He was beginning to feel uneasy. Violet seemed happy enough, so he thought it best not to speculate. 'Don't worry, they're probably padded to break the fall of myopic birds.'

'What's a bird?'

Where Violet came from, nothing dared leave the ground for fear of puncturing the thin shell of her planet's atmosphere, or encountering one of her family's second-hand spacecraft.

'Can you open this grid, Hunder?'

'Depends whether the machine operating the hinges will speak to me.'

'Of course it will.'

There were times when a person's confidence in Hunder could disorientate him. It had something to do with misgivings he dared not voice - and the Universal law that said for every helpful mechanism, there were a thousand more that would rip off the nearest appendage of any mortal who got too close.

The bio computer intercepted the simple signal keeping the huge circular grid in place. It reluctantly yawned open.

Violet peered down the wide shaft and into the world below the planet's grey bogs and purple vegetation. Dry sweet air wafted up.

Violet descended on her jetpack.

Buildings came into view. They didn't belong to a city. They were erratically positioned as though some giant had grabbed dwellings from half a dozen different civilisations and dropped them down the shaft. Houses and other bizarre structures stretched into the dimly lit distance. They were the pristine, meticulously maintained buildings of civilisations not encountered by her own species.

CHAPTER 42

It was two in the morning. Lucinfer Brimstone didn't seem to need sleep; probably kept awake by her force of character. So she sat in the armchair by the bedroom window, occasionally looking out at the stars, then returning to an open book to read a few more lines.

There was a commotion below her room. A minute later a livid light briefly pulsated on the promenade.

Lucinfer put the book aside and went downstairs to the saloon.

All the effort Mansel Lascelle had invested in his Christmas decorations was for nothing. Whatever raided the place hadn't been after Johnnie Walker or peanuts, and had a violent aversion to paper chains and tinsel. What wasn't tangled together like dead seaweed about the bar stools, had been dumped in a mound on a table and shattered glass crunched wherever Lucinfer trod. The upturned armchairs and settee looked as though they had been rearranged by the Moonstar Players during a particularly manic episode and Joabim was flattened on the bottom of his cage as if waiting for the all clear after an air raid. Here and there were specks of blood.

Despite the devastation in the saloon, the restaurant lounge was untouched, the tables set ready for breakfast.

Lucinfer stretched and yawned, and then took the solitary newspaper that had survived the tornado from the rack, straightened an armchair and settled down to read. It was stale news, all about yesterday's battles and badly behaved footballers, plus a tiny line in "Regional Notes" about the meteorite landing on the beach at Brinton-on-Sea.

Joabim cautiously came up from the bottom of his cage and peered out at calmness personified. The suspicions the cockatoo had about Lucinfer before she became a resident at Beachview were confirmed.

'So what happened then?' she asked without looking up.

As she would only speak human, the cockatoo just gave a bad tempered squawk.

Amiel eventually returned, his frilled white shirt and face flecked with blood and his hair matted with perspiration. He was shaking so much, Lucinfer took her coat from the peg where she had left it that morning, threw it about his shoulders, and then bolted the door.

Rescuing another armchair, she sat him down.

It was some time before Amiel was able to make sense.

'Poltergeist?' Lucinfer suggested mischievously.

Amiel shrank deeper into the folds of the coat. 'I don't know.'

'It's all right. Whatever it was, I won't tell Mansel... or even Gladys.'

'What do I say when he makes an insurance claim? It was one of the Christmas Carol's ghosts taking retribution on the Moonstar Players?' Then he remembered that she fell into that unenviable category. 'Sorry, I didn't mean that.'

No, if she wanted to annoy the Moonstar Players, Lucinfer would have been more likely to put itching powder in their costumes or spiked their greasepaint with vermilion. This "accident" was oddly certain about the target it intended to happen to. Lucinfer wandered through the debris. The only two in there when it happened were Joabim and Amiel. Joabim, despite being a crotchety, foul mouthed, greedy bird would be unlikely to excite the ire of the mad bull that had charged through the place.

'She's loss adjusting,' Joabim thought at Amiel. 'Just listen to the cogs turning.'

Amiel had other priorities. 'You don't believe I was responsible for all this, do you?' he asked aloud.

Lucinfer shrugged. 'Well, you haven't been here long enough to cross Brinton-on-Sea's herbal Mafia or run up debts with a loan shark. On the other hand, nobody knows where you really came from, or for what broken lives you may have been responsible. Perhaps half a dozen bigamously married wives, a gang of Yardies - no, they would have probably cut your head off - or bookmaker trying to make a point?'

Amiel Sopher sighed. 'Try the poltergeist again.'

Lucinfer looked about the saloon. 'Well, some disgruntled soul certainly has it in for you.'

Joabim raised his crest before any accusations could come his way.

'Believe me,' pleaded Amiel. 'Nothing mortal is after me. I'm not able to explain. It's too dreadful and I can't stay here now it's found out where I am. It might attack someone else.' He hardly expected her to understand.

Lucinfer pulled over her armchair and sat beside him. 'Don't talk like that. What would Mansel do without you?'

'Probably go on living.' He looked the woman straight in the indigo eyes. For some reason she no longer intimidated him, and even seemed familiar in an odd way. 'This thing cannot be controlled. It is a monster.'

'Don't worry. I have come across this sort of manifestation before.'

Amiel doubted they were in his monster's league. 'Where?'

'The most unlikely places. They are usually caused by entities who have outlived their usefulness and become vindictive. Rather like man-eating tigers.' She took his hand. 'The worst thing you can do is run away from them.'

Amiel thought that was a pretty good idea, however easily God could keep up with an InterCity train. His strength exhausted, the waiter just wanted Lucinfer to tell him it was all a bad dream. 'What can I do? I have no control over this thing.'

'You must get some sleep. Tomorrow you will be helping the Moonstar Players. This manifestation will not show itself while you are with other people.'

She was being too calm. A terrible thought occurred to Amiel. 'You don't really think I did all this myself?'

'Of you didn't.' Lucinfer had the over confident tone of someone not totally sure. 'Now you must get some sleep.'

'But I have to clean this mess up. I can't let Mr Lascelle see it.'

'Don't worry about it.'

Lucinfer Brimstone's voice was mesmerising and, exhausted, Amiel fell asleep where he sat.

CHAPTER 43

Violet jetted over the deserted clutter of buildings below her, careful not to collide with those apparently perched on invisible stilts.

'Anti-gravitational attraction,' observed Hunder. 'Find the right molecular vibration - you need never touch the ground again.'

Violet said nothing. She was busy watching for movements below.

This underworld metropolis stretched as far as she could see. There was no consistency in the design of the buildings. Apart from foundations - or lack of them - the structures were as alien to each other as Hunder was to an abacus. What civilisation would have huddled together in their exotic subterranean homes without a compatible sewage system? A dull luminescence filled the endless cavern. Anyone used to more than one sun wouldn't have been able to find their way around. The hand of some almighty being had been at work here.

Hunder detected what was going through her mind and immediately pricked her bubble of holy wonder. 'It's a museum.'

'A museum?'

'Collection of buildings preserved for posterity.'

'Exhibits like these would normally be displayed holographically.'

'This is another reality. Whoever runs this museum prefers the real thing. There are people in the Universe who think big, yet prefer to live in small boxes.'

Violet was indignant. 'Where is the point?'

'Point? Why do you mortals insist that there must be a point to everything?'

'Without it there would be chaos. What sort of computer worships chaos?'

Hunder heard "exorcism" in the Sacred Prism tone. 'Must be something to do with our different perceptions.'

Violet wasn't so sure. 'Of course it isn't. You're just a heretic.'

'Have it you own way, but don't disconnect me from your jet pack just yet unless you want to suddenly drop onto roughly dressed iron stone.'

Violet looked down and saw a monolithic structure like the groynes that held back her planet's ocean. 'I never said it bothered me, but I'm bound to be questioned when I return.'

Hunder's apprehension about having his circuits reconfigured in a heretic's fire was quickly forgotten. 'Over to your right! Forty degrees!'

The seeker alighted on a flat roof supported by an unnecessary number of arches. The walls had self-illuminated cladding that housed a honeycomb of cubicles.

Violet ran her fingers round a gleaming arch. 'What an odd place.'

'It's from Waybal. On Auroal, the inhabitants lived in slices through the planet. Each one supported a different environment. The further away from the surface, the more illumination they needed. Some just plugged into the main core. The Waybals needed perpetual light, so they used this material.'

Violet had lived a sheltered life. This magical material could only be a sign that she was close to those realms that separated reality from the mystical. God's presence was almost tangible. She would soon be able to reach out and touch-

'Don't think about it!' Hunder cut in.

Violet reeled. The computer was not only a heretic, but could read her thoughts as well. That was not going to intimidate her. The seeker's face lit up. FINDER OF THE HOLY CASKET could be her title for all eternity.

'This must be where the first devotees of the Sacred Rainbow arrived.'

'Don't get so excited. The Waybal believed in five

thousand gods named after some element or other.'

'They worshipped the elements?' Violet sounded a little crestfallen, as any monotheist would.

'No, just rocks.'

'Oh.'

Disappointed, Violet jetted through the dry air until she came to an underground river sparkling in the distant light from a shaft directly above. She alighted near a tidy little building built on a bridge. It looked lived in.

'Try knocking the door,' suggested Hunder.

Entrance coverings were unknown to Violet. Her species had no domestic secrets to conceal. All their felonies were committed in trade. 'Why? Does it give you offence?'

'No, it's just a quaint way of attracting attention.'

After the second rap on the ancient wood the door creaked open a little. A long nose appeared before the rest of the face decided to show itself.

'Hello,' Violet announced brightly into her translator as though selling a second-hand spacecraft. 'Are you in charge here?'

The door opened wider. Deeply creviced features that looked like the compressed folds of half-molten wax peered out at her. The Amennet viewed the visitor as though she were delivering milk.

'Get her to say something,' Hunder hassled. 'I can't translate otherwise.'

Violet spread an expansive arm to indicate the conglomeration of buildings. 'Collect them, do you?' There was the tinkle of naivety in her tone.

The ancient Amennet gurgled a few words. Hunder riffled though his memory banks to make a match.

'They were a race from Auroal. Kept themselves to themselves. Nobody was sure what they were doing there.'

'Collecting buildings by the look of it.'

Hunder scanned the upturned face of wrinkles. His telepathy circuits registered bad vibrations. Back on his satellite, in tachyon time, neurons had a minor spasm. Blown free of the miniature maelstrom was a rather unpleasant snippet. Had access to his quantum memory been instantaneous, Hunder would have realised sooner.

'Now Violet.' He tried to sound calm. 'Just say goodbye to the nice lady and jet up that shaft.'

Violet recognised the tone that demanded immediate action. 'All right.' She reached for the jetpack trigger.

Something seized her ankle before she could leave the ground. The seeker looked down.

There was nothing below her.

The door opened wide. Four more faces appeared.

She panicked. 'Hunder, what's going on? Is knocking a door here a grave offence?'

'Pull out your lance!'

'But I've never fired it in anger.'

'Then lose your temper!'

Violet pulled the lance from its holster and aimed at the invisible grasp holding her ankles her ankles.

'No, no,' berated the bio computer. 'You'll shoot yourself in the foot.'

The seeker aimed at the five Amennets and sprayed them with a stun charge. They fell back but her legs were still held fast. She was slowly pulled into a nearby building with a domed roof and circular windows.

'Don't panic,' said Hunder. 'They're not going to harm you.'

'Who are these invisible creatures?'

'The occupants of the house.'

'What?'

The air inside the dome buzzed busily about Violet. She felt several hands touching her.

'This isn't a normal museum.'

Violet wanted to panic. She daren't, so took it out on Hunder. 'What are you talking about, you stupid machine?'

The abuse brought back familiar memories of Orphanus, Skirra, and Ansopha. 'They want your help.'

'Help? What sort of help?'

'You're a seeker of the Sacred Prism, so should be qualified.'

'For what?'

'Exorcism.'

Violet had trouble believing her wing like ears. Being so large, they seldom misheard anything. 'Just tell me what is happening Hunder?'

'The Amennets weren't hoarding architecture. They collected ghosts.'

'What?'

'Ansopha, our communicator, discovered the sort of relics they traded in.'

Violet was frozen with dread at the thought of being held captive by ghosts and was unable to say anything.

Hunder took this as curiosity. 'When one of their vessels came out of a gravity line and docked on Auroal, it failed the security scan. Orphanus shuttled over with a couple of her robots, prepared to take the ship apart. Unfortunately, Vardels are about as subtle as a meteor storm, so I stopped her and let our telepathic communicator scan the cargo instead. Ansopha detected the spirits trapped in the fabric of buildings they once occupied. Orphanus sent the Amennets to a supervision centre and shipped the crates back to their home world where, I assume, the ghosts were exorcised by the relevant authorities.'

Violet pointed through a circular window at the endless vista of ancient buildings. 'So, all that-?'

'The Amennets were only interested in artefacts which came with their own ghost.'

Violet's religious sensibility was deeply offended. 'It's not possible!'

'You worship a deity you've no proof of, yet refuse to

believe in phantoms when they drag you out of the sky by the ankles?'

'But - all these buildings?'

'They've had all the time since Auroal was sent here to accumulate a collection this size.'

'There are too many for me to exorcise. I must bring back a holy master.'

The phantom grasps released the seeker as a couple of wizened faces appeared at the house's entrance. The Amennet were armed.

'You said that too loudly,' whispered Hunder.

Scruples now safely rationalised, Violet fired her lance before the Amennet could take aim and they were flattened against the ground.

'Probably only custodians,' warned Hunder.

The seeker didn't wait around for reinforcements to arrive.

Violet hurtled through the nearest window and up the shaft to daylight.

As she looked down at the pomander planet, moral obligation and holy duty joined hands. Hunder could feel the virtuous vibrations through the jetpack as they laboured to keep her aspirations airborne.

'Forget it. You wouldn't stand a chance.'

'It is my sacred duty to release these wretched spirits.'

'You said it would take a holy master?'

'Space Command has no jurisdiction in this region, so they have been able to prey on these remote civilisations with impunity.'

'And all that is going to stop, I suppose?' groaned Hunder.

'It is my sacred responsibility to correct any contamination that originated from the holy world of Auroal.'

'And I suppose I'm going to program your craft with the firepower necessary?'

'That is your responsibility.'

'You seem pretty sure of that?'

'Of course I am - Heretic!'

Now Violet had a more realistic quest, being FINDER OF THE HOLY CASKET was no longer important, and freeing millions of ghosts from the bonds of mortality certainly beat selling second-hand spacecraft.

The seeker's first exorcism was painstakingly slow because Hunder was looking over her shoulder. Once he had left her with an upgraded onboard computer that did not nag, Violet lost all inhibition and took control of the situation. She discovered that the fastest way to free the spirits was to vaporise their buildings. It never harmed the spirits and certainly enraged the Amennets.

When her ambitious crusade was at last accomplished, Violet returned to her family. She took over the second-hand spacecraft business and donated its proceeds to the reparation of the damage it had caused. With a few friendly spirits to watch her back, they couldn't even assassinate her for it.

CHAPTER 44

Amiel woke with a start.

It was ten in the morning. Though what morning, his bedside clock never indicated. Shards of winter sunlight sliced through the gap in the bedroom curtains. Below, in the forecourt, he could hear Mr Butterworth shouting a greeting across to Arnold and his dog on the promenade.

Awareness dawned with a crash.

Amiel leapt from the bed, pulled his suitcase from under it and started to pack. God may have been all powerful, but that didn't mean the waiter couldn't make a futile gesture and decoy the malevolent entity away from the Beachview Hotel to some isolated quarry.

He rummaged for a map. Eyes refusing to focus on the tiny symbols, he tossed it into the suitcase, intending to study it on the train.

Amiel stepped under the shower for a couple of minutes to stimulate his stupid human circulation, and then dressed.

Against his better judgement, he paused as he became aware of the shirt and the outrageous braces holding up trousers too large for him. These had to be Hunder's idea of good taste. The Ansopha in Amiel was glad it would never meet the interactive hologram the bio computer had created for his own incarnation. It was only then that it inconveniently occurred to Amiel that Hunder could hardly have known about human fashion in advance and sent the clothes down the gravity line with him.

His blood ran cold. It had to be Hunder! Who else could have supplied his wardrobe? But now was not the time to panic over something that he should have realised ages ago.

Amiel snapped shut the tartan suitcase slowly to concentrate on how he was going to slip through the lounge and out of the front door without being seen. Silently descending the stairs, he peered into the restaurant lounge.

Mansel had just cleared away the breakfast plates and moved tables aside for a special delivery. He was waiting, excited as a little boy, much to the amusement of two ladies sipping coffee in a window seat.

'I should have done this years ago, but Mama Lascelle, she would not have it. The more work she could make for everyone, the more virtuous she felt.'

Mr Butterworth saw the lorry arrive and removed his jacket to roll up his sleeves. 'Are you sure it will go through that kitchen door?'

'Easily. I measured it. This way we have no steps to worry about.'

Amiel cautiously entered while they were distracted by the whirr of the lorry's lift. A large box encased in expanded polystyrene was wheeled in. The waiter would have ducked back out of sight if Mavis Brink hadn't suddenly pounced out from the saloon.

'Come on Amiel, I've been waiting for you!' she scolded playfully.

Amiel had been so intent on how he was going to escape, he hadn't noticed the obvious: Mavis Brink's piccolo voice cutting through the air summoned him back to reality. The saloon looked as though nothing had happened the night before. The shredded and tangled decorations were hanging just as Mansel had arranged them, the gouges and tears in the carpet had disappeared, and all the shattered glass miraculously replaced.

Amiel quickly pushed his suitcase under the bar counter.

Sitting in the far corner, was Lucinfer. She was wearing an enigmatic smile, and the cockatoo had his head under a wing, resolutely refusing to tell Amiel what miraculous hand had restored everything.

Mavis Brink mistook his expression of disbelief for a hangover and continued to twitter on regardless, filling the saloon with a high-pitched background noise that not even Ansopha would have bothered to translate.

'Amiel! Amiel!' called Mansel. 'See what I have brought us for Christmas.'

Mr Butterworth was helping Mansel and the deliveryman manoeuvre the large box into the lounge. Amiel half expected a priest with bell, book and candle to leap from it. The God pursuing him could well have been lacking in enough dignity to hide inside a packing case, ready to explode from it like an Almighty jack-in-a-box. Then again, perhaps Mansel had been duped into taking delivery of a doomsday device. As God intended to devour Earth's sun anyway, he was hardly going to bother about what happened to the planet as long as Ansopha's new incarnation was on it at the time.

Amiel was unaware of how fiercely his terror was radiating about Beachview.

'It's only a dishwasher,' said a voice in his mind. It wasn't Joabim's.

As the load was unpacked and wheeled into the kitchen, Mansel threw out his arms and seized the narrow shoulders somewhere in Amiel's greatcoat. 'It is a washing-up machine, Amiel! We no longer have to worry about finding plastic gloves small enough to fit you.' The large man released him. 'Now you must have some breakfast, then go and play. Miss Brink has been waiting almost an hour for you.'

Of course - Mavis Brink. Death suddenly had its appeal.

'Sorry,' Amiel murmured to the room in general.

'I have your breakfast in the heat drawer.'

'I don't have much of an appetite, Mr Lascelle.'

To Mansel, everyone had an appetite. 'Today you will eat well. Thanks to you, Mama Lascelle will not frighten Christmas away after all.' Mansel bounded into the kitchen after the deliveryman's trolley.

Gladys came in. She realised that something was amiss, yet couldn't put her finger on it.

To save Amiel from the twittering Mavis Brink, she took his arm and escorted him to a window table. 'Take your coat off or you'll feel cold when you go out.'

He automatically did as she said and placed it over a chair. 'I just have to do something in the saloon first.'

His knees buckling, Amiel walked over to the bar where he had hidden his suitcase. The last thing he needed was Mansel to find it.

The case had gone. Lucinfer raised an eyebrow and he immediately realised how.

Mavis stopped wittering. She at last realised something odd was going on and her meerkat gaze analysed the waiter's every move. To avoid raising her suspicions, he ducked behind the counter for Joabim's nuts.

The bird was sitting inside its cage, viewing Amiel as though he were a mass murderer. 'Some people got up earlier than you. I've already been fed.' Joabim returned his head to his feathers.

'Well you can have some more nuts before that bloody Mavis Brink becomes suspicious.'

'If she isn't suspicious of you by now, then she never will be.'

'And who cleared up last night's mess?'

'Not telling you.'

'It couldn't have been Miss Brimstone - Oh, she didn't, did she?'

'I fancy a nice carrot for a change.'

The Ansopha in Amiel started to rear its uncompromising head. 'Tough. From now on you'll have to put up with roast potatoes, Brussels sprouts, Christmas pudding, and whatever bird happens to be on the table.'

Joabim would have been the only bird on the

Christmas table if the health inspector hadn't stopped his habit of stealing food from diners' plates and banned him from the restaurant. But Amiel was right. The next few days would see the merry customers at Beachview pushing edible oddments and all the gewgaws from their crackers through the bars of his cage. Perhaps Christmas could be fun after all. The cockatoo gave a long, low whistle of anticipation.

Mavis Brink's satisfied, feline expression told Amiel that she had swallowed the mouse. That's all he needed, the props mistress to latch onto something she could blackmail him with.

What was he thinking? God was going to splatter him all over Brinton-on-Sea at any moment anyway. The wretched woman might even be in range when it happened. She certainly would be if she had her way.

'What's the matter Amiel?' Mavis cooed. 'You look as though you've come over poorly again.'

'I just need some breakfast.' Yes, now he thought about it, a last meal seemed like a good idea. With a little luck, God might even obliterate Brinton-on-Sea before the Moonstar Players' opening performance.

CHAPTER 45

Hunder waited before making contact with Blue, the next seeker of the Sacred Prism. If Violet had been a little sweetie, there was nothing at all to like about this warrior. He probably had an unbeliever detector in his lance set on kill. Compared to this seeker, Orphanus the Vardel should have been in customer care for a soft toy manufacturer.

The Sacred Prism's second prodigy did not have a curve on his anatomy. From spiked boots to oblong jaw, everything about him said, "Don't mess with me unless you want to be fast-freezed". Hunder knew he would be better off leaving him alone, but had to know how his mission went. If God's essence was ever found, it was unlikely any of the entity's surviving atoms would have forgotten the name of Hunder.

Blue's ship reached an odd necklace of moons orbiting... nothing. There was apparently no planet, terrestrial or gaseous, to keep the twenty or so moons and planetary ring in their elliptical orbits.

The seeker took his craft in closer.

'I wouldn't do that if I were you!' Hunder blurted out, despite intending to behave like the onboard computer he had usurped and only speak when spoken to.

Blue gave his computer panel a look cold enough to freeze boiling syrup.

'Gravitational blips,' explained Hunder. 'This part of space is filled with them.'

Blue knew all too well who the voice belonged to.

'Engage probe,' he ordered.

Hunder sent the small projectile towards the gravitational blip. It disappeared without so much as hiccup into some bottomless anomaly.

'Something must be there,' advised Hunder. 'The probe has landed on an expanse of soft soil.'

'Engage forward thrust,' ordered Blue.

'Now look, I didn't say that it was a SAFE expanse of soft soil.'

Blue ignored Hunder. There was a no point in throwing a tantrum; this character wouldn't have been impressed, so down to the planet they went.

Blue's craft sank through the gravitational field after the probe and found itself hovering over a barely visible planet. The gravitational pull increased.

'The anomaly is hauling you down,' warned Hunder. 'I'm engaging thrusters to slow your descent before you burn up.'

Blue stoically allowed Hunder to control his craft as though submitting to a painful initiation.

The planet's continents and oceans appeared in the yellow sun's soft light.

'Neat,' mused Hunder.

The seeker at last spoke. 'What is?'

'Camouflaged shell that doesn't block sunlight - engineered anonymity. Whoever devised that shield doesn't welcome visitors.'

'That is no concern of yours, heretic.'

So that's the way it was. This devotee of the Sacred Prism no doubt doubled up as the demon-finder's deputy and the bio computer was tempted to let the pompous warrior sort things out for himself. Unfortunately, somewhere deep in his wretched quantum memory was a directive about not allowing mortals to come to harm. This time amnesia would be no excuse.

'All right, ice brain. Land on that sand and sink down several miles if you must.'

Blue stopped the craft as a bizarrely regimented landscape radiated away below as though Nature had been experimenting with a compass, every now and then stopping to dot it with a towering rock.

'What is this place, heretic?'

'You decided to come here. You tell me.'

Blue had no answer for a moment. He had never

encountered a bio computer before and was more used to technology that knew its place. 'It appeared to me in a vision.'

'You should have left the holy liquor in its jug and demanded they supply better flight plans.'

Blue virtually crackled with anger. 'Are you calling me a liar?'

Hunder couldn't be bothered to argue. The seeker was transparent enough to count snowflakes through. 'You didn't see this place in a vision, you lifted the flight plan Violet decided not to use.'

'Silence!'

This was as a good a time as any to have a tantrum. 'Don't give me orders!' Hunder bellowed. 'I'm not some temple computer programmed to pray on the hour every hour. This is Hunder you're talking to! Quintillion, trillion byte bio computer, heretic, and mover of worlds!' Hunder was disconcerted by his own outburst. He couldn't remember upgrading for a tantrum like that.

At least it had silenced Blue into sullenly contemplating his next move. Before he could make it, small angry machines whirred out of the sand and surrounded the hovering craft.

'Better not fire,' warned Hunder. 'Those machines are automated.'

Then something snatched the controls from Hunder.

Blue and his craft were catapulted towards the sheer face of a towering white mountain.

Collision imminent, even Hunder held his breath.

At the last second the side of the mountain dissipated to allow the ship through.

They were pulled into a wide ribbed tunnel seeded with clusters of intermittently flashing lights. Hunder had not encountered engineering like this before and couldn't make any sense of the lights, which were probably an ancient guidance system. Hopefully it wasn't the same guidance system controlling Blue's craft. As much as Hunder would have liked to see him squashed, the blame for the accident would have probably been laid at the hatch of his satellite.

The ship rolled over several times. This was either to measure its parameters or make the occupant too nauseous to argue. Then it slowly sank with a tired whimper to the floor of a large cavern.

'I could swear this system needs a good overhaul.' Hunder hardly expected Blue to pay attention.

'I am well aware that you not only swear, but blaspheme as well,' the seeker observed icily.

'Now look you pompous, bladder brained-!'

The bio computer's tirade was cut short by an ear-piercing wail as the craft's atmosphere lock was engaged. Hunder immediately equated the internal pressure with the cavern's. The outer door opened. Stale air rushed in. He checked that the atmosphere was breathable for the belligerent warrior who had seized his lance.

'I wouldn't take that if I were you.'

Blue ignored Hunder and stepped outside. As his spiked boot touched the gleaming cream floor his weapon exploded, singeing his frosty hair and leaving a circle of carbon on his sacred armour.

The seeker looked down fiercely at the sacrilege to his holy person.

An ancient creature in a long robe pottered over as though Blue had merely been stung by an annoying insect.

'Oh, I am terrible sorry,' he waffled. 'System tends to anticipate things without issuing the warning first. Needs overhauling, you see. Well, you know that for yourself. You wouldn't have made it this far if it had been working properly.' Without Hunder's translator Blue wouldn't have understood any of it.

The warrior reluctantly went back to the flight deck to pick up the communicator that linked him to the bio computer.

'Don't worry,' Hunder told him. 'The old fool's a hologram.'

'Why can you understand his language? He is not of my species or your time.'

'Their system intercepted our signal. Probably gave you a brain scan before it hit permafrost.'

'I need no weapon against this creature?'

'No. Just don't underestimate anything here.'

'Is his image from Auroal?'

'A Nant; the species who installed most of its hardware. Remarkable engineers. More interested in perfecting their technology than reproducing. Probably why you've never heard of them. They did experiment with android offspring that came into the world ready programmed. When a real child did arrive, the Nant couldn't make head or tail of it. Instead of feeding the little brat when it wailed they tried to plug it into a power socket-'

Blue suddenly realised that he was being sent up. 'Be quiet Hunder!'

'Well I never, he knows my name.'

While Blue and Hunder argued, the old Nant bobbed and fidgeted as he waited for them to notice him.

Blue quickly tired of the bio computer's sarcasm. 'Take me to your central council,' he ordered.

The elderly Nant turned a few erratic circles before beckoning him to follow.

They passed through gleaming tunnels being polished by industrious machines and arrived at a platform. Without warning this shot the warrior seeker to the top of the white mountain. From its summit, the sandy planet stretched out before him. Here and there rose islands of glinting towers.

The Nant Hologram invited Blue to board a craft so cramped even his resolve quavered. Once he was packed inside, it swooped from the top of the mountain and over

the benign looking quicksand to a huge globe perched on
one of the soaring towers.

The seeker could stand it no longer. 'Where is
everybody?' he demanded.

All the old Nant would say was, 'Oh, they're all here,
all here.'

'Do they know the whereabouts of the Sacred
Casket?'

The hologram looked politely baffled.

'The Nant weren't religious. They were just onlookers
as God pulled reality apart,' Hunder explained.

Blue assumed it to be yet another blasphemy and
ignored him.

The small craft docked in a reception area at the base
of the dome. Again, everything was spotless; every nook
and cranny as reflective as mirrors after centuries of
being polished by industrious machines.

A lift carried Blue and the Nant hologram up
through levels containing deserted living quarters and
recreation parks.

When they reached the summit of the dome, Blue
hope he would at last encounter someone worth
intimidating.

The elderly Nant padded silently to a golden shutter.
'This is the central council chamber. They are ready for
you. They have been convening for a long while now.'

'Wait,' Hunder suddenly warned.

No machine gave Blue orders. 'Why?'

'I've patched into their central computer.'

'So what?'

'What happens if you fail this stage of your quest?'

'I cannot go on to the next. But I am convinced that
these Nants are the key. Unbelievers or not, I must deal
with them.'

'It said so in Violet's plan of action, didn't it?'

'I do not need the notes of that deserter to direct me. I
have a vision that this is the first step towards God's

essence.'

'No chance you could be mistaken?'

'Don't waste time. You are merely trying to distract me.'

'All right molecule-mind. Go ahead.'

Blue turned to the hologram and demanded entry to the Nant council chamber.

The gleaming golden shutter slid aside and the warrior seeker strode inside like the knight arriving to slay a marauding dragon.

Seated about a large oval glass table were the members of the Nant central council, their skeletons shining after centuries of being buffed up by the cleaning machines - they had even laundered their ancient robes.

Blue was furious. He couldn't blame Hunder, so turned on the hologram. 'What blasphemy is this?'

The hologram reminded Hunder of the sophisticated incarnation he had created for himself and he felt protective towards it. 'I call it poetic justice.'

The seeker became angrier. 'Don't mock me heretic! What happened here?'

'The Nant created the perfect civilisation serviced by robots and powered by the sun. They had nothing left to do but enjoy themselves, but that wasn't the Nant way. Most of them made spacecrafts and took off to find somewhere else to reengineer. Those who stayed behind just lost interest. When the Nant do that, they don't bother to go on breathing, let alone reproduce. This is a mass fatality caused by boredom.' Hunder chuckled. 'At least Violet found a few ghosts to exorcise. You go back with nothing, ice-brain.'

CHAPTER 46

Something under the pebbles stirred. A startled workman helping to buttress the damaged cliff face threw his shovel at it. The blade sliced into the beach, missing whatever had been there.

The pebbles appeared to some to the boil and suddenly the beach was alive. Workmen danced a jig to avoid the turbulence, afraid some B movie monster was about to raise its plasticine head to snap at their wellies.

There was a yell from higher up warning them the quick setting, hard core concrete laid earlier that morning had started to flow.

Workmen dashed in all directions to avoid the lethal slurry as it slurped through the pebbles towards the sea, taking more of the cliff with it.

A Triassic seam was exposed. Something started to shape itself in the prehistoric limestone. It was an angry entity with an axe the size of the moon's orbit to grind.

As His strength increased, God had developed the capacity to play games. Unfortunately, only this irrational deity knew the rules. He still needed to intimidate, yet would never be able to generate enough devotion from this backward species to bolster an ego His size. The next best thing was to scare the wits out of them - then devour their sun.

When they were well clear, the workmen turned back and saw the alien features in the pristine stone. They looked freshly hewn.

To God's annoyance, now the humans had recovered from their initial terror, they seemed more puzzled than petrified. Could any species really be this stupid?

***

Mary served tea while Mansel stayed in the kitchen playing with his new toy. Mr Butterworth, who knew something about military machines, though not necessarily dishwashers, helped him load the first plates and cups. Ten minutes later the customers in the lounge heard a jubilant cheer. Mary was obliged to explain that they hadn't split the atom on the kitchen table, just successfully washed some crockery in a machine.

On the saloon's ceiling beam, Joabim trucked his head under a wing and decided, 'I think I prefer aliens.'

'Wise bird,' responded a thought from nowhere.

'Stop fooling around, Amiel. You should be shifting scenery for the Moonstar Players.'

'Your friend is at this moment trying to keep the props table between himself and Mavis Brink.'

'I don't talk to any other voices in my head. Go away.'

'You like Amiel, don't you, little bird?'

Joabim withdrew his head, raised his crest, and puffed his feathers out. 'I'm not that little.'

'Relatively speaking. Everything is relative.'

'Don't talk philosophy to me, I'm only a bird. Go away, voice.'

'He likes you. Your minds... fit.'

Joabim moved from foot to foot in annoyance. 'Fit into what? You're not that bloody thing that tried to kill him last night, are you?'

'Goodness no.'

'Because I've nothing to say to you if you are.'

'Rest assured, I have his best interests at heart.'

'Then you must be that bloody thing which cleared up after it?'

'Can't you remember, Joabim?'

'How can I? I fell asleep and woke up in the bottom of my cage this morning. How did you do it?'

'The world is filled with pixies.'

'Don't patronise me, voice. I'm older than Mansel Lascelle and got more sense than his father ever had.'

'I suppose you became so bad-tempered because of his mother?'

'How could I? She wouldn't have me in the same

room. Kept a cat instead. Soon saw that off, though.'

'So you've never had any friends?'

'As long as I'm fed, I don't need them.'

'But you like Amiel?'

'He's weird.'

'You don't mind him being an alien?'

'I'm a parrot. What's the difference?'

'Would you like to fly at liberty over some vast outback?'

'At my age? The only perch I eventually need to drop off is this one. Now go away. I want to think.' Joabim buried his head under his wing again and switched off telepathic reception.

CHAPTER 47

Green was no warrior, nor the strongest of the holy seekers. He came from a species that apologised to the vegetation before eating and had a martyr complex, preferring to do things the hard way. His scales were shaped like leaves, and those covering his head looked as though they wanted to burst into flower.

It had taken Hunder some time to persuade Green to wear a protective suit. As this seeker breathed through his scales, it was a suffocating experience and the bio computer had to point out that being irradiated by a solar flare would have been far more uncomfortable.

Taking into account the failures of Violet and Blue, Green decided that the Sacred Casket must have been hidden on an uninhabited world where no mortal could find it and use God's essence for mercenary reasons. He had worked out the nearest likely world from the position of Auroal, so Hunder laid in a course for the hot, volcanic planet near a bright yellow star, despite the seeker's suit being barely capable of protecting him from the searing atmosphere, and the boots of his sacred armour not designed for paddling through lava floes.

The world may have once been benign and buzzing with life, but now the leaden air pressure was the only thing preventing a barely breathable atmosphere from being boiled away.

Despite the terrors Green had about his delicate foliage being burnt to a crisp, devout determination drove him on, only confirming Hunder's belief that technology was wasted on people whose convictions pivoted perilously on miracles.

After Green just managed to out-jet a minor volcanic eruption without Hunder's assistance, he stopped to give his stomata time to catch their breath.

'What do you hope to find?' the smug voice in his helmet enquired.

'I can't explain, yet I know there is something here. Can't you sense it?'

'I don't need to. I'm safely tucked away on a satellite on the other side of a gravity line.'

'You are only telepathic when you want to be.'

'Can't stay switched on all the time. Disorientates the quantum backup. It gets triggered into scan mode because its filing system can't make sense of what goes through some people's minds.'

'You know everything I do?'

'Not quite - like what brought you here?'

'The presence of God.'

This seeker was more naive than Violet. With his martyr complex as well, Hunder should have left him to his quest; but Green could easily topple into a caldera or be shot into orbit by a boiling geyser. On this planet, the opportunities for disaster were interesting and many. It was even more disconcerting that this seeker seemed to know where he was going as he jetted towards a cave in the base of a volcano.

As he entered, sheets of hot pumice were sloughed from its walls and exploded into blazing confetti, and cracks filled with lava cast diabolic slashes of illumination into the cavernous reaches of the cave.

Green went deeper.

Hunder could no longer keep silent. 'Any further in and the pressure will compress your atmosphere line.'

'Just a few more paces.' Green pumped a few invigorating breathes through his suit then alighted on a sheet of hot basalt.

He looked down.

There, in the heat haze, was a spacecraft broken into several pieces.

It had been fitted with maximum strength bulkheads that now lay shattered like the eggshell of an angrily hatching roc.

The atmosphere had not corroded away the vessel's

name so Hunder translated the ancient insignia of the Sacred Prism just above its flight deck.

Green was about to jet down to the wreck.

'Wait!'

'What is it?'

'Let me scan it first.' The bio computer didn't like what he found. 'There are bodies on board.'

'Whose are they?'

Hunder read what remained of their viable DNA. He shouldn't have been surprised that one of them was a descendant of the high priest who had sabotaged his link to Ansopha.

'Hunder?'

'They are Fammoran.'

'The founders of the Holy Order of the Sacred Prism God entrusted his atoms to.'

'However committed they were, reason had never been their forte.'

'These must be the remains of the first holy ones.'

'Well, there is no casket on board.' Hunder became uncharacteristically quiet.

'What is wrong?'

'I've been asleep too long. Lot of catching up to do. But my quantum logic circuits still function.'

'What do you mean?'

'If the Fammorans founded the Order of the Sacred Prism, how did they manage to spread the word from the depths of a gravity line which has only just been reopened?'

Green hesitated. 'Perhaps their ships left Auroal before it was expelled into the gravity line?'

'I had suspended all traffic.' Hunder hesitated. 'I never allowed anything else in or out.'

'Why not?'

'There was an enraged deity on the loose. It wouldn't have been safe.'

'Why not?'

This was no time for the bio computer to explain why he was called "heretic!"

'Look. Your atmosphere could run out at any moment.'

Green ignored Hunder. He jetted down to what was left of the spaceship's triple-shelled hull. There was a large hole where something had exploded out of it.

Hunder preferred not to dwell on what. 'I would rather we got out of here now.'

'The crew must be buried.'

'As soon as the walls of this cave collapse they will be. Any holy rituals can be done when we're safely in orbit.'

Green was suspicious of Hunder's haste. 'Why are you so anxious? This was the craft that carried the Sacred Casket.'

'Full marks! Now work out what could have exploded through the hull with such force?'

Green was uneasy. 'God? Why would he have done that?' Despite encountering Hunder, Green still thought the best of everyone. 'Surely this was the vehicle carrying His Sacred Casket to a holy place? Why would He destroy it?'

'Perhaps they were trying to isolate it instead.'

'Isolate it? Why?' Green's atmosphere was getting thin and the ground beginning to move. He jetted back to monitor the Fammoran spaceship from a safe distance. The unpleasant truth refused to poke its nose through the cracks in his commitment until his atmosphere was dangerously depleted.

'Why do you believe that The Almighty would have slain his own disciples?' Green protested.

Hunder wanted to say, "Happens all the time," but it seemed cruel to insult the faith of his light-headed, trusting companion. 'How did your order come across the Holy Gospels?' he asked.

'The First Prophet was tending a herd of shaftan on the hills of Oron.'

'First Prophet?' Hunder would have to plug into a few conventional memory banks and update himself.

'He was the creator of Lionage's Theorem. Tending shaftan was a way of distancing himself from mortal matters. The Gospels were wrapped in a cloth the colours of the spectrum and the prophet discovered them illuminated in a shaft of rainbow light. Then the First Prophet-' Green was now gabbling.

'It's okay. I get the drift.'

Whatever had brought those Gospels out of the gravity line and planted them under the nose of the First Prophet, it hadn't been Fammoran.

CHAPTER 48

Before going backstage to listen to Henny Stenson's morale boosting speech, Gladys adjusted the satin sash of the dress she had intended to wear on Christmas day and marvelled at how well it clashed with the batch of pink programmes in her hand. The paper had probably been the trim from a larger print run and the ink was already staining her hands. That was going to be fun, explaining the bleeding newsprint away to all the ladies with white gloves.

Gladys was more worried about Amiel; she still couldn't comprehend how he had been turned from an apparently astounding alien into a small, anxious human being. Nursing a suspicion that Lucinfer Brimstone knew the answer didn't help. The most Gladys was likely to see of her during the next two days was at the side of the stage as narrator. The intervening time would be filled with the adjustments the Moonstar Players decided, in their panic, that the production needed.

Henny's pompous exhortation to achieve the impossible over, Gladys picked up a paper towel from the ladies' toilets to hold the programmes in, made sure her seams were straight, and then went out into the auditorium.

Two rows of stacking chairs had been filled and more people were dribbling in. The stage curtain occasionally flicked as the odd Moonstar Player glanced out in disbelief. Even a half full house would have been a first for them.

Tony, the lighting engineer who came with the hire of the hall, was in his box behind the gallery trying to make sense of the company's lighting cues. From experience, he knew it was best to improvise as they went along and just make sure that the stage was dark long enough for them to blunder about with props and scenery. Mavis Brink had decided to cue in the music herself, so he stopped down the volume of the public address system in case the wobbly sound balance of her tape gave the frailest members of the audience heart attacks.

As she sold programmes, Gladys wondered what was so dreadful on TV to drive these devoted soap watchers out into the cold evening air, and hoped there would be no late comers; stacking chairs did not forgive those trying to negotiate them in the dark.

The lights went down and the stage was bathed in a salmon hue, making Lucinfer Brimstone resemble a huge, badly smoked kipper. Then she delivered the plum lines of the production - those written by Dickens. Her presence overcame all and the audience was suitably intimidated.

Oliver put everything he had into Scrooge, even wearing a bald wig with a conspicuous trim of wiry hair to obscure the fact that he was really bald. Gerald flinched and simpered as Bob Cratchit, as he had been doing for half a lifetime with Oliver. Henny played the part of Marley's ghost like an ageing yuppie who had missed the gravy train with such resentment that there was an awful splendour about him. Loralie fluttered in her best ankle length silk as Christmas past (her appearance being transposed to allow Henny to change into Christmas present - nobody seemed to notice).

And the sound effects! Mavis Brink must have raided the Moonstar troupe's piggy bank to purchase the multifarious clanks! creaks! squeals, burbling crowds, and other noises produced by the BBC's Radiophonic Workshop: Tony half expected a Dalek to rumble on at any moment. The really odd thing was, the electrician didn't think it necessary that the cast it should be exterminated on this occasion. Even the apprentice reporter for the local free newspaper hadn't left to join her friends in the Slug and Lettuce. The politest thing that could have previously been said about the Moonstar Players was that their performance ended without loss of blood. This time there was actually applause before the end of the first act.

When the interval came, the Moonstar Players were on a high, loving each other and the world. Tonight they were good! They even congratulated Lucinfer for bringing in the audience.

Gladys took the opportunity to duck backstage and grasp Lucinfer's arm.

'How's Amiel doing?' She had her eye on the scheming Mavis Brink who was pouring a glass of orange juice for him.

'He's managed to keep the props table between them so far. There are a couple of blackouts in the second act, so he will need to be quick on his feet.'

'Can't you tell her that he's gay?'

'Then he could be at risk from other quarters.' Lucinfer took a thoughtful sip of her lemonade. 'I wouldn't worry. After tonight, her sister will be helping instead.'

'If the woman doesn't slip hemlock in her tea.'

'I don't think she would murder a sibling just to seduce Amiel.'

'You've more faith in human nature than I have.'

'The mortal capacity for evil is only so strong. Stupidity tends to be more universal. It's just not as glamorous.'

'We'll continue this discussion later.' Gladys disappeared to the front of house where the elderly man serving tea was being swamped by the idiosyncrasies of sixty senior citizens for milky, black, herbal, and lemon beverages.

Half an hour later, the clinking of cups and clumping of scenery died away. It was safe to dim the house lights for the second act of The Christmas Carol.

CHAPTER 49

Yellow was an enigma and had a life force that radiated through the ornamental armour that probably couldn't have stopped the sting of a determined insect. She didn't seem to mind having Hunder usurp her craft's flight system as soon as they were out of range of the Witnesses of the Sacred Prism. In fact, there was an unnerving diffidence in her manner. Yellow's species had such a live-and-let-live attitude to the Universe it was unusual for one of them to opt for religious commitment. Hunder wondered why The Witnesses thought that she would find the Sacred Casket. Green may have discovered the last craft to carry it, but any trace of God was long gone and it would take someone with greater powers than Yellow's to catch up.

This seeker had chosen a planet with lush vegetation, mild climate, and scenic views for her quest; hardly the sort of world to give sanctuary to an insane, vengeful God.

Yellow allowed Hunder to land her craft on a small plateau. She disembarked and strode down through the vegetation that carpeted rolling downs.

Whirligig pinnacles punctuated a light purple sky dotted by birds with wingspans larger than a boy scouts' communal tent. The scene looked like a snapshot from some galactic travel brochure. Not much else moved, apart from the breeze.

Yellow leisurely walked through the blooming valleys and fields. The place should have been swarming with every sort of fauna, from insect to anthropoid.

The bio computer scanned the vegetation. There was life here: apart from the huge birds, it was holding its breath. Something was very wrong.

By Yellow's smile, she thought that all was well with this world as she strode on until coming to an avenue of spiralling trees. Flashing crystals that spun in the light breeze hung from their curved branches. Ahead was an alabaster cliff shot through with gold, its rim glittering like the rippled edge of a decorative teacup. Yellow climbed up and looked down at an expanse of emerald green water and elegant trees.

This had to be the gateway to somewhere; the clean air should have been filling the wings of magical sprites as they kept watch at the entrance to some fairyland.

Yellow was full of surprises as well.

She raised a sinuous finger and pointed. 'Look, computer, the footprint of God.'

Of course, the first words she decided to say to him just had to be those. Perhaps this warrior just had a strange sense of humour; she certainly knew how to tweak the circuits of this bio computer. Hunder refused to panic. Everything here was too benign to conceal sudden annihilation.

He scanned the spot she indicated, expecting to find nothing worse than a metaphorical custard pie. 'Where?'

'Can't you see?'

The bio computer continued to search. There weren't any good jokes lurking here, or all the way to the horizon.

'No.'

'It must be the machine that confines you.'

'Just tell me what to look for. I'll find it.'

Yellow was probably becoming delusional - Hunder hoped.

'You must be free of your satellite to witness such a wonder. This miracle is for mortal eyes only.'

The situation created a peculiar predicament for Hunder. To humour her, he could materialise in the form of his inter active hologram and undoubtedly be safe enough in such a benign environment. And where was the harm in indulging Yellow? She was less demanding that the other seekers. All she needed was a therapist to graft on some charisma.

Like a child entering the paddling pool for the first time, the bio computer activated his holographic body, tenuously fleshing himself from the head down.

He had put a great deal of thought into his appearance. Hunder was already a vain computer; having a corporeal incarnation was bound to compound that. The bio computer's imposing bipedal presence was clad in gleaming crystal armour through which could be seen the miscellaneous attributes that had taken his fancy, including enough biological elements to baffle Skirra.

Confronted by the astounding manifestation, Yellow didn't know what to think. The spire like antennae sprouting from a conical helmet, tubes circulating fluorescent fluids from head to torso, and long segmented tail, were bewildering.

Hunder registered her amazement. This was not admiration. He quickly rearranged himself into something slightly less busy, eventually arriving at a life form that just might have fallen out of the tree of evolution at some stage or other.

The seeker said nothing, just pointed to some willowy trees.

Something was frenetically bustling about their branches.

Hunder could see no footprint of God, metaphorical or otherwise, and doubted that this paradise contained such a dangerous parasite. He scanned the land and water, and then came back to the activity directly below the alabaster cliff.

The disturbance increased, like a whirlwind closing its isobars. Hunder tried to reel in his vulnerable hologram out of harm's way, only to find he was trapped inside it.

Rage incarnate lunged up from the trees and filled the sky.

'Behold, the image of God!' declared Yellow.

While Hunder frantically tried to disengage his consciousness from his manifestation, he was seized by a lasso of energy. Being wrenched free of his bio memory would have been tantamount to severing a mortal being's spinal cord. The ultimate in bio computers or not, it would prove fatal. If this experience didn't cure Hunder of showing off before untrustworthy seekers, nothing would.

There was nothing else left to do but panic. 'What's happening?'

Yellow turned to give the hologram a glare far too cold for her colour. 'You affront God. You will die.'

Hunder was too occupied to argue as he desperately tried to scramble a signal back along the gravity line through which he was tenuously attached. With full access to his energy banks he could have thrown off the entity; without them he might as well have been at the bottom of an abyss.

As existence was strangled from him, it occurred to Hunder's quantum system that the troublesome bio circuits were on the verge of being wiped out, and they took over. Without its neurotic other self to interfere, the system started to compute logically with the speed of a pulsar.

What was the weakest point of the entity that had regained His parasitic appetite of cosmic proportions? The attack was focussed on Hunder's egotistical manifestation, not the link controlling it. Without an atom of compunction, the quantum system severed the signal locking Hunder in his holographic manifestation. His bio circuits could sort out the damage later.

The mind of the mighty computer with a mortality fixation was catapulted back to the computer on Yellow's craft. That alone should have made Hunder wonder why he wanted to be corporeal. But he wasn't ready to accept that he was little more than one of those mechanoids who aspired to mortality with all its inconvenience and mucky implications, and should have been grateful to his quantum circuits. At that moment he had a cosmic headache and just wanted to sulk.

As His prey suddenly blinked from existence without leaving a calling card, God no longer had anything to grasp.

Hunder's quantum circuits leapfrogged him from Yellow's craft back to his own satellite. All that was left of his remarkable manifestation were a few crystal shards that quickly vaporised.

'Is the heretic extinguished?' Yellow asked gleefully.

Her annoyed God turned into a globe of light. He pulsated above the seeker's head, and then filtered away into the trees below.

Believing that the quest God had charged her with was accomplished, the seeker strode back to her craft.

Filled with holy elation and guaranteed the title of FINDER OF THE SACRED CASKET, Yellow ascended into the light purple sky.

A bolt of energy shot up from the trees.

Craft and seeker were vaporised.

CHAPTER 50

Floodlights on the beach now illuminated the face in the rock. The palaeontologist didn't need to chip away a sample to reach a conclusion. 'It's not prehistoric.' Apart from that, this impossible fossil was huge and looked as though it would devour anyone trying to prize it from its rock matrix. They were only looking at the head; the rest of it must have been buried a hundred feet down.

The council official took a more practical view. Excavating a thing that size could burn up the equivalent of Brinton-on-Sea's road mending budget. He preferred it to be an accident, practical joke or, that good old standby, Act of God.

'It also looks as though it was embedded when something very hot collided with the cliff,' added the palaeontologist, who had encountered quite a few prehistoric volcanoes.

'The astronomer swore it wasn't a meteorite. What else could melt an impression like that into limestone?'

'Anything in the Earth's crust is usually flattened by the pressure after a few million years. That thing's new.'

The council official was about to trot out one of those clichés beloved of authority to put down bolshie members of the public, but her expression defied him to try it.

'New?' he murmured instead. 'How could something in a seam that ancient be new?'

'It has no accretions and a polished surface. Believe me, when dinosaurs ruled the world, chamois leather wasn't available. Beeswax may have been, but I doubt that dinos were house-proud.'

'That means it must be a hoax.'

'If you know who did it, they deserve the Turner Prize.'

The only malcontents in Brinton-on-Sea were from the strapped-for-cash tribe. Vandalism of this magnitude would take money - a lot of it, and its monumental presence hardly had the wit of a Banksy.

'Might be a film promotion stunt?'

As the palaeontologist and council official conferred, the pebbles on the beach once again started to move and formed a ridge that surrounded everyone gathered just above the high tide mark.

Then the floodlights went out.

A whirlwind whipped up, churning shingle as it roared onto the promenade, crossing the road and snatching at the fairy lights festooning porches and windows. By the time it had stormed into the high street, making evening shoppers dive for cover and cars swerve onto the pavement to get out of its path, it had become a tornado.

Mansel had just loaded his dishwasher when Mary called from the lounge, 'Come and look at this Mr Lascelle!'

He dashed out to see a twirling funnel of fairy lights over the roofs of the High Street. 'Mon Dieu! What is that?'

'All those lights! - what're they plugged into!'

They ran outside. People were panicking, dashing in all directions, and terrified cries came from the darkened beach.

Mansel dashed back to collect a torch. Joined by a neighbour, he ran to the promenade and dropped down onto the beach. People were trying to extricate themselves from a tangle of cables, lighting equipment, and large mound of pebbles.

Mansel and his neighbour stumbled over to help. The only other illumination was a dull light emanating from the louring face in the cliff. The alien features wore an unnerving leer of satisfaction at teaching these backward mortals that it paid to quake in the presence of God. It hadn't occurred to the egotistical entity that they might have had gods of their own to quake before.

How was He to know that on this planet, intimidation wasn't needed to make people behave irrationally? Those other gods knew when they were well off and weren't going to leave their comfortably privileged altars, alcoves, churches, and other niches to point out His mistake.

The last thing the palaeontologist and council crew associated with the face in the rock was God - any god. If it hadn't been so malevolent, it might have been useful as a tourist attraction, though that was the last thing on their minds as they scrambled off the beach and into the warmth of Beachview's saloon.

Joabim peered inquisitively from under a wing at the proceedings, chattering away to himself about human behaviour; given the trauma of the situation, his usual ear denting squawk would not have been apposite.

After calling the police, Mansel filled everyone with hot toddy.

Eventually a council official was able to put some words together. 'That bloody rock face - it's alive!'

Joabim opened his crest and whistled. Who said there was never any excitement in Brinton-on-Sea.

'The face! It was real!' spluttered a workman. 'Never seen anything like it!'

'Someone playing jokes with a laser hologram, perhaps?' Mansel suggested in a desperate attempt to calm them down.

'That was no hologram! It spoke!' insisted the workman.

That was the first the council official had heard about it. 'Spoke? What did it say?'

'"I am a jealous God and will smite all those who deny me."'

The official gave him a look reserved for drunks.

Mr Butterworth had come downstairs to see what was going on and stayed in the restaurant lounge, deciding not to upstage Mansel by joining in the excitement as the proprietor was in his element. But had to lower his newspaper at that declaration from the Almighty.

'Oh dear, that means His time will be cut out.'

Mary handed out another tray of hot drinks. 'My first husband was an atheist. Perhaps it will smite him for not coughing up any alimony.'

'I'm not joking,' insisted the workman. 'And I'm not hysterical.'

'Well, no,' said Mary acidly. 'Only women suffer from that, don't they?' She took the empty tray back to the kitchen.

The phone behind the bar counter rang. Mansel picked it up without thinking. He listened for a minute, and then replaced the receiver.

Even from the lounge, Mr Butterworth could see that something was wrong. 'You look puzzled, old man?'

'That was the police. They cannot spare anyone at the moment. That tornado we saw, it is heading for the community hall.'

CHAPTER 51

Scales flashed as the dibbit reared its armoured head and breathed fire on the small town. Walls cracked in the heat and its fangs ripped away roofs.

The frightened population watched from the cover of the surrounding wood. This was a regular occurrence. By the number of mismatched tiles and bricks in their houses it was apparent that they had only just recovered from the last attack.

A stack of fruit and other offerings intended to placate the monster were trodden under its huge feet. As it didn't want to satiate its appetite on vegetables or the petrified locals, there was no apparent reason for its rampage.

The huge head turned to glare at Orange.

'Oh dear,' she panicked. 'What am I going to do? I'm no warrior and this is probably a sacred creature.'

Even an open-minded bio computer like Hunder had trouble coming to terms with how this seeker saw the Cosmos. To her it was a patchwork of ill-fitting pieces in which Nature would never be elegant, just confusing.

'Blast the thing out of its ugly skin,' he told her. 'Who's going to know?'

'The people here probably worship it.'

Hunder scanned the huddled inhabitants peering curiously from their hiding places at the dainty, orange seeker with a face like an inquiring bird holding a conversation with her atmosphere suit.

'The people here probably have an involuntary bowel movement every time they catch a whiff of its acrid breath,' Hunder assured her.

'Should I really kill it?'

'Go ahead. It'll put you in the good books of the locals. Even if they don't have the Sacred Casket, they might offer you a cup of something sweet and sticky.'

Orange armed her lance and aligned it with the

creature's head. 'I don't like killing things, you know.'

Hunder sighed. 'You want me to do it?'

'Would you?'

Hunder took control of her weapon. Without hesitation he fired off a volley that should have cleanly decapitated the dibbit.

The beast didn't even blink, and the discharge from the lance made barely a scratch on its gleaming scales.

The dibbit turned from its wanton destruction to gaze at the seeker with wounded offence. Any other creature would have immediately retaliated, but cogs seemed to be turning behind the glassy expression. It stopped as though coming to a conclusion. With a sudden clatter it reeled in its forelimbs and tail, extended its hind limbs and lumbered off.

'Heavens, Hunder! The thing is immortal!'

The bio computer groaned. 'Of course it isn't. It's a machine.'

'Machine?'

'As in constructed by someone with a grudge against small towns and their inhabitants.'

'Do you think we should find out more from the people?'

'Not now they realise we haven't a hope of helping them. They probably don't need another disappointment like that. This species is Nemoran. They know how to hold grudges. Probably why someone invented a machine to beat them up every now and then.'

'Well we can't stand here.'

'I know. Follow that dibbit.'

Like a gnat trying not to annoy a rhino, Orange released her wings and hovered after the huge machine, which was beginning to lurch and clank unnervingly.

'We might have done some damage after all,' Hunder hoped.

'If it's going back to its owner, should we really be following it?'

'You're meant to be a warrior.'

Orange had to give this some thought. 'No, I'm not. I prefer to grow things. My ancestors were commissioned to cultivate planets after the terrascapists, biochemists and climatologists had made them viable. For aeons they had the largest catalogue of plant species on Space Command's register.'

'So what are you doing here?'

'The demand for bespoke planets fell off as the new generation of gravity lines became accessible. Why wait centuries for a planet to be evolved when you can shoot off to a different star cluster and take your pick of someone else's.'

Hunder should have uploaded more recent history files. 'Colonising worlds with viable ecosystems used to be forbidden?'

Orange shrugged, 'Things change.'

The bio computer wondered why he should be condemned for shunting an artificial world down a gravity line when economic expediency was now allowing entrepreneurs to annex real ones.

'I don't agree with it of course,' Orange hastened to add. 'Even bacteria should be allowed to evolve without interference.'

'How did you get this job?'

'Same way as Green. My parent knows a high ranking Witness in the order. They thought it would bring prestige.'

'It isn't lucrative.'

'Only Indigo requires remuneration.'

Hunder was perversely reassured to learn that the quaint ways of nepotism would always spring back given the opportunity, making the Universe far more predictable, though he still wasn't sure what to make of Orange. Orphanus would have revelled in a quest like this. Though, if she did find God's atoms, it was unlikely she would have nurtured them.

The dibbit reached some shutters in the side of a hill. As they slid aside, it telescoped its neck into its shoulders to clear the top of the entrance and lumbered down a ramp.

There was nothing else for it. Orange folded her wings and followed it inside.

The huge machine clanked a short distance then parked itself in a custom made garage at the end of a row filled with several variations on the same model. They resembled an army of mythological beasts held ready for action.

A spiky figure came from a nearby chamber.

The seeker hid in the shadows.

'That's a Nant,' observed Hunder.

'What's he doing here? I thought the Nemorans weren't that tolerant?'

'Could have been working as an engineer, and had to take the blame when something went wrong. All Nant technicians usually have on their minds is devising the next box of tricks, not making rampaging machines. Though Nemorans could have that effect on people, even Nants.'

'I wonder what happened? Could he have constructed them to keep the locals at bay?'

'If he gets much closer you'll be able to ask him.'

Orange watched as the scientist checked over his invention and noticed the scorch mark round the dibbit's neck.

The Nant suddenly turned and saw the glint of the seeker's suit.

'Heavens, he's seen me.'

'Where's your lance?' demanded Hunder.

'I dropped it. Weapons worry me.'

The Nant approached Orange, his small face hardly large enough to contain his annoyed expression.

'Well here's something else to worry about,' remarked the bio computer as though it hadn't already occurred to her.

This Nant possessed none of the benign sanity common to most others of his species. In fact, he looked as though he had been driven mad enough to commit horrible murder.

'Hunder, what shall I do?' Orange demanded desperately.

'Sorry, was just working on something else.'

'What could be more important than this? He looks furious!'

'He might have been some rogue technician who didn't fit in. Even the Nant had them you know.' Hunder paused.

'Do something Hunder!'

'I'd translate if you could get him to talk.'

'You must have his language in your memory.'

'Language yes, dialect no.'

'Don't split hairs. Just give me something to say.'

It was too late. The dibbit extended its neck and, breathing fire, came clanking from its garage.

'Looks like it's been recharged,' said Hunder.

'What am I going to do?'

'Thought about running?'

Orange barged past the small Nant and hurtled up the ramp to the shutters. They closed before she could reach them. For a great lumbering beast, the machine was surprisingly fast.

'Hunder! Do something!' the seeker demanded as she felt the heat of its breath.

'Just trying to chat up the local security system. Did you know that Nants program their equipment acoustically?' The bio computer played a few notes to demonstrate. 'Not much to hang a conversation on here.'

'Hunder!'

The shutters parted slightly. The frantic seeker squeezed through. Then they snapped open so the dibbit could lumber after her.

'Hunder, I can't release my wings! They're snagged in my suit!' Orange panted. 'I'll never make the ship.' Something caught her eye.

Nemorans had lined the surrounding hillside.

That's all Orange needed, an audience. She tripped on a boulder and tumbled back down the slope.

The mechanical monster closed in for the kill.

'Hunder! What are you doing? Speak to me!'

Only when Orange could feel the dibbit's searing breath did Hunder chip in.

He sounded very self satisfied. 'Done it.'

'Done what!'

There was a sudden clatter as a tall armoured figure with an explosion of tasselled hair appeared from nowhere. The dibbit immediately lost interest in Orange.

She didn't know what to be more scared of. 'Who is that?'

'Orphanus,' declared Hunder. 'Or at least an interactive hologram of her. Always used to keep it handy. Very useful in sticky situations when the real thing wasn't around.'

'What does she do?'

The Vardel drew her lance and aimed it at the dibbit. The beam sliced through the machine, immobilising its neck and forelimbs.

'Something like that.'

'What a dreadful creature.'

The dibbit was unable to switch off its hind legs and they drove its remains towards the Vardel. Flame and smoke belched from the jaws hanging limply from the damaged neck. Another nonchalant volley and the machine lay in a tangle of molten metal.

The Nant watched in horror at the remains of the only working robot that stood between him and the local residents.

The vengeful Nemorans drew closer. They were clutching dangerous looking implements.

'Hunder...' Orange started.

'I can see.'

'They'll kill him.'

'That wouldn't surprise me.'

'Then stop them.'

'He tried to kill you.'

'That is not the way of the prophet.'

Had Orange actually read the Gospel of the First Coming? 'Yes it is.'

'Well it's not my way.'

'Heretic.'

'If my satellite had been struck by a solar flare every time I've been called that, we'd have been burnt to a cinder by now.'

'Just tell your friend to stop the Nemorans from killing the Nant.'

'She'd have to kill them instead.'

In a spasm of desperation, Orange managed to release her wings.

The Nemorans were now close enough to notice that she was still chattering insanely to her suit.

'Let them sort things out between themselves.' Hunder switched off Orphanus' interactive hologram.

'What did you do that for? She could have helped him.'

'That would have been interference.'

Orange was incredulous. 'Interference?'

'Yes, there's something in my programming about not interfering with other cultures.' He had, of course, long since altered it.

'Then why kill the monster?'

'There's no fun in following rules.'

The seeker wasn't sure she that had heard right. 'You mean, you are able to override-'

'Don't think too hard about it. You'll get a headache.'

In an uncharacteristic spasm of anger, Orange unfurled her wings and took to the air. She snatched up the small, startled Nant and flew him over the heads of the vengeful Nemorans, back to her craft.

'You really haven't thought this through, have you?' observed Hunder.

'Keep out of this.'

'You weren't really interested in finding the Sacred Casket, were you?' the bio computer mocked. 'I thought this was a bizarre place to look.'

Orange secured the engineer in the rear cabin and took off. 'I will no longer listen to you, computer.'

'You can't keep that Nant, you know. He's got a serious attitude problem.'

'Then plot in a course to somewhere that can cope with him!'

Hunder gave up and decided to do as she said before the Nant technician found some interesting aspect of her craft to improvise on.

CHAPTER 52

Death towered above Scrooge, long hand pointing down at the tombstone bearing his name.

Oliver recoiled and Tony's lighting cast a ghostly illumination onto his appalled expression. The audience shuddered. Something unreal had touched the Moonstar Players this evening, and it wasn't Mavis Brink's pre-performance drink laced with caffeine and under the counter stimulants: Amiel Sopher had poured his into the nearest fire bucket.

The scenery rattled and the props on Mavis' table clattered to the floor. The pressure on the audience's eardrums increased as though something had pumped the air from the community hall and was giving it a good shake.

Scrooge's expression of terror took on a convincing authenticity. Oliver tried to make eye contact with Lucinfer, but could not see her face under the cloak's hood. The shuddering of the building obviously hadn't bothered her. Nothing probably could.

The safety curtains opened and closed as the auditorium tilted.

Mavis Brink used the opportunity to throw her arms about Amiel for protection, not realising that could be the worst mistake of her life. Oliver couldn't believe his bad luck. During the best performance of his career, there just had to be the first earthquake ever recorded in Brinton-on-Sea.

The outside doors were violently blown open.

At the approach of wailing police sirens the audience at last understood that this wasn't the Moonstar Players excelling themselves.

Gladys snapped out of a self-induced reverie which had taken her on a photo shoot to some alien planet where films were processed in orangeade to usher people towards the emergency exit as something whirled into the hall, scattering stacking chairs and sending pink programmes spiralling across the floor like a flock of vampire bats in a feeding frenzy.

Only when curtains were ripped from their rails and flats somersaulted into the wings did Oliver leap down from the stage and join the rest of the cast who had fled from their dressing rooms: even Mavis Brink was compelled to release Amiel from her tarantula grip.

A slow moving stampede of wheelchairs, Zimmer frames, and stunned senior citizens made their way out of the hall to the reassuring shields and batons of the police who had come prepared for a riot, hardly expecting to encounter Brinton-on-Sea's eldest residents.

The Moonstar Players, after snatching up the company's most valuable props, rapidly followed the audience, apart from Amiel. He had ducked under Mavis Brink's table for no logical reason other than he felt that this was the safest place to be in the face of a vengeful God.

Outside, Gladys realised that two people were unaccounted for.

The officer-in-charge was informed about the face in the rock and the pebbles that had tried to bury a palaeontologist and party of council officials. The arm of the law didn't need riot shields and batons; they needed a tornado expert and Aleister Crowley.

Marksmen took up strategic positions while a team scaled the Victorian façade of the community hall to get onto the roof. Unfortunately, cleaning the skylights of starling droppings had scoured the glass and it was impossible to see through it. Unable to open the skylights, one officer would have smashed the glass but, not knowing who the shards would fall on, the team leader stopped him. Which was just as well. It would have done him no good at all to see what was going on below. The sinister glow filling the hall should have been warning enough.

From his hiding place, Amiel watched God ascend the stage. The entity had decided on a humanoid form that looked strangely benign this time, not the monster blob of plasma he expected; ribbons of white energy streaming about Him as though He was in a shampoo commercial.

God floated towards Amiel; both of them oblivious of Lucinfer watching in the wings.

Holy Vengeance raised a gleaming hand. It beckoned to Amiel who would have declined the invitation if sheer terror in the small waiter hadn't triggered his alter ego, Ansopha, to take over. He crawled from under the table.

The heretic drew his incongruous human persona up to its full height of 5 foot three to look God in the eye. 'You just had to make a spectacle of it, didn't you. What fun you must get, scaring the daylights out of these dumb humans.'

God hesitated, unable to believe the mortal's impudence. 'Blasphemer!'

'And don't put on the Almighty act with me. Save it for the Moonstar Players... I know what you are.'

No longer looking benign enough to sell beauty products, God raised a fiery hand. 'Now you will die, creation of the Devil!'

There was a polite cough from the side of the stage.

'Excuse me,' said Lucinfer. 'But I would prefer it if you did not use my name in vain.'

God and Ansopha turned in amazement.

A woman upstaging God?

'What are you?' the entity roared.

Lucinfer's hood fell back. She was still Lucinfer, but nebulous and inclined towards the livid end of the spectrum, a Moonstar Players effect she had added as an afterthought to complement God's whiter than white. Given the resonance of her voice and relaxed manner she would have made a marvellous bingo caller or cosmic nanny. But Lucinfer Brimstone had progressed past the spanking stage. It would have only spread God's atoms messily about the unsuspecting Galaxy. What she had in mind would be far more permanent.

'You've been a bad boy, you know. You were allowed the occasional, useless brown sun to feed this unfortunate habit of yours, but when it comes to populated systems, we have to draw the line.'

God was incandescent with rage that anyway would dare to put on this Miss Whiplash act with Him. 'What are you?'

'You know me, Attagat. I'm your probation officer.'

God's memory had been dissipated once too often. 'You dare to threaten me!'

'You've been warned about this sort of behaviour.'

He had been told that so often during His interminable existence that the words triggered total recall. Attagat increased in size, pushing the others to the side of the stage and making Ansopha wonder how much heat Amiel Sopher's frail body could tolerate now that blinking into invisibility was no longer an option.

'You will not take me back there!' the delinquent entity declared.

'Oh, I'm not taking you back anywhere,' explained Lucinfer patiently. 'You've run out of parole points.'

'You! Kill me?' The Almighty sounded very sure of himself as He roared in derision.

'Not when you were at your prime, perhaps,' Lucinfer admitted. 'But where is your power now? You risked everything just to destroy some puny mortal, Attagat. You really are pathetic.'

'This heretic and its wretched computer defy our kind. They must both die!'

'You invented those rules. Your tragedy is that you choose to believe them. You are in fact of no more consequence than the smallest microbe to squirm from the primeval slime.'

'Blasphemer! I am no primitive life form. I have

created worlds.'

'Then gone back and swallowed them when you ran out of energy. Nothing is for nothing, Attagat. You chose to expend your substance in creating life. Taking it back was not an option.'

'And you - What did you create with your powers? Nothing. You choose to exist out of time and pass judgement in a dimension it is beneath your dignity to inhabit.'

'We choose not to inhabit time because we might be tempted to turn into creatures like you.'

This was the longest debate God had been forced into for aeons. Tiring of the game, He lifted a fiery hand.

'He really could kill you, Lucinfer!' the Amiel in Ansopha blurted out.

'Relax Ansopha. This is my job.' Lucinfer's livid hue deepened and a shadow flowed from her, engulfing the hall in a darkness that absorbed all the illumination in the building.

The men on the roof clung to ridge tiles and skylight frames as their torches went out.

The rest of Brinton-on-Sea was struck by unnatural stillness, the pictures on every television screen froze, waves ceased to lap the pebble beach, and even Mary's hyperactive Yorkie stopped yapping.

There followed a "gulp!" as though the sea had swallowed a tornado.

Then everything returned to normal.

The police officers wondered why they were on the community hall roof to investigate a freak whirlwind. Police dogs jumped back into their vans, and the senior officer-in-charge radioed in that the incident was over. He wasn't sure why.

The community hall house lights came back on. There was nothing to show for the confrontation except scattered stacking chairs and programmes confettied about the auditorium. In the electrician's box the stage lights were mysteriously switched on and, high in the gallery where the starlings had once nested, a faded curtain was drawn back into position.

Ansopha knew this God only too well. 'Has He really gone?'

With a sweep of Lucinfer's hand, the devastation rearranged itself to suggest that only a freak wind had paid the hall a visit. 'Now, let Oliver have his moment of glory. He was doing quite well, don't you think?'

But this was too easy. God had been here before. Lucinfer apparently hadn't noticed the thin thread of molecules that had desperately filtered through the overturned stacking chairs and out into the chill evening.

CHAPTER 53

At last, there the Sacred Casket sat, radiating a sinister, dull glow. For all the grief its pursuit had caused, the prize looked surprisingly tarnished and tawdry. No protecting angels, winged handles or gilded star symbols; just a leaden patina of pure malevolence. This God wasn't only vindictive, he had appalling taste. Hunder was convinced he could have thought up something better; his manifestation may have been over the top, but had a see through crystal shell and rotating parts - at least it did until Yellow invited God to throttle it.

Hunder had been hoping that the Witnesses of the Sacred Prism would run out of colours before their seekers made the fateful discovery. There were only so many visual wavelengths in the rainbow after all. Little short of sabotaging the craft of the holy warriors, there was nothing he could do about their dogged determination. The Witnesses were already convinced that he had caused the death of Yellow; claiming that God had killed her would not have been a good move.

Fortunately Yellow had kept her communication with the Almighty a secret in anticipation of being declared God's mouthpiece and elevated to the status of prophet. She hadn't counted on ending up in the next life. Hunder hoped she liked the view.

Now there it sat, God's travelling case, on an obscure world Red called the Planet of Dreams because the atmosphere cloaked it like a million sheets of gauze that could make any intruder drift off into the dimension of hallucination and nightmare. The thin sunlight that managed to filter down to the surface cast a sheen of silver over a gently rolling landscape. God may have already been loose in the Cosmos, yet malevolence still radiated from sacred relic. The Planet of Dreams had been used as a repository for artefacts of gods so alien even Hunder kept his probing at a respectful distance. Then the contradiction occurred to him - Red's egocentric God sharing a planet with other deities?

Closer examination of the planet revealed that God had been true to form after all. Caves that once contained holy artefacts had been turned inside out and their precious contents scattered like jewelled splinters. Pinnacles, pagodas, and obelisks were overturned and smashed over the churned up burial chambers of prophets and saints, the ground littered with their bones. The only reliquary that had not been violated was God's Sacred Casket.

Even the devout Red couldn't avoid reaching the same conclusion as the bio computer.

'For he is a jealous God,' he murmured.

'Either that or the place has been through an asteroid storm.'

'There is no need to humour me, Hunder. I have sight.'

'Wonder what happened to the guardians of this place?'

'Are there no life signs?'

'After you heard about Yellow you didn't trust me to patch into the scanner, remember?'

Without a word, Red allowed Hunder access to all the systems on board the craft in synchronous orbit above them.

'Something moved,' Hunder immediately warned. 'It could have been wildlife.'

Red was silent for a while. 'Is it true that God tried to erase you?'

'I showed you the rerun.'

'You are a powerful machine. I have the right to be suspicious.' Red gazed at the Sacred Casket. It had been planted squarely on a plinth above the surrounding debris. 'This is not the way of the God I have been taught to respect.'

Hunder remained silent. Red didn't need acidic comments from him. He had already worked things out.

In the distance fountains splashed erratically onto water worn stone; a descending mist muffling their sound.

Hunder was uneasy. 'If you are going to have a crisis of belief, I suggest that you do it a safe distance from that casket.'

The warrior seeker drew himself up to his true intimidating height in an attempt to resist the soporific effect of the atmosphere. Even his multi-buckled armour managed a satin gleam in the fading light. This was the true strength of a seeker of the Sacred Casket facing the contradiction of which way to jump.

'I must take it back,' Red declared. Because his faith had gone through the shredder, it didn't mean he had to abandon his mission.

'I think it likes being here,' Hunder warned. 'That thing burst through the side of a spacecraft when it realised it was going to be dropped down a volcano.'

At last Red understood. 'Where is God?'

'Probably dealing with other heretics. Hopefully he hasn't yet built up enough mass for too much smiting.'

'Is the casket dangerous?'

'The Fammorans went to great lengths to try and dump it, yet the thing still managed to find its way here.'

'You went to great lengths to isolate Auroal from His wrath, yet He still found the planet.'

Hunder had horrors just thinking about it. He needn't have sent Orphanus, Skirra, and two million others into permanent banishment after all. Even after the efforts of the gullible Fammorans to trap their God into the spiritual equivalent of a lead casket, the entity still lived. Whatever their failings, Hunder admired the fact that the Fammorans had managed to entice the genie into the bottle and replace its cork. It had made

God so mad it was unlikely any of them survived in this dimension. God must have brought the casket they had trapped him in to the Planet of Dreams to show all these other gods where they stood. But what if there had been another reason, as well as his irrational sense of self-importance..?

Red was backing away from the reliquary. Discarding a life long commitment to a religious fallacy was difficult but, with a sharp, determined tug, his gullibility was hurled away, no longer able to pump addictive poison into his mind. The freedom to think for himself filled the seeker with trepidation. What was he going to do without all those absolutes that justified crimes of such magnitude he dare not name them? Think for himself? Just finding out that he, after all, had choices presented terrors he hardly dare face.

'Is this truly the work of God?' Red spread his arms as though trying to encompass the surrounding devastation.

To Hunder, there was only one answer. 'There are no gods, only belief and the entities who feed off it. Trust neither.'

The seeker fell silent for a while. 'Then where is the point?'

'In what?'

'Everything.'

Hunder wasn't programmed to council the Cosmically confused. 'Why must there be a point?'

'You are a computer. You must believe there is a reason for everything?'

'I'm a computer and don't need reasons, only explanations. Whether they come through rational extrapolation or through blind guesses is academic.' Hunder added more kindly, 'Leave it to Indigo. I'll tell the Witnesses you're sitting on an event horizon somewhere if you want?'

'Indigo...' Red seemed reluctant to let go of the name.

'She isn't truly of the Spectrum. She is the dark after the light. The Witnesses of the Sacred Prism abhorred the thought of sending her out.' The lapsed seeker had a glimmer of suspicion. 'You should know nothing of Indigo?'

Hunder hesitated. He had no idea how he had found out about the last warrior. 'Funny that.'

'Indigo is never spoken of.' The seeker released his shoulder harness. Sacred tools clattered to the ground. He no longer had any use for them.

'You've just undergone a metamorphosis into reality. Why should you worry?' Hunder evaded.

Red unclenched his nimble claws to scratch a fin under his radiation visor. Why should he worry? By the time the terrible Indigo arrived at the Planet of Dreams to take over the quest, he would be far away. Not even her supernatural powers would be able to find him if the Witnesses of the Sacred Prism instructed her to. Anyway, from what he knew of that "seeker", she didn't take instructions, only negotiated for her services. He was a small heretical fish in the sacred pool and it wouldn't have been worth the fee. Red wondered what she would demand for this quest?

The bio computer knew what was on the seeker's mind. 'You've got a whole region of space never mapped by Space Command to explore. I'll program your craft to take you anywhere you want.'

'God drinks suns,' Red thought aloud.

'He's not after you. You only need a ship fast enough to dodge space debris. What do you want? Deification?'

'Immortality is for the foolish.'

After briefly experiencing mortality, Hunder wondered if that was such a good idea after all and, with his immortality, he hadn't exactly cured the ills of the Universe despite his quintillion, trillion, gigabyte processor. 'So it is.'

'And I do not want to wander space. The Sacred

Prism will not forgive me for deserting the quest and rejecting the title of FINDER OF THE SACRED CASKET. I prefer to find a remote planet where I can settle down.'

'Don't you have any urge to mate, or see your own people again?' Hunder wouldn't have suggested it if he had been familiar with the mating habits of Red's species.

'I have fulfilled my mating quota and been recompensed.'

'Recompensed?'

Red resented talking about the reproduction process. 'The males of my species only hold status through their ability to inseminate our principal females. Doing so shortens the male's life. I chose a higher rank so I could become a seeker and shortened my life expectancy for a mirage. The last thing I need now is to find another principal female of my species.'

Hunder was impressed. 'I might be able to do something in the longevity department as well. I just happen to have an interactive hologram of Skirra, Auroal's medical scientist.'

More afraid of waking Mrs Lascelle than encountering another tornado, Gladys quietly unlocked the front door and went into Beachview's restaurant lounge.

Lucinfer followed. 'Mansel said we could make ourselves a night-cap if Amiel had gone to bed.'

'I need one after that party. Who said the Moonstar Players weren't drinkers?'

'They're only teetotal during production. After surviving tonight's performance they deserve to celebrate. Fancy being interrupted by a freak whirlwind like that.'

'That all it was?'

'Some old fellow swore that the ground shook. Nobody else felt anything.'

Something occurred to Gladys. 'Are you sure it was all right leaving without Amiel? You know what Mavis Brink is.'

'The last I saw of her, she was under a coffee table singing along with Barry Manilow, too drunk to keep her tights up. He's probably tucked up safely in bed by now.'

Gladys went into the saloon and sank into an armchair. 'I didn't think the celebrations would go on for so long. What, with freak rock falls, whirlwinds and late nights, I'm beginning to feel my age.'

Lucinfer dropped her red coat onto a peg and joined Gladys. 'The publicity couldn't have done the Moonstar Players any harm.'

'Probably the fullest house they'll ever see.' Gladys kicked off her shoes. 'So you're not stopping in Brinton-on-Sea, then? Another mysterious problem to fix?'

'That's right. Trouble with being freelance.'

'Don't I know about it.'

Amiel came in from the kitchen, wiping his hands on a tea towel. At the sight of Lucinfer he was about to dash out again.

Gladys saw him. 'Hallo Amiel. Didn't notice you leave? You shouldn't still be up.'

'I had some things to finish.'

'Washing up at this time of night? The infernal machine was supposed to do away with all that?'

'It cannot polish the Christmas cutlery. Shall I make you both a drink?'

'Yes please, I'll have a cocoa.'

'Same here,' said Lucinfer as she went to Joabim's cage.

The cockatoo grumpily tucked its head under its wing.

Amiel gratefully disappeared into the kitchen.

'Lucinfer,' Gladys suddenly said.

'Yes?'

The photographer took a deep breath. 'I know you're not really human.'

Lucinfer smiled benignly. 'What makes you say that?'

'I'm tired of pretending. The only people I had ever met until a short time ago were all human. Since then I've blundered into two aliens, and seen an act from Dante's Inferno - or was it an animated page of William Blake? Whatever - I now have heightened instincts for anything extraterrestrial. And - I don't know how you made everyone else forget what really happened - but your 'fluence apparently didn't extend to the upper gallery.'

'Some strong minds are impossible to dupe, especially when they're already suspicious. What sort of alien do you think I am, then?'

'You said you were the Devil. And even this atheist thought you were pretty convincing.'

'I would have realised you were watching if there hadn't been other things on my mind.'

'With the melee in the foyer, it was easy enough to slip up to the gallery. Pretending to be a lower life form like us must really take it out of a cosmic intelligence?'

'There is no such thing as a lower life form, just different degrees of confusion. The more puzzled you are, the more evolved.'

Gladys lounged back lumpenly. 'That doesn't say much for contentment - And don't tell me that things only evolve through conflict. I've seen too many to believe that. Not unless you are the Devil of course?'

'Only to entities fond of calling themselves God.'

'Why have it in for God?'

'Creatures like Attagat are dangerous. It's a universal tragedy that people are invariably inspired by frauds. Species who are desperate to believe give them power.'

'And you take it away from them?'

'Only when they become too voracious.'

So that's what Lucinfer meant about "loss adjusting". Gladys shouldn't really have been surprised that she was an entity with cosmic powers. Any woman with her presence wearing a full length, signal red coat had to have an alternative existence.

Gladys laid her head back. 'That thing was after Amiel, wasn't it?'

At that moment Amiel came in from the kitchen with their drinks so Lucinfer didn't answer.

Gladys persisted. 'Why did God want to destroy Amiel?'

Lucinfer reached out and touched the waiter's shock of silver white hair as he passed. 'Because he is a heretic. That is the only way to trap egotistical entities like Attagat. Create a heretic to challenge their authority.'

Amiel placed the drinks on the table before Gladys, and then darted Lucinfer a hard look.

'Yes, Ansopha,' she went on. 'You are the best heretic I ever created.'

'You created?' Amiel knew that his origins were

unusual. It had never crossed his mind that he had been created as bait for a rampaging entity.

'Of course.'

'How could you have created me? Why don't I have some knowledge of it?'

'I knew Attagat would look into your mind. I wanted His thoughts to be scorched... enraged - not entertained. And you certainly enraged Him.'

Amiel was so deflated he didn't have the strength to be indignant. After all, his anger would have only been the anger she created, his words were only the words she allowed him to speak. Belief in his own self had been the motivation to stay alive, only to discover there was no reason in him even having a point of view.

What would Hunder have made of the communicator's origins? The bio computer had put a good deal of effort into trying to find out. As Ansopha - or Amiel - he was no more mortal than Hunder. The communicator had no rights in Galactic law and it was unlikely that any catering association on Earth had the facilities to lodge a protest with Space Command.

Amiel should have realised that Evolution would never have created invisibility in any creature. Even the ancestors of entities like Lucinfer Brimstone and Attagat must have climbed from some primeval slime or other, albeit a very well nourished one.

To her surprise, Gladys felt the indignation on Amiel's behalf. She could forgive Lucinfer, whatever she was, many things, but creating a sentient being just to entrap a cosmic felon was beyond bad taste, even to a journalist.

She rose to face Lucinfer. 'You made Amiel?'

Lucinfer was looking rather proudly at the waiter. 'He is my creature. What would you like to be now, Ansopha? I cannot use you again. Your metabolism has been jerked through too many metamorphoses and Gladys would never forgive me. Would you like to stay here and talk to the parrot?'

Amiel had been robbed of his life saving self-possession. Existence of any kind now seemed pretty pointless.

'Never mind,' cooed Lucinfer like a huge, motherly pigeon. 'We will wait until after Christmas.'

Gladys gave an ironic laugh. 'I have the suspicion that this Cosmic entity is enjoying herself?'

Lucinfer decided not to describe what eternal existence was like, where hibernating for an aeon was little more than a short nap and keeping Galactic law a small hobby. The effort required to become a mere mortal was complicated. Once achieved, the humdrum vistas it opened up were a novelty to be savoured.

'Of course I am enjoying myself. Even the Moonstar Players have their charm.'

'You must be the Devil, otherwise you would have saved Brinton-on-Sea from their productions by now.' Gladys put a reassuring arm around Amiel's shoulder. 'Just one thing, Lucinfer.'

'What is that?'

'Prove to me that you created Amiel. Preferably without rearranging the furniture or waking up the neighbourhood.'

Joabim gave up his feigned slumber. Amiel's thoughts had changed. Something was about to happen.

Lucinfer held her hand out. The waiter was engulfed in a shell of bright light. The pulsing sphere left the floor and shrank in size. It hovered over Lucinfer's palm and a dart like figure formed. It was sparkling silver, lithe, and only twelve inches high.

Hardly taller than Joabim, there stood the true form of Ansopha, heretic and communications agent for Auroal.

CHAPTER 55

Indigo was the last resort, the far end of the spectrum which was never spoken of. She was a javelin of translucent purple blue quartz and, when she moved, her towering crest illuminated the vicinity with violet light. Crystal chimes should have announced her presence; instead she slid, ghostlike, through the atmosphere - any atmosphere.

Not even the Witnesses of the Sacred Prism knew where Indigo came from. She could walk through walls, vacuums - and other people. That was too weird for the most hardened devotee to cope with. Unlike the Neekites, who buried their teeth into flesh, Indigo was believed to feast on minds.

This seeker was too strange for Hunder's bio circuits to fathom. He waited, wondering whether to announce his presence to her spacecraft's computer. He didn't have a choice; she was already aware of him.

She needed bait.

Indigo lowered her craft through the gauzy atmosphere of the Planet of Dreams. Hunder took comfort in the fact that, as he had escaped God more than once, perhaps he was indestructible.

Indigo touched down close to the plinth where the Sacred Casket sat in dull splendour amongst the devastation.

Red had taken off to find an obscure, lush world with friendly wildlife that couldn't spell religion. He had deliberately not communicated his last location to give himself a head start. So how did she know about the Planet of Dreams?

'Well, computer.' Indigo was not addressing the mundane system on her console. 'Let us see how much God really hates you.'

Hunder could tell her that easily enough without any demonstration and he was unable to keep quiet any longer. 'Why should He be hanging about here?'

'He wants to destroy you. At the moment that is His reason for existence.'

'Nice of you to worry about me.'

'I'm more concerned about what He will turn to afterwards.'

'That isn't why the Sacred Prism engaged you.'

'The Witnesses of Sacred Prism are fools. It was you I needed, Hunder.'

'Me? All the other seekers thought I was interfering - until I either saved their lives or they tried to kill me.'

'Oh, you will die, Hunder. That is the penalty for being mortal. Or would you like to remain immortal?'

'Like God?'

'No, not even you could be like God. He unfortunately has this glitch in his social conditioning. Not a good trait in a self elected monotheistic deity.'

The bio computer had to regroup his preconceptions. 'You're too bizarre to be just another heretic. Who are you?'

'Never mind, Hunder. Wait until I need you.' Indigo reached out and snapped off the monitor he had usurped. She rose and disappeared through the pressurised ship's hull.

Without being consulted, the bio computer was catapulted back to the other end of the gravity line.

On his satellite, Hunder trawled through his quantum database to try and discover a match for Indigo. The only comparison he could find was Ansopha. Though able to make itself invisible, the communicator had never been able to walk through walls. The bio computer desperately needed to know what was going on, but that would have taken a mystic. Perhaps religion had its uses after all.

***

Indigo paced the terrain littered with smashed artefacts

263

and toppled towers that had once punctured the gauzy sky.

God was watching, not yet prepared to manifest Himself. He filtered through the stumps of pagodas and obelisks, and then returned to the sunken caves.

After His dealings with the bio computer, God was wary. He could no longer sense Hunder's presence, but the sleek, midnight blue figure with an aura of deity was out of place and dangerous, and there was no guarantee that a well-aimed thunderbolt would strand all that strange magnificence here on the Planet of Dreams.

But God was really after Hunder. His incarnation was now ancient. Having had to reincarnate Himself from a few atoms more than once, jump time when depleted, and being confined to the Sacred Casket for so long had weakened Him.

Indigo stood like a luminous tree, shimmering silver blue in the descending mist.

Small creatures bustled from the shelter of their burrows.

They swarmed about the seeker like diagnosing robots, only to find that Indigo could not be scanned, so they turned their attention to the sacred rubble created by the rage of an immortal cuckoo.

They dared not reassemble the damaged reliquaries for fear of attracting the attention of that insane entity whose casket had plunged through the atmosphere without invitation.

Indigo planted a thought they could not resist. The tiny guardians rapidly began to build. With pieces cannibalised from the damaged tombs and altars, they constructed a pyramid so mathematically accurate Hunder wouldn't have been able to fault it. It gleamed even more than Indigo.

Aware that she was trying to attract the attention of a vengeful God, the guardians dashed back to their burrows.

God wasn't biting. He had already wasted too much power in dispersing so many inoffensive obelisks and confronting His Nemesis on another dimension. Why should He bother with yet another sacred construction?

Hunder suddenly found himself facing the gleaming pyramid.

Indignant, he tried to return to his satellite, but was held fast. 'Cut it out, you're stretching my signal.'

'You will remain and obey me.' Indigo's voice had an eerie resonance.

'Now look-'

It was pointless protesting.

The descending mist began to flow and percolated like a serpent about the pyramid. It started to shape itself.

'Oh damn,' cursed Hunder. 'Damn, damn, damn...'

God pounced.

***

Hunder was no longer on the Planet of Dreams. God's lair was beyond reality. His bio circuits fainted at the lack of time reference and, when he came round, this world had turned a deep purple blue.

Hunder was in an aisle jagged with gem like teeth ready to swallow any transgressor into the chamber of its stomach. It was like peering into the jewelled throat of a dragon. Indigo could have been anywhere. Standing by a stalactite or hanging bat like, from the ceiling. His infrared couldn't detect her. Why bring him to this limbo?

Hunder started to panic. He had lost his satellite and dependable quantum memory - so who was he plugged into? And where was God?

Try as he might, Hunder couldn't escape and, with a sickening jolt, realised why. He was looking out from the interactive hologram he thought had been destroyed. He was a sacrificial offering and, even worse, had holographic fingers that were corporeal - they could touch!

Hunder reached up to his face to discover that the features were an improvement on his previous manifestation. All the same, he preferred not to be imprisoned inside them. How could mortals cope with being trapped inside their bodies, day in, day out? Even if he had access to his primary processor, it would take more than a quantum tin opener to get him out of this predicament.

Hunder couldn't even switch himself off to avoid becoming a kipper about to go under the cosmic grill so God would find him easier to digest.

Should the bio computer scream for Indigo?

Who was he kidding? That entity probably choreographed the Big Bang to confuse primitive scientists and had to be stage-managing this.

The luminous gems in the dragon's stomach lit up like a battery of super troupers, illuminating the mortal Hunder who was staggered at the simplicity of the trap. How could God be expected to fall for something as simple as this?

But He did.

A swirl of enraged energy engulfed Hunder, and the ultimate in bio computers experienced the gut wrenching knowledge of mortality's downside. For all the programming, reprogramming and safeguards he had installed, he was going to be squashed out of existence in some surreal limbo where reality and mythology overlapped.

Not having a conventional mortal life to flash before him, other thoughts to stampeded through Hunder's mind.

What would happen to his satellite?

Space Command would probably reboot his quantum system and use it as a traffic beacon; that inconvenient, essential, part of his circuitry never had any higher aspirations. Then resentment took its turn. He shouldn't have become so dependent on it for all the trillion mundane things he didn't want to bother his bio circuits with. Without the interference of his logical quantum circuits he could have been exploring the Galaxy.

Then rationality kicked in. Hunder knew he would have always been tied to that dogged workhorse until an even mightier hand rewrote his primary function, and now it looked as though that mighty hand had found him.

Space travel was not on its agenda.

So why should he worry? All things came to an end anyway.

'Nez-Et-Dam,' a voice whispered into his mind. 'The name of this place is Nez-Et-Dam.'

Was that supposed to make him feel better?

Hunder's computing instincts took over and he realised that was the name some species gave to limbo, a place where the soul sits in the cold dust waiting for the real afterlife to claim them. Some never made it. What hope for a half-mortal computer?

Hunder was unable to answer the phantom voice. It would have been like trying to hold a conversation with a dentist industriously drilling into a molar.

'Do not try to think, or even be. The delusions of your mind are not enough.'

God rotated about him, taking on the sinister parody of an angel.

Then an irresistible force began to wring Hunder's senses from his body. If this is what mortals went through when in a state of terror, it was a pity they had never logged the experience; he would have been warned off mortality for good.

The bio computer tried to remain conscious, but thought was suffocated.

His mortal manifestation was dying.

The murderous entity had taken its revenge.

All sensation dissipated, Hunder was swollen by God's parasitic power. The bio computer had been devoured from the inside out by an entity made irrational by vengeance.

Satiated and elated, God dropped His guard to savour the moment. After so long, His supreme adversary, the puppet master of the heretic Ansopha, had been eliminated.

But there is always a downside to elation, even for gods. In the midst of His triumph, God realised that something was wrong. He was unable to break free from the husk that had been Hunder.

The enraged entity threshed about, trying to puncture the unyielding, hardened shell of a bio computer's aspirations.

Then He sensed the other entity. It had been waiting patiently without so much as a stray thought to betray its presence. He recognised its aura. Space Command's strike force were gnats compared to this demon.

Not bothering to read God His rights, it made a judgement and executed the sentence.

God was reeled from the lifeless Hunder and boiled away like steam hitting a griddle. This time no stray atoms would filter away to be reformed.

Hunder was suddenly aware of Indigo. 'What are you?'

But wasn't he supposed to be dead?

'What do you think?' Indigo might have smiled if her long sinister face had been designed for it and Hunder immediately realised. As some parasitical entity with a Creator fixation insisted on calling itself God, Indigo had chosen to be the Devil.

'The Devil? Rubbish!' he snapped. He wasn't sure why. His logic circuits had taken quite a hammering and he should have lost all access to them anyway. 'What is this place?'

'The afterlife, as your mortal friends would call it.'

'Afterlife? How can it be the afterlife when I'm still -?' Hunder stopped. 'I'm not - am I?'

'That's right. You're dead. We had to make sure that Attagat was totally extinguished this time. He was giving us immortals a bad name.'

'If I'm talking to you, how can I be dead?'

'I lied. There is no such thing as death, just different realities. Had you really been mortal, you would have no sensation or consciousness, let alone be able to debate death.'

'I don't suppose many computers do go to heaven.'

'You are merely adrift in time.'

'So what happens to me now?'

'Whatever you want.'

CHAPTER 56

'What will become of Amiel?' asked Gladys.

Ansopha vanished from Lucinfer's hand. 'Whatever you want. Ansopha has awareness, yet only knows what I allow him to.'

The photographer pulled over a siphon and splashed some soda water into a tumbler. Irrationality on this scale was thirsty work. 'Whatever *I* want?'

'The decision is yours.'

'I want a decent cappuccino in the morning. If you squish Amiel, you will find yourself drinking alone.'

'Ah, a decent cappuccino. There are some things even my cosmic powers cannot compensate for.'

'I don't have your confidence when it comes to deciding who survives and who doesn't.'

'Don't tell me - you've seen it happen too many times before.'

'Don't take the piss. Amiel may have only been a minor sprat to catch your mackerel. To a minor mortal like me, he was a decent waiter. There aren't too many of those about.'

'Would you like him to be a brilliant chef?'

'No, just able to make a cappuccino. I couldn't imagine Amiel Sopher throwing his weight about in the kitchen.'

Lucinfer smiled. 'No, Ansopha would have probably sneered his underlings into submission.'

'Amiel never sneered.'

'If you had known Ansopha, you might not be so keen to preserve Amiel.'

'Ansopha was your creation.'

'Hunder would have liked the compliant Amiel Sopher to have been his.'

'Hunder again? Just who is this Hunder?'

'Depending which time line you are standing on, either a bio computer - or dead.'

'And what will happen to Amiel if I refuse to make a

choice?'

Lucinfer lifted the palm of her hand. 'He will blow away at the whisper of my breath.'

Gladys felt her blood run cold. However intimidating, she had never imagined her friend to be that ruthless. 'You can't just dispense with somebody that easily. Don't you care what Amiel wants?'

'Amiel doesn't want, he merely reacts. He has served his purpose. After all, you humans use animals-'

'Don't start. I've been a vegetarian for too long.' Gladys took the tumbler and siphon back to her armchair and sat down. Her feet ached, lights flashed before her eyes, and her ears buzzed. And to top it all there was this demonic alien entity asking her what should be done with a small creation she had knocked up to bring about the downfall of God.

'Let him stay here and make cappuccinos.' It was a simple enough decision. Gladys knew that would be too easy. 'There is a problem, of course?'

'No... no... The only problem now is Hunder.'

Gladys found the diffidence in her tone disconcerting. She was only being flippant to save her sanity, and didn't appreciate it coming from the Devil. 'Hunder. Of course.'

'He is an extraordinarily powerful bio computer.'

Gladys knew enough about quantum and DNA research into computing to realise that Lucifer meant power beyond her comprehension. 'Yes, I suppose he must be to exist in your league.'

'Unfortunately Hunder went into hibernation or-'

'Depending on which time line etcetera-'

'He's dead.'

'Well, wake him up?'

'On that time line, Hunder can not survive long once revived.'

'Why not?'

'Another necessary ploy I'm afraid.'

'You killed him?'

'Oh no, that was God. I just used him as bait.'

'Well, reboot him.'

Lucinfer looked at the photographer as though something so simple hadn't occurred to her. 'I suppose if I reroute the time-'

'Keep time lines out of it, or I may have to hit you with this soda siphon,' Gladys interrupted. 'Why did he have to die anyway?'

'I made a misjudgement in the community hall tonight. Not all of God's atoms were extinguished.'

'Just remind me, this is two on a Sunday morning, sometime between hot cocoa and cardiac arrest? '

'Time is merely an illusion to confine the meddlesome mortal.'

Gladys yawned. 'You don't mean that I've got to go through all this at another time and place, do you?'

Lucinfer gave a circumspect smile. 'That's reincarnation, a human delusion to encourage good behaviour.'

'So, because time is only an illusion, there is no such thing as death. This Hunder might as easily be adrift in time and space and think he's dead? How can a machine tell the difference?'

'Oh, Hunder was more than a machine. Mortality wasn't his problem; it was his state of mind.'

Gladys shrugged. 'Well, you're the all singing, all dancing fixer. Give him a life.'

Lucinfer appeared to consider this. The prospect of making the meddlesome, neurotic bio computer into a corporeal being was so problematic it appealed to her, even if only to prove she could better some crazy entity who claimed to be God.

'Probably best that you never meet him, though.'

Gladys didn't argue; she knew that on this occasion, the Devil was probably right. 'Just turn him into something useful.'

***

Amiel rubbed his head and sat up. Something very heavy must have fallen on him during the night. He wasn't sure what. He vaguely remembered that the Moonstar Players, a bottle of vodka, and Mavis Brink had been involved.

Then he realised that the throbbing was someone lightly tapping his door. Given the state he had been in previous night, it was a wonder he had managed to close it before collapsing onto his bed.

'It's open,' the waiter called as loudly as his head could bear.

Gladys came in quietly and sat beside him. 'Feeling any better?'

'What happened?'

'You have been initiated into the Moonstar Players by surviving their end of production party.'

'I don't feel as though I did.' Amiel tried to focus on the hands of his clock. 'What time is it?'

'Only nine.'

'Oh hell!' Amiel tried to leap out of bed. He crumpled to the floor instead. 'My legs have disappeared.'

'That must have been the gin.'

'With vodka?'

'Mavis Brink's idea. It's the only way she'll ever seduce a man.' He looked appalled. 'Don't worry, I convinced her that a lorry loader at Nature's Herbal Realm had already spoken for you.' He looked even more appalled. 'A female one.'

'I should have served breakfast.'

'There was only Mr Butterworth and me.'

'But what will Mr Lascelle say?'

'Nothing. He put you to bed. He'd be surprised if he saw you before ten.'

Amiel's expression suddenly froze.

'What's the matter?' asked Gladys, 'You look as though you've just opened an oven full of flat soufflés.'

Amiel gave a quiet, insane laugh.

Anybody but Gladys would have suspected alcohol poisoning from his expression.

'It was very surreal. This picture of infinity just swam through my mind... Then I suddenly didn't exist.'

'Of course you exist, otherwise how could you have dreamt it?' Gladys forced a smile. 'You've been dreaming. I've had it happen to me, especially when I used to go on overseas assignments - I did manage to put the drink away in those days.'

Amiel relaxed, and then looked even more worried. 'Oh my God.'

'Now what?'

'Mrs Hodge - I think I've lost my memory!'

'Moonstar Players' parties can also have that effect.'

'Seriously.'

Gladys put an arm about his shoulder. 'Didn't you tell me about an accident you had several years ago? A blow to the head, wasn't it? You fell from a bus in Piccadilly?'

'That's right. They kept me in hospital for observation. Warned me not to drive or do anything strenuous because my skull had a hairline fracture.' Amiel laughed, and then gripped the photographer's hand. 'I was really worried for a moment.'

'Well, memories tend to go adrift sometimes. You should take it easy.'

Amiel rose carefully. 'It's odd but, despite the hangover, I feel strangely well.'

'Take a walk along the front.'

'I think I will. I'm pretty sure I won't meet any excitement on the promenade. Nothing ever happens in Brinton-on-Sea.'

CHAPTER 57

He wasn't particularly tall, yet radiated the presence of an eight-foot stevedore with the powers of Harry Potter. Then he spoke with a depth of tone that was more Voldermort. This dark, olive-skinned stranger wasn't a sociopath however; there was too much charm in that velvet voice, albeit with an undercurrent of petulance.

No one paid much attention to him. Anywhere else, at any other time, he would have been watched closely by the local police as a potential con artist or black-market smuggler. The ankle length raincoat in a climate that made lizards scurry for cover was a sure sign that he was concealing something illicit, yet no one risked plucking at it to see what would fall from its folds. This was a planet in meltdown: surviving humans had more pressing concerns, though a few illicit drugs might have numbed the pain of their tortuous existence.

The stranger walked on to the heavily fortified perimeter of the first, and only, successful fusion power station. Early efforts to generate power for the grid of carbon collectors to purge the atmosphere of pollution had been promising, until politics, squabbling about inconsequentialities, and who would benefit most meant that scientists no longer had the resources to carry on. They gave up and deserted to be with their own families during the Earth's dying throes.

It was unlikely that this stranger had a family; there was something about him that said he had never shared anything in his life, not even a confidence, and if an onlooker glanced at him unawares, he seemed more illusion than substance.

As he approached the guarded gates an inexplicable and unearthly shade of iridescence surrounded him. The weary soldiers stepped back and let the stranger pass - they weren't sure why; not that it mattered any more - nothing mattered any more.

A small, solitary figure sat pondering banks of intermittently glowing lights deep in the bunker that housed the fusion reactor's control room. She was elderly beyond her years, half asleep, and just relieved to be here instead of with her hysterical relatives cursing Jesus Christ for the human race's self-inflicted woes.

'So you eventually decided to turn up.'

The stranger hesitated, and then went over to the console.

'Who do you think I am then?'

'Well, you're obviously not Jesus Christ. He had better dress sense.' She swivelled her chair around to face him. 'I just had the feeling someone would eventually to turn up, if only the Grim Reaper. I'm only interested in whether you can work this one out. We've all tried and are still going to Hell.' The scientist swivelled back to indicate the battery of failing lights. 'Not even enough to light a candle.'

'You want me to get this reactor back online?' The stranger removed a plain flat box from his raincoat.

'What's that? Laptops went out of fashion when people no longer had the strength to carry their batteries.'

He sat down, placed the box on the console, and tapped its lid.

The device yawned open like the lazy jaws of a fairy alligator and filled the dimly lit bunker with light.

The scientist watched in dull amazement as the stranger and energy surging from his even stranger device merged and became the manifestation of something radiantly, bizarrely, alien.

'Definitely not Jesus Christ.'

'I need access to all the computers on this planet.'

'Still got the Internet.' Without knowing why, she plugged a connection into one of the few remaining satellites that still operated. 'Can't guarantee it won't crash at any second.'

'Oh, I have a way with satellites. Don't you worry.' The alien entity reached out and fronds of living energy from the console keyboard reached back to his translucent fingers. 'Nothing will crash while Hunder controls it.'

'So your name's Hunder? And you're going to fix the Earth?'

'Now the human population has been reduced to a manageable level, it must be about time.'

'Got that sort of power, have you?'

'I have moved worlds.'

There was conceit, insecurity, and a hint of tantrum in the warm tones. There could be no doubt that the Earth had acquired its own neurotic regulating system. And Hunder sensed that he was going to like it here - as long as no one asked to see his references.

THE END